The
Victim Donor

The
Victim Donor

A Novel

Ken Corre

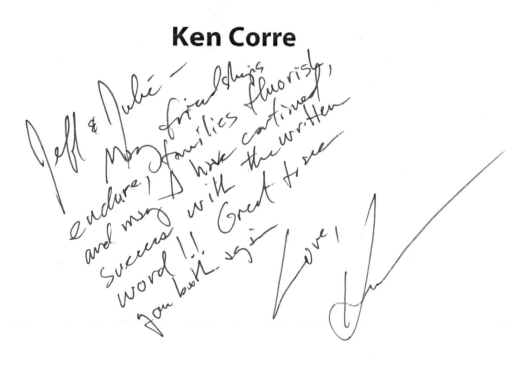

iUniverse, Inc.
New York Lincoln Shanghai

The Victim Donor

iUniverse books may be ordered through booksellers or by contacting:

iUniverse
2021 Pine Lake Road, Suite 100
Lincoln, NE 68512
www.iuniverse.com
1-800-Authors (1-800-288-4677)

This is a work of fiction. All of the characters, names, incidents, organizations, and dialogue in this novel are either the products of the author's imagination or are used fictitiously.

ISBN-13: 978-0-595-40659-3 (pbk)
ISBN-13: 978-0-595-85025-9 (ebk)
ISBN-10: 0-595-40659-9 (pbk)
ISBN-10: 0-595-85025-1 (ebk)

Printed in the United States of America

Acknowledgments

I would like to thank my beloved family and cadre of loving friends for sacrificing precious time together so that I could pursue my writing. I am also grateful for the editing skills of Ed Stackler; the editors and staff of iUniverse; the exceptional medical mentors in my clinical training and for the multiple untold positive influences throughout my life.

Chapter 1

John Harris woke to his watch alarm. He lay on his side, facing away from Cheryl. The first memory that surfaced was of their argument the night before. He got up and quietly headed toward the bathroom. Despite having just awakened, he was ruggedly handsome in his husky, five-feet-ten frame.

John allowed minimal time for a shower, a shave, and breakfast in order to maximize what little sleep he got during the week. Cheryl operated with a different sort of efficiency. In their walk-in closet, she had already laid out her clothes, including her ironed white coat with *C. Harris, MD, Pediatrics* embroidered on it in red thread. The lapels were adorned with little animal pins, the type that kids at Utah Memorial Hospital found disarming; her stethoscope was looped above one of the large pockets. Her black bag sat on the floor beneath her outfit.

Like John, their two boys had never laid out their clothes ahead of time for school. The two girls had done so since the tender age of two—and without any prompting.

John simply grabbed one of his suits, a shirt, and one of a number of ties. It was Wednesday, and he needed to bring his tennis racquet and workout clothes for a lunchtime game ... that was, if he got a lunch break. John ranked highly at his brokerage, but the hours were killing him. And if the hours didn't prompt his surrender, then his superiors would. Not one of them earned John's respect at any level. In fact, John thought that if his boss were in a crosswalk as John's car approached, John would be faced with one of life's great dilemmas: which pedal would he hit?

Before leaving, John took a risk: he approached Cheryl's sleeping body, kissed her cheek ever so gently, and whispered an apology into her ear. She gave him a brief hug with one arm and fell back asleep. Her clock displayed 4:17 AM.

On his way outside, John mulled two questions. How long could he continue to wake up at 4:00 AM? And was this what old age was like—mutual love, but precious little lovemaking? How could that be? He and Cheryl were only forty-one.

The movement beyond his Range Rover caught his eye. Three deer and a fawn grazed on the foliage. They suddenly stood perfectly motionless, their ears perked, as they fixed their gazes on John. John paused as well, briefly, and then beeped his car remote. The deer fled with large leaps on delicate legs. The beauty of his surroundings was always in the back of his mind. He felt fortunate.

John started up the Range Rover and reversed his path from the night before, down the mountain. He could see his house in the rearview mirror, illuminated by motion lights triggered by his departure. He held up his coffee mug in a mock toast. He could not wait to return.

Not wasting another second, he hit the automatic dial on his cell phone and listened to his voice mail. There were a number of messages, but no big clients had called him. No panic attacks in the wee hours … good.

The piano music on his stereo resumed where it had left off the day before. John settled in for the drive. Soon he would be sitting in front of a TV monitor, taking calls and scheduling meetings, his fingers tap dancing on his keyboard. Another day, another several dollars.

No other traffic was visible on Highway 18. In a few more miles, the road would begin to coil. Sometimes, depending on his mood, John would play rock and roll as he entered the mountain twists. That day, he stuck with classical as he passed the Curves Ahead sign—an unnecessary warning. He knew the highway well enough to drive it by feel.

It happened as he came out of a particularly sharp curve. John barely saw the flashing lights in time to apply the brakes.

A small car lay on its side in the oncoming lane, near the steep drop-off. A large truck sat some thirty feet ahead on the right, close to the mountain, with its hazards flashing. As John stopped on the shoulder, a flashlight beam struck his windshield and bathed his face. Squinting, John could just make out the familiar khaki trousers of a U.S. forest ranger. When the ranger lowered the flashlight to the ground, John could see a third vehicle just beyond the large truck—a forest-service pickup with its lights flashing. John thought it odd that as the flashlight dimmed, the ranger smiled at him. A quick glance at the upended car did not reveal any bodies or body parts. No blood.

The ranger approached the car, and John lowered the window.

"Good morning," the ranger said. "There's been a bad accident here. I'm expecting a tow truck and ambulance soon."

"Can I help in any way?"

"Could you please put on your emergency flashers and remain in your car?" The ranger flashed his light around the interior of John's car. "It's safer than stepping out on the road." The ranger's light returned to John's face. At that moment, a figure popped up next to John's window and thrust something into the left side of John's neck.

The hiss of pressurized air being released was the only sound John heard. Before he could register the face under the dark camouflage paint, John slumped forward into the steering wheel.

As the horn started to honk, the ranger pushed the executive in the Range Rover back into the seat, reclined the seat enough so that he would not fall forward again, set the parking brake, and turned off the engine.

The back of the large truck opened, and two more men in fatigues and camouflage directed the truck driver to back up closer to the Range Rover. The men pulled a wide ramp out from underneath the back of the truck. A miniature, caged Caterpillar forklift drove down the ramp toward the overturned car.

The ranger signaled for the men to hurry. A hook and cable spooled from the dimly lit recess of the truck's cargo bay. One of the men attached the hook to the underside of the Range Rover.

While the others kept busy with the toppled car, the ranger drew a silenced pistol and approached the man lying supine under the Range Rover, then shot him in the chest and abdomen. He quickly holstered his weapon and turned toward the others; no one had heard a thing.

The truck driver, dressed in civilian clothes, joined the ranger at the overturned car. Before a word was uttered, both the truck driver and the ranger drew their silenced weapons and shot the other men in the head, then placed all the bodies in the overturned car.

The truck driver climbed into the forklift, backed it up, and approached the car. The forks of the lift slid under the car, and with some lurching and straining, it sent the car over the edge and hundreds of feet down the mountain. Even with binoculars, the car would not be visible from the road. The ranger smiled.

The forklift and Range Rover were secured inside the truck. The ranger donned a backpack and then removed a hose from its side. He began rinsing down the roadway, starting with the blood from the shootings. When the fluid came in contact with the blood, it steamed and sizzled into vapor. The paint on the roadway from the overturned car was similarly erased, along with the tire marks from the tractor.

Finished, the ranger flung the backpack as far from the road as he could. In the predawn stillness, he put on a second backpack and quickly rinsed the previously doused areas with copious amounts of another liquid. This time, there was no steaming. He threw that pack over the edge when he finished, satisfied the dense wilderness below would prevent the evidence from being discovered for weeks—perhaps months. By then, the corpses would be unrecognizable. Nature would see to that.

The ranger ascended the ramp in his forest-service pickup, secured it behind the Range Rover, and stripped away his ranger uniform, revealing civilian clothes. He joined the driver in the cab, and the truck pulled away, gradually reaching the speed limit. The beads of sweat that had gathered on his brow from the precision and importance of the events that just transpired evaporated in the rush of morning air.

Chapter 2

An hour later, the truck driver parked in front of an unmarked hangar on the outskirts of Utah's Larchmont airport.

A ten-passenger private jet waited inside the hangar. Two armed soldiers in khakis stood outside the jet ready for action. The jet door opened to form an accordion of stairs as the truck backed into the hangar. A large, bearded man, with piercing black eyes and an automatic rifle slung over his Middle Eastern clothing, descended from the jet. He and the two men from the truck opened the truck's cargo bay and squeezed past the ranger's pickup, approaching the Range Rover. The executive behind the wheel remained reclined in the driver's seat, unconscious. His head was cocked to one side, and drool ran from the corner of his mouth. He appeared at peace with his predicament.

"Fuck, fuck, fuck." The ranger smacked the Range Rover's roof. "We don't have enough room to get him out the door without hurting him."

"Is that what they teach you here in America? 'Fuck, fuck, fuck'?" The large, bearded man shook his head and chuckled. "Get the pickup truck out of here now. You can put it back after. Lower the seat-back all the way and push him over the seat."

"You" he commanded the driver, "pull the pig up and over from the back. And hurry. We don't have time to take his vehicle out too."

Moving the dead weight of the flaccid body proved to be of monumental difficulty, even for two strong men. Slowly the limp form was inched to the middle and then to the back of the Range Rover, his head bobbing freely and hyperextending backward as he was heaved over each seat.

A Caucasian woman in a nurse's uniform looked on from the aircraft's entrance as John's body was hauled from the truck and carried to the stairway. The three men moved John roughly up the steps to the jet doorway.

"Idiots, you'll hurt him." The male voice from within the aircraft spoke in a French accent. "You'll bruise him internally."

The nurse darted inside the craft as the men struggled to move the limp body up the final few stairs and into the cabin. Bullets of sweat coursed down the bearded man's forehead. He gave the French doctor a look and then slowly lowered his precious cargo to the floor. With the ranger's help, the large man lifted and secured the unconscious man in a seat. The nurse and doctor took over.

As the nurse started an intravenous line in the executive's forearm, the doctor listened to the chest through his shirt with a stethoscope and nodded; his heart and lungs sounded good. The nurse deftly secured the line with white tape and hung the bag of sterile feeding solution from the ceiling of the plane.

While the nurse took the blood pressure, the doctor turned on a machine. A wire ran from the machine to a clip on the executive's finger. After a few seconds, two LED displays lit up. One showed a heart rate of 101 beats per minute; the other showed an 02 saturation reading of 96 percent.

"Excellent," the doctor said.

"Blood pressure: 110/72."

"Good, good, very good," said the doctor, who thought he saw the slightest smile at the corner of the man's mouth. "He's not nearly deep enough." The doctor shined his penlight into his patient's eyes, lifting one upper lid at a time. "OK, put 80 milligrams in the chamber and run it in at 5 milligrams per hour, and let's hydrate him with 200 ccs per hour of normal saline, with 20 milliequivalents of potassium chloride per liter."

Deep in sleep, but before the new medication was started, John was an undergraduate again. Cheryl, his premed girlfriend, made him smile. They had moved in together during their second year of school, risking their families' disdain. He was white, she was black, and their love had been intense enough for both of them to plunge in regardless of what anyone might think. They spent their days and nights in three ways: studying, making love, and watching *Saturday Night Live*. There was no time for anything else, but it did not matter. Graduate school came, and the relationship deepened. They were so lucky to be accepted to their respective graduate schools on the same campus. And she turned out to be a superb physician. He saw it with his own eyes and heard it year after year from her colleagues and patients.

The nurse drew medication from a small, brown bottle and squeezed the malleable chamber. The chamber filled from the bag above it, turning off the intravenous drip below it. She injected the medicine into a port at the top of the chamber and shook it to mix the contents. The tubing led to another nearby machine. She set its digital display to 54 cc/h.

"OK," said the doctor, "we're all ready to go. We'll start the blood work as soon as we've leveled off."

He looked at the large Middle Eastern man and nodded, acknowledging again that everything was ready to go.

The two soldiers who had guarded the jet outside entered and took seats without a word. The bearded man closed the hatch as, outside, the ranger left with the truck, making way for the jet's departure.

As the jet taxied toward the runway, the bearded man reached for the executive's back pocket. He slid the dreaming man's wallet out and flipped it open.

"John Harris," he said aloud. "Big American executive. Big fancy car."

At cruising altitude, the doctor and nurse unbuckled their seat belts and made their way to the converted wet bar that held a microscope and two complex-looking machines. The nurse brought out a large, plastic toolbox and opened it. Inside were medications, syringes, tourniquets, intravenous solutions, empty test tubes with colored caps, and other sterile medical packages. As the nurse plucked out a syringe, a tourniquet, and several test tubes, the doctor calibrated the machines.

The nurse cut away John's jacket and shirtsleeves and applied the tourniquet. Several large veins in his arm bulged; she smiled, knowing that she would not have difficulty getting blood from this patient. The guards watched with interest as the nurse placed a needle at the end of a syringe, then plunged the needle into a vein. A tiny spurt of blood shot out from the skin as the needle pierced the vein. The nurse withdrew the plunger, flooding the syringe with its crimson load. The two men laughed nervously, unnerved by the simple letting of blood.

The nurse filled several vacuumed test tubes and gently rocked to them to mix the blood with the invisible chemicals lining the tubes.

Without a word, the doctor took the tubes, turned around, and ran his science project. The machine clinked as it carried out its analysis. While the doctor scrutinized the printout, the nurse prepared for another medical procedure.

The guards watched as she unbuckled John's belt, then unbuttoned and unzipped his pants. Despite his dead weight, she was able to work his pants down to his knees. She did the same with his underwear, exposing his genitalia in a matter-of-fact way. To her, John's was just another set of genitals, just one more part of the anatomy. Today, however, she was getting paid more than usual for her work. Substantially more.

The guards sat forward to see what was coming next. The nurse opened a sterile kit containing gloves, cotton balls, soap, jelly, drapes, a syringe filled with clear solution, an empty screw-top cup, and some long, thin tubes. She tore open a packet of dark brown soap and poured it onto the cotton balls. After the nurse placed the sterile drapes around John's most private part, she used each cotton ball individually to wash John's penis, starting with the tip and then moving down the shaft toward the pubic hair. In this way, she annihilated bacteria prior to inserting the tube through the penis into the urinary bladder. An infection would not be tolerated.

As it happened, the cleansing process sexually aroused the comatose patient. The nurse could feel John's penis enlarging and hardening long before his erection became obvious. Although she knew this was a normal reflex, she became embarrassed in front of the strangers and tried to cover the erection with the drapes. The men laughed like schoolboys, joking in their native tongue and grabbing their own genitals.

The nurse tried to ignore the men whose joking now clearly involved her. Holding John's erect penis in one hand, she dipped the end of the thin, opaque rubber tube in K-Y jelly and introduced the tube into John's urethra.

She pulled John's pants up again without any help, letting the tubing and bag protrude from his zipper. The bag was already collecting urine as his kidneys purified his body of its naturally occurring wastes. The nurse took a urine sample and carried it over to the doctor.

The doctor extracted one drop, placed it on a slide, and looked at it through the microscope.

"Perfect," the doctor said. "Just as expected." He smiled at the two soldiers. "So, where are we headed?"

They looked straight at him expressionlessly and said nothing. His smile quickly faded, and he returned to his seat and buckled up.

Chapter 3

Many hours and one refueling passed before the terrain below could first be appreciated. A major change in geography had clearly occurred. From its earliest visibility, an off-white plain seemed to stretch to the horizons. The doctor and nurse silently tried to place the landscape beneath them. Their concentration drifted further and further from their patient as they gazed out the window more intently with the plane's descent. They did not see the expected increase in topographical resolution that should have come with the descent.

Their concentration was broken by the shriek of an alarm. Each recognized it immediately, while the guards, grabbing their weapons and looking about the cabin in surprise, did not.

The doctor rapidly assessed John.

"He's desaturating. His pulse ox is 88 percent," said the nurse.

"Give me the oxygen and I want you to draw up some antidote."

"What does this mean?" asked the bearded soldier.

This time, it was he who was ignored.

The doctor ripped open John's shirt and, placing his stethoscope on each side of John's chest in rapid sequence, listened for both the presence and depth of breathing. The nurse reached under her seat and handed an oxygen mask to the doctor, who put it on John's face.

"*Merde!* He's too sedated," he said as he turned off the IV machine. "You ready?"

"Almost." The nurse opened the toolbox and concentrated on plunging another needle into a small vial.

"You're going to need to dilute that or draw up a small portion. We cannot have him wake up. He must remain sedated until after ..." said the doctor, sweat mounting on his brows.

"After? After what?" asked the nurse.

The guards looked with piqued interest, but the doctor did not respond.

"Okay, we need to give 0.5 milligrams to start with. Do it now!" John began to vomit. The doctor pulled the mask off John's face and turned his head to one side with his left hand. With his free hand, he managed to turn on a suction machine on the floor.

The nurse brought out an unusually thin, calibrated, hypodermic syringe while the doctor suctioned the liquid vomit out of John's mouth and re-applied the oxygen mask.

"Here, give this," said the nurse as she handed the syringe to the doctor and drew up more solution into a larger syringe.

The doctor paused, silently searching his memory. Would he give this into the muscle or the IV? If he gave it IV, would he need to chase it with some fluid, or would the bolus injection of it be enough? A series of other questions followed. Why had she handed it to him? Did this nurse that he met only yesterday know her business? What might the consequences be if they lost their patient at this stage of the preparation? He began to perspire freely.

"I'm the doctor, you're the nurse. Now give it and hurry."

She delivered the minute but precise amount of antidote into a side port of one of the IV lines, close to the patient's skin. The closer to the patient, the quicker the medicine was received. She then flushed the line with another syringe to make sure John received all the medication immediately.

The doctor observed John's chest heaves and then listened to the lungs.

"Yes, much better, I think. Wait two minutes and then take off this oxygen mask and lets see if he desaturates again." The physician silently crossed his fingers. "This is the best estimate we can do without actually being able to measure tidal volumes or inspiratory force or carbon dioxide levels," he said primarily to himself. This was the first time he had been in a life-threatening situation outside of the hospital.

The nurse instinctively took out an ambu-bag manual breathing device in anticipation of the need to help John breathe. This made the doctor even more nervous, as he looked back and forth between his watch and the patient. He did not like this situation. In particular, he did not like the other men sharing this tiny space with him. He understood the need for their presence. But they were just so ... crude, and unprofessional.

"Two minutes." He replaced the stethoscope as the nurse removed the mask.

"Eighty-five percent. Heart rate is only forty-seven!" she cried as the piercing sound of the heart monitor alarm returned.

"Give him another zero-point-five milligrams," he barked back. He grabbed the ambu-bag and mask, dropped to his hands and knees, disconnected the tubing to the mask now on his patient's face, and attached the tubing that ran from the end of the ambu-bag. He replaced the bag and sealed the mask tightly to John's face, using one hand to hold it there while the other one rhythmically squeezed the bag. Each squeeze was associated with an exaggerated rise in John's chest wall. For the moment, the doctor was actually breathing for him.

The nurse repeated the process of injecting the antidote and flushing it to get a rapid effect.

The doctor felt a sinking, uneasy feeling in his stomach. There was no one-to-one relation between the sedative he had given John and the antidote he was now giving. Although he found comfort in knowing he could continue ordering doses of the antidote to the desired effect, this increased the possibility that John might reach a state of consciousness with a significant awareness of his surroundings. It had been made excruciatingly clear that his patient was never, *never*, to regain any level of awareness prior to his final destination. There was no equivocation. Mistakes would not be tolerated.

The doctor tried to stay calm, assuring himself that all would be fine. But he was only human—and medicine was, and always would be, far from an exact science.

The nurse reached into the box and pulled out a bottle labeled Atropine to speed John's heart rate. As she began to open it, the doctor snapped, "We won't be needing that. The problem here is ventilatory, not cardiac."

After a few more minutes of forcing John to breathe, he removed the bag and mask from John's face. With his stethoscope on the patient's chest, he watched the monitors. The breaths sounded adequate, and the saturation now hovered in the normal range. The heart rate was about seventy—also normal.

The doctor wiped his brow. "OK. Let's back off on the drip to 3 milligrams per hour."

To be safe, the doctor left the suction device hissing next to John's head.

In the moments after the antidote had been given and before the sedative drip was reestablished to the desired effect, John had undetectably reached a significant level of consciousness. Before he faded again, his mind struggled with the mixture of remembered events and the clouded input his senses were now relaying. He saw brief flashing images of an overturned car. But … he hadn't seen a body. Where was the body in need of an ambulance? And who was the Middle Eastern ranger? Not only had John never seen him before, but he had also never even seen a non-Anglo ranger. And some of the voices he now heard sounded foreign … maybe Arabic. His brain struggled to put it all together.

He then heard something much louder: the whistling of air past his ear, a sort of hissing. The brisk rush of air suddenly brought his mind vividly back to the events and his state of mind on the night preceding his abduction.

It was as if he were there again, if only for a moment. He sat behind the wheel, his suit jacket slapping in the wind on its hanger behind his seat. His tie was loose; his pants were unbuttoned and unzipped to make room for the mild paunch of middle age. John's head relaxed into the headrest as the leather seats engulfed his tired body. His hair, sparse in the typical areas, seemed to dance with the music.

The winter forest aroma that was carried into the Range Rover's cabin cleansed the senses. The scent of moist soil combined with pine and aspen fragrances soothed the soul. This, in combination with the CD of a collection of mellow songs played pianissimo, completed the dichotomy of his life; the first half was the high-powered office job he had just left.

His Range Rover raced up Highway 18 toward home. The headlights reached into the darkness, occasional orange reflectors breaking up the monotony of white stripes on the two-lane road. The stars were brilliant that night, with the kind of clarity that stirred no awe in county folk, but rendered city folk speechless.

John turned onto his property, past the sign with an *H* angled inside a circle that marked the entrance to the Harris ranch. Partway down the long driveway, the car triggered an infrared sensor that lit the rest of the drive and the front of his home and rang a bell with a single dull chime, inside the home. Circling in front of the house, he pulled up next to the family minivan and his wife's Jaguar. Before he turned the engine off, the front door of the house burst open, and two Irish setters and four children bolted out to greet him. Cheryl stood on the porch, watching and laughing. She wore jeans, a plaid shirt of John's, and cowgirl boots. The baggy shirt did not manage to hide her pedigree or her slender, tall figure. She looked relaxed, beautiful, and content. Her perfect teeth complemented her clear, taut skin.

As John stepped down, he let his unbuttoned pants drop to the ground. The entourage stopped their advance toward him just long enough to scream and laugh.

"What? What's the matter?" feigned John.

The group swapped kisses and hugs, though Eric would allow only a hug; maybe it was his age, maybe his pimples … maybe both. The children broke away and ran back to the house.

Two-year-old Nicole had a big smile on her face as she waited in her mother's arms on the porch. The three of them shared a big hug. Nicole, sandwiched between the two, began to laugh.

"Mommy and Daddy are the bread," said Cheryl, "and Nicole is the … bologna!"

"Yeah," said Nicole, laughing again.

"So, to what do I owe this unusual greeting?" asked John.

"Well, John, you've been working a lot lately, and I think they really miss you. Hey, Nicole, show Daddy the moon."

Nicole searched the sky carefully, picked out the crescent orb, and pointed. "Moon."

"Very good," they told her.

"Shall we go in?" John asked.

Nicole shook her head. "Daddy, walk." She attempted to push herself away from John and shimmy down his body.

"Oh, you want to walk? OK."

Beautiful Nicole was growing up so fast. How could he have ever been hesitant about having a fourth child?

In the family room, the two oldest already had Nintendo joysticks in hand. Michael peered over their shoulders, equally absorbed without the stimulation of his tactile senses. For the time being, he was an indentured observer.

"OK, guys, it's time for bed." John looked at his watch. "In fact, it's past bedtime."

No one budged; their concentration was fixed on the television.

"Ahem!"

No response.

John put Nicole's hand in Cheryl's, grabbed the TV-remote, and depressed a button on the top. The TV went blank.

The kids went berserk, finally turning to look at John. "Hey!"

John held up the TV-remote and blew on it as if it were a smoking gun.

Eric started to reach for the power button on the TV.

"Don't do it," warned John. "You guys need to go to bed. It's late. You know the rules." It usually was difficult for him to be stern when he had not seen the children all day; however, he was convinced the consistent discipline would pay off when they grew up.

"Oh, Dad," came the reply, in melodramatic unison.

It took the usual hour to get the four children to bed (but not necessarily to sleep). No matter what John and Cheryl tried, the one-hour barrier could not be broken.

Exhausted, the couple met in the master bathroom. Cheryl had made it there a little bit before John. He passed by her en route to his sink on the other side of the bathroom. She stood barefoot at her sink, wearing a terry-cloth bathrobe, as she quietly flossed her teeth. Her hair was pulled up in some sort of device on top of her head with a pair of big plastic claws, and she stared absently into the mirror. Her eyes blinked, but in between the blinks, it was doubtful that she saw anything. Her brain may have subconsciously registered the spaces between her teeth, allowing the navigation of floss. She was elsewhere, as she always seemed to be at this time of night.

For a moment, John sat with his backside against the sink counter, watching her. She was still so very attractive to him, in body and soul. In terms of the former, he had wanted to nail her since the last time they had made love, a week or so ago. If she knew he was looking at her at that moment, he imagined she would think to herself, *What a sight—in a bathrobe, no makeup!* But to him, she was the most beautiful creature on earth.

"What are you looking at?" she asked.

"Oh, nothing. Just thinking about my long day."

He couldn't explain the white lie. As Cheryl turned back to her sink, John walked over to her, lovingly put his arms around the waist of the woman he dreamed about, and kissed her once on the back of her neck.

She did not turn, but she knew exactly what he was getting at. There was no response ... no participation, no compliance. John turned and walked back to his sink, the mounting passion he had felt waning.

Cheryl sat in bed, reading. She did not look up as John returned. He removed his terry-cloth robe and got into bed nude, as always. It bothered him that she did not take visible notice of him. If she were naked, he would appreciate her—at all times.

As he slid under the covers, he became precipitously more aroused. In an effort to be cute, he nudged his head onto her lap and under her book.

She ignored him and continued to read. He wondered if this were a subtle yes. His experience told him no, but his passion told him that he did not care what his experience had to say.

As John rotated his head ever-so-gracefully over the top of her soft thigh, toward what lay just inside of it, he could feel her quadriceps muscles tighten just before she dropped her book on his head.

"I'm sorry. I'm just not into it right now," she said.

"When?" he asked, rubbing the point of impact on his scalp.

"When, what?"

"When do you think, reasonably speaking, that you might be into it again? Sometime this year?"

"Whoa … low blow, John. That's uncalled for. You don't get your way, so you start putting me down. Now I know where the kids get it."

The viciousness of her last comment startled them both, although she did not apologize.

John's posture stiffened as he rolled away from Cheryl and prepared for a fight.

"Fuck you," was all that came out of his mouth.

Cheryl remained silent, refusing to act out her anger.

John realized they were both enraged far out of character. Where had all the love gone?

Cheryl took some deep breaths and turned to look at John. He lay on his side, facing away. The sheets were rising and falling at a rate that perfectly paralleled his anger.

"John? John? Honey, could you turn around, please?"

He did not shift or speak.

"We need to talk about this," she said.

"I'm all ears," he said without turning.

"From where I'm sitting, you look like you're all back," she joked.

John turned, but did not smile. "I don't get it," he said. "Why should you be mad at me? I didn't do anything wrong."

"Mad?" she said. "Who says I was mad?"

"Do you really expect me to believe you dropped that book on my head accidentally?"

"I wasn't mad …"

"But you are now, right?"

"A little."

"A little?" he repeated.

"I just don't feel like I know you."

"Ah, there it is. Here we go again. That just pisses me off. Know me? How can you not know me? We've been together twenty years, married sixteen of it. Every fucking time my schedule goes to shit, you hold me personally responsible. How can you go cold so quickly on the one you love? I just don't get it. Where did all the passion go?"

"I've spent all day with kids and kid-oriented things, went to the office in between, saw other people's kids for four hours, and then rushed home to be here for our crew when their school day was over. We've done homework. I've made dinner. We've had baths. If you don't think homework is a bitch, think again. You're never here for homework. When was the last time you were here for dinner?"

"Wednesday," he said hesitantly. "I've been on the road since 4:30 AM, going to meetings, making sales, and so on. I've spent the day with people I cannot stand. I've listened to people and smiled when I really felt like throwing them off the roof of our building. I hate my boss. The brokerage business is torture to me. Despite all this, I gladly helped put the kids to bed … and despite all this, I still want you."

"OK, calm down … by the way, do we have a good life-insurance policy on you?"

"Not funny. Don't try to lighten things up here. I've had an incredibly hard day too. Every day, lately, is a hard fucking day. At least you like your work. I can't help it if I'd like some loving from my wife when I get home. Is that too much to ask?"

"When you say it like that, it sounds perfectly reasonable. Here, let me just spread my legs, and you just hop on board and have a great old time." She threw off the covers and started to cry.

"Jeez, what are you crying about? What have I done now?"

"It's just how I am," she said. "I feel the need to communicate … connect … before I can get intimate. It's not a disease. It's just not the way *you* do things. Maybe it's the difference between men and women. I don't know. I don't know how to change it, or if I even can change it."

"You didn't used to be that way."

"I'm not sure what decade you're referring to, but before, we did not have children, a home, bills, or a tenth of the worries. So, you might be right. I can't remember that far back. But back then, we had only each other. Now we have each other, several kids, two dogs, and all this shit. Welcome to adulthood. I wouldn't trade our kids for anything, but it takes its toll."

"Look, it's fucking 10:15 PM. I gotta get up in less than six hours. I can't believe we always get into this so late at night."

"Why not? It's the only time we have to ourselves to communicate."

"Now ask yourself honestly: Wouldn't it have been so much better to have just made passionate love and gone to sleep?"

Cheryl just looked at him incredulously.

"OK, OK. Just kidding. Good night."

The landing was uneventful, despite an arid, thirty-mile-per-hour cross-wind. There, in mid-January, temperatures eclipsed eighty degrees. The airport looked more like an old military base; barbed electrical fence surrounded it. The few small buildings were dilapidated. There was no flight tower, but a radar device rotated next to the single runway, which led to a large Quonset hangar. The jet looked out of place in the humble surroundings, as did the sophisticated tank positioned to the side of the hangar. Men in turbans and linen robes stood heavily armed at all portals.

The jet taxied inside the hangar, where three vehicles waited: an ambulance and two black Mercedes, with small flags flying from small chrome poles on the hoods. Medics brought a gurney out of the ambulance and met the jet crew at the stairs.

John was carried to the gurney with the IV bottles temporarily taped across his abdomen. The doctor and nurse watched and winced as though their most treasured piece of furniture were being carried by children.

The doctor and nurse joined John and the medics in the ambulance, raising an IV pole from the side of the stretcher and re-hanging the bottles on it.

One IV tube was run through a small machine with an LED readout that matched the one in the aircraft. Once the EKG monitor and pulse oximeter were reconnected, readings resumed, and the numbers remained in the normal range.

The doctor reexamined John briefly but thoroughly and nodded at the two guards. "Look," he said. "The patient has been out for a long time now. I need to prepare him for our final destination ... wherever that is."

This time, an answer came, and without hesitation: "We'll be there in less than an hour."

Chapter 4

"Thank you for calling Locke, Stocker, and Granitelli. This is Ms. Harrington. How may I direct your call?"

"Donna, this is Cheryl Harris, trying to reach my husband, John. I'm only getting his voice mail; he's not picking up his cell phone."

"Hmm. I don't know why no one picked up. The office must be empty. Tell you what: hold on, and let me check it from this end … Nope. Lois is gone and his office lights are out."

"What? That makes no sense. Let me speak to Mr. Mankin, please."

"Sure, I'll transfer you."

"Thanks." Cheryl waited anxiously, already beginning to wonder if something awful might have happened, and already reassuring herself that she was being ridiculous.

"Harvey Mankin's office."

"Hi, Harvey, how are you? This is Cheryl Harris."

"Cheryl? Wow, I haven't talked to you for …" A conversation ensued, with his hand obviously over the receiver. "I'm sorry about that. How the heck are you?"

"Just fine. Listen, have you seen John today? As you know, Lois is usually long gone by now, that lucky lady, and he's not answering his phone. I wanted to see if I could meet him for dinner."

"You two have a little tiff?"

"Harvey! Now, did I forget about some big meeting this evening or something?"

"No, no. I haven't seen him today. He missed our usual AM meeting, but that happens to all of us once in a while. Missed a tennis game with Bob, too. Hold on … let me go check his desk. Be right back."

"Could you? I'd appreciate that."

There was no response; Harvey was already on the move.

It had been difficult for Cheryl to ask for Harvey. John's miserable boss at brokerage and his wife had been over to the house a few times, so that John could entertain and kiss butt. Cheryl had advised John after their last visit that life was too short to have to spend an evening, or even a portion of an evening, with two pompous assholes like the Mankins.

"Cheryl?"

"Yes."

"I'm baffled. I don't see anything on his desk that would suggest he was in today. Now you got me thinking. I'm sure there's a logical reason for this. Tell you what. Give me your number again, so I don't have to look it up. I'm gonna ask around, check his parking spot. OK? I'll call you back in ten."

"Thanks. I'll be getting the kids ready for sleep, so it may ring a bit, but I'll pick it up."

"Hi, Cheryl. I can't find anyone who has seen John today. Lois didn't make it in either. I just spoke with her at home … car troubles. But—"

"Harvey, I don't mean to interrupt, but what the hell do you mean he didn't show up at work today? He had no appointments outside. Has he ever *not* shown up at work?"

"Well …"

"Come on, Harvey. Be honest."

"Well, not often. But from time to time, we've got to meet or entertain clients … that type of thing."

"Sure, but he would never leave town without telling me, not to mention his secretary. Christ, she makes his flight arrangements. Now, yes or no—do you know where he could be? I'm really worried."

"Don't panic, now. There has to be a reasonable explanation. There always is."

Nausea blossomed deep in the pit of Cheryl's stomach. A sour taste developed in her mouth—a taste she had hated since the first time she vomited as a child.

"Well," she said, "if you figure it out, please call me immediately."

Cheryl closed her eyes, fought back tears, and tried to concentrate on everything John had said over the last forty-eight hours, even the innuendos. The only notable circumstance that registered was that they had fought briefly the night before over her understandable lack of interest in making love. There was nothing else. He had said nothing about any meeting, about anything outside of work. She knew him too well to have missed anything subtle.

"Dammit, John … where the hell are you?" she said aloud.

"Hey, Mom," said her eldest son, Eric, with Erin in tow.

"What?"

"You just said, 'Where the blank is Dad?'" Eric smiled devilishly.

"Yeah, you used the d-word and the h-word," said Erin.

"Oh, I'm sorry, honey … that wasn't right, was it? I apologize. Listen, Eric, you and Erin need to go to bed now. I'm not going to be able to help, but I'll try to come by and tuck you two in. Look at me. No messing around. Into bed, lights out. Thank you, guys."

"What about Dad?"

"Oh, you know what? He's running really late. You'll have to see him tomorrow. By the way … did either of you talk to Daddy today?"

"No."

When the kids had thumped their way up the stairs, the smile disappeared from Cheryl's face, and she hurried into the kitchen. She thought for a moment before picking up the phone.

"Hello? I need to speak to the Larchmont Police Department."

From the kitchen, Cheryl could see the lights on the driveway and the front of the house go on with the associated single ring of a bell. It was what Cheryl had been waiting for. Could John finally have made it home? She ran to the front door, opened it, and stood on the front porch, struggling to see past the bright headlights. The plain police car circled and parked next to her car, just as John would have. It was 10:37 PM.

Two men in their mid-fifties exited and approached the porch. Both wore generic suits. Weapons were not obvious, but surely present.

"One of you must be Detective Marley," said Cheryl disappointedly. She had forgotten that she left the front gate open.

"You must be Mrs.—I mean, *Dr.* Harris. I'm Detective Marley." The taller of the two shook her hand. "Thank you for leaving the gate open for us."

Cheryl found Marley serious, strong looking, and fatherly, which comforted her. His dress was professional, and he was very matter-of-fact in his posture, movement, and tone.

"And I'm Detective Panzer," the other man said.

"Nice to meet you," she said. Panzer appeared portly, relaxed, and somewhat disheveled. "Would you like to come in?"

They followed Cheryl to the living room. All took a seat. Panzer took out a pad and pen, but Marley spoke first.

"I want to let you know a few things before we start asking you a bunch of questions, some of which may seem irrelevant and even too personal. OK?"

"Sure."

"OK … first off, a missing-person report has not yet been made. Before we leave, we need the most recent picture of John that you can supply us with. We've checked all the ERs, and no one has been checked in under the name of John Harris or John Harris III all day, as of about an hour ago. If he does show up in any of them, we'll be called immediately. This is my card. My beeper is active twenty-four hours a day … I'm sorry, Doctor. Are you OK?"

"No, I am not OK," she snapped. "My husband's gone. This is absolutely out of character. I'm worried. I'm really worried!" The detectives looked directly at her without breaking eye contact, to let her know that they were with her. She softened. "I'm sorry … I'm so upset."

"No, no, it's quite all right. We understand. That's why we're here." Marley handed her a tissue. "May we continue?"

She nodded as she blew her nose.

"The state police report no accidents. County sheriff and Larchmont police have nothing to report. Forest rangers, AAA … nothing. So, when was the last time you saw him?"

"This morning … well, last night, really. I think I remember him kissing me this morning, but I may have been dreaming." She closed her eyes. When she opened them, hoping to awake from her nightmare, the two detectives were still sitting in her living room.

"Did he say anything unusual?"

"No. Well … we kind of had a fight … but no. Nothing."

"What did you fight about?"

"Are you serious?"

"Absolutely," Marley said. "I think you can imagine how that would be an important question."

She paused, then answered, "It was nothing earthshaking. The bottom line is that he's been working his tail off at work, and there has been … slight tension and distance in our relationship."

"Slight?"

"Yes. We had a short discussion-slash-argument about this, as we do a few times a year. It's part of the process of getting close again."

Marley leaned forward. "OK … bottom line, Dr. Harris: Were you guys having marital difficulties to the point that he would consider leaving you? I do remember you telling me on the phone that you had four kids."

She looked incredulously at him, and then at his partner. "Without question, no." She realized she was going to need to leave her emotions elsewhere, as when she worked with a seriously ill child. She had to get the work done and suppress the awful, personal feelings. Like most physicians, she was good at it.

"Can you think of a reason, any reason, your husband would want to leave you?"

"No. We have a wonderful relationship … a wonderful family and home life. This is his sanctuary. He wouldn't run from it. No."

"OK … can you think of anyone who would want him dead?"

"No!" she answered, her voice breaking momentarily. She regained her composure. "Detectives, despite being professionals, my husband and I are normal people. Nothing fringy. No drugs. Nothing kinky. No weird friends. No BS. No skeletons in the closet. No enemies. No financial problems. No neighbor disputes."

Detective Marley nodded, but couldn't seem to summon a smile. "It's late. We'll be done soon. Just a few more questions along this line. In the years of your relationship with John, can you think of anybody your husband has intentionally or unintentionally pissed off?"

"Like what? Like who?"

"Like … someone at work, say. An old or current secretary or co-worker with a grudge. Any incidents, no matter how slight or unimportant they might seem."

"No. No one. John's good in that way. He doesn't alienate people."

"What kind of work, exactly, did your husband do?"

"*Does*! What kind of work *does* my husband do."

"I'm sorry," said Marley as his face began to flush. It was a sizable slip for a man who prided himself at being both accurate and sensitive to the needs of his customers.

"He's a stockbroker. You know—trading, stocks and bonds. He works for a big company, is fairly high up. Doesn't own it."

"Can you tell us his daily routine, please?"

"He gets up very early Monday through Friday, because of the time difference with New York. You know ... the New York Stock Exchange. He gets up around four or four thirty and gets into work around five ... five thirty at the latest. He rarely makes it home before seven thirty at night. John's weekends are mostly his ... ours. The exceptions are the rare occasions that he has to go out of town on business. Thank God that doesn't happen very often. We vacation four weeks a year. Is that relevant?"

The officers nodded.

"Now," Marley began, "you said Lois told your husband's boss that she didn't make it to work today because of car problems, right?"

Cheryl just nodded.

"Do you know her home phone?"

"No."

"At the risk of being nosy and offensive, could your husband be having an affair with her?"

"No." Cheryl's insides went numb.

"Again, forgive the question ... but has your husband ever had an affair?"

"No!"

"I'm sorry. But can I keep going with the real personal questions and just get them out of the way?"

She nodded again.

"OK. Are you having, or have you ever had, an affair?"

"No," she said, looking directly into his eyes.

"Who does the accounting in your family? You know, the simple stuff: checks and balances, savings, bank accounts?"

"I do the bulk of it. I use Quicken on the computer."

"Oh, yeah. Good program. My wife uses it too," said Panzer.

"For you and John?"

"Yep."

"Have you noticed any irregularities? Any unusual deposits? Unusual payments?"

She thought for a moment. "No."

"Does all the money come through you before it gets deposited, regardless of the source?"

"Yes, with the exception of his pension. That's invested in pretax dollars, before he gets his paycheck. He, of course, decides where the investments go."

"He's your broker. OK. Do you have a life-insurance policy?"

"On me personally? We each have a life-insurance policy."

"How much is his?"

"Something on the order of 1.2 million."

"Who is or are the beneficiaries?"

"Me and the kids on his."

"Does John play any regular sports? Company teams, you know, that type of thing?"

"No. I mean, he plays tennis as often as he can … which isn't much."

"Does he have a regular watering hole?"

"I wish. His schedule is so tight during the week, there's just no time for it."

Without warning, Cheryl found herself crying again. She just shook her head as Detective Panzer slid her another tissue.

"Take a minute," Marley said gently, "and then maybe you can take us on a tour of your home."

After a short while, Cheryl stood. "Well, obviously this is the living room. Isn't it lovely?" she asked, laughing and crying at the same time. She looked at Detective Marley. "I want my husband back."

"You know, Doctor, I want to get him back for you. Something's wrong here. But we don't know that foul play is the answer. We cannot officially call it a missing-person case until twenty-four hours has lapsed or we have concrete proof of something happening to him. Nonetheless, we will do our best to find your husband. Rest assured."

For some reason, Cheryl was not reassured.

After viewing the house room by room, the detectives said good night and checked out the toolshed and horse stables with their flashlights. The Harrises owned several acres of land, but a nighttime search would be futile. Besides, at that stage of the game, it just was not necessary.

As the detectives walked back to their cars, the lights went on in the front of the house and along the driveway. At first the officers thought their footsteps had triggered the sensor, but a BMW sedan pulled into sight and looped in front of the house. The lone driver opened the door, and the car pitched as a heavy, well-dressed man got out.

The detectives identified themselves.

"I'm Harvey Mankin, John Harris's supervisor," said the man, examining their IDs. "Have you found John?"

"We're just getting under way."

The front door opened, and Cheryl came out, almost running.

"Harvey, any word?"

"No. I wish. Just came by on my way home to see if there was any news."

"Doctor, would you mind if we took a few minutes alone with Mr.... did you say Manken, M-a-n-k-e-n?" Marley asked. Panzer had his pad out again.

"Yes, close enough."

"Uh, sir, we need the accurate spelling."

"M-a-n-k-i-n."

"Harvey, come on in after, OK?" Cheryl said. "I'll put on some more coffee."

The detectives waited until Cheryl was out of earshot.

"Do you have the slightest idea of where John is?" Marley asked.

"I sure as hell wish I did."

"Any hypotheses?"

"Not really. How about you boys?" Harvey answered sarcastically.

"Like I said, we're just getting under way. Did you miss that?" Detective Marley's shot got no reply, so he continued. "Has anything like this ever happened before with John?"

"No."

"How long has he been working under you?"

"Oh, about seven years."

"And you guys do stocks and bonds, roughly that kind of stuff, right?"

"Roughly, yes."

"Dr. Harris told us about his no-show at work today ... the car not being there, the whole thing. Do you have anything to add, no matter how small of insignificant it may seem?"

"No. Not that I can think of."

"Is John in any sort of trouble?"

"What?"

"You know—drugs, financial, that kind of thing."

"Not that I know of," he replied, shaking his head from side to side.

"Does he function independently of you, or are you aware of all his dealings at work?"

"He's in a high position, but let me put it this way: I'm aware of all the financial dealings of those below me on a daily basis."

"Any problems—illegal-type dealings, major dollar losses, maybe—that would piss a client off?"

"Knock on wood, we've done very well for our clients over the years. We're a publicly held company, so we're scrutinized from the outside as well as inside. John Harris is clean."

"How about you, Mr. Mankin? Are you clean?"

He paused before answering. "Crystal."

"That's a good one," said Panzer. "I saw that movie too."

"Mr. Mankin, I don't want to get into a pissing match with you," Detective Marley interceded. "We're here to find John as quickly as possible. If you think of anything, see or hear of anything, please call us immediately." He handed Harvey his card.

When Mankin left, the detectives looked at each other.

"You sure pissed the fat boy off," said Panzer.

Marley smiled at the thought. "I don't think we burned down any bridges. We just set him straight, right?"

"What you mean *we*, white man?"

Marley just shook his head, his smile fading more quickly than was customary. It was late, he was tired, they had no leads, and he had a bad feeling they wouldn't be closing this case anytime soon.

Chapter 5

The procession passed through several miles of gently rolling, virgin sand dunes. Viewed from the side, the edges of the dune ridges carved perfect arcs across the lower sky. Unlike most deserts, this one lay under swarms of oil rigs, each moving rhythmically, if not in concert, with the others. A large city loomed in the distance.

If John were awake, he would have been appalled by the stark contrast between his Mercedes-heavy entourage and the squalor of the people it drove past. The air-conditioned environment in which John traveled belied the poverty of the country the ambulance belonged to.

In the heart of the city, the caravan entered a three-story hospital building and proceeded down a gated and guarded ramp under the building.

The ambulance backed up to an entrance, and two armed guards in camouflaged fatigues opened the rear doors. The nurse moved the IV bottles from their hanging position on the roof of the ambulance to a self-contained pole on the gurney. The gurney, deeply sedated stockbroker aboard, was removed from the ambulance and rolled into the hospital, with the doctor and nurse in tow.

They entered a service elevator and took it to the top floor, where security was even more intense. A man who appeared to be in command spoke loudly and castigated the team for running late.

To the right stood two large doors, with big, bright red Arabic letters covering each. They opened, and behind them stood soldiers dressed in surgical attire: blue paper pants, tops, foot covers, hats, masks and sterilized weapons. The large, bearded guard from the jet steered his team in their direction. He

was careful to stop without crossing the large, red line on the floor that demar-
cated the germ-free space beyond.

In English, he said, "We must relinquish our passenger at this point."

Words were exchanged in Arabic with the door guards.

John was moved onto a new gurney and wheeled away, the doors closing
behind him. After a few minutes, an unarmed man came out in a similar scrub
outfit. He had a stethoscope-like device with only a single earplug pinned to
his shirt. He addressed the nurse and doctor in English. His American accent
contrasted sharply with the foreign surroundings.

"You're late. Were you able to follow the sedation protocol and preparation?"

"Wait a minute," said the doctor, trying to keep his voice level. "You mean
to tell me they send out the anesthesiologist, not the surgeon? I don't get to
speak to the surgeon?"

"Keep it down!" the anesthesiologist said in a sharp whisper. The accent
sounded Texan. "Is this your first time? These people are fanatics. They see shit
entirely different than us. Be careful, be gracious, be humble … or you'll find
yourself dead." He quieted his own voice as if by example. "Now, yes or no on
the sedation and prep?"

"Yes."

The nurse simply looked on in horror.

"Did you have to give anything more than the sedation medication?"

"We had to partially reverse it once about an hour and a half ago," the nurse
said.

"Yeah, but he didn't wake up, and he didn't need to be intubated," added the
doctor defensively.

"Pre-op labs?"

The doctor reached into his coat and handed over the printed results. "All
normal."

"I's and O's?"

"3.2 liters in, 2.5 out," replied the nurse.

"Perfect. Well, I gotta go. Best of luck to you all. And … remember what I
told you."

He turned, opened one of the doors, and entered the void.

John's limp body was moved from the stretcher onto an operating table surrounded by three scrub nurses, the anesthesiologist, and two more guards in
scrub suits. The floors were lined with sparkling white tiles that ran halfway up

the walls and radiated sterility. Huge surgical lights adorned the ceiling. Although there was no ceiling glass for scholastic viewing, the operating room rivaled that of any major teaching center, contrasting starkly with the rest of the hospital.

On one of the walls to the side of the operating table sat an elaborate, small Plexiglas bath of sorts that bubbled with oxygen and circulating water.

The nurses used large shears to cut off the rest of John's expensive suit. The pieces were pulled out from underneath him as he was rolled from side to side, then tossed into a plastic trash bag. The anesthesiologist approached while the nurses changed his leg bag to a much larger urine-collection bag that hung from the underside of the front of the table.

The anesthesiologist frog-legged John's flaccid legs and placed a thermometer probe in his rectum. He removed the previous cardiac leads on John's chest and placed his own; wires connected these to a machine at the head of the table. Another chrome device was taped over John's throat, just below the Adam's apple. The anesthesiologist walked back to John's side and looked at his left arm.

"May I have the A-line tray, please?"

A nurse rolled up a stand with an opened kit on top. The anesthesiologist plucked the gloves from the top and placed them on his hands. The doctor used a dark, liquid soap to cleanse the palm side of John's wrist. He palpated the thumb side of the wrist with his left index finger and guided a needle through John's skin, just below his finger. He hit bright red blood quickly. The doctor advanced the clear sheath over the needle and into the artery. When he removed the needle, blood shot out the end of the sheath and almost halfway across the room. The nurse quickly connected a line to the sheath with a screwing motion.

"Go ahead and calibrate that and give me a pressure reading, please."

After less than a minute, she said, "101/73, good wave form."

"Excellent, thank you. OK, call for the IVP."

The doctor picked a huge syringe and injected its contents slowly into John's IV. The anesthesiologist knew the thick solution would course into John's veins and quickly find its way to his kidneys. As the syringe emptied, a portable x-ray machine was rolled into the surgical suite, and an x-ray film was placed below John's back. About one minute after the dye was pushed, a single x-ray of John's abdomen was taken. The machine and its technician disappeared as rapidly as they had appeared.

"Let's intubate him, and then you can go ahead and start your prep," the anesthesiologist said.

John was kept on his back. The doctor, standing at the head of the table, grabbed a preselected clear tube about fourteen inches long. Coursing through the middle of it was a malleable metal rod that allowed the tube to be bent into just about any shape desired. Looking at John's external anatomy, the anesthesiologist sculpted the tube into a suitable configuration. A chrome instrument placed in his other hand was reminiscent of a miniature scythe, with a light at its tip. Looking ready, he calmly called an order to one of the nurses.

"Go ahead and give the paralyzing agent now, please. Anectine."

Soon, John would stop breathing.

"Cricoid pressure, please."

The lighted metal instrument was gently inserted into the back of John's throat. His head was slightly lifted off the table by the force applied to the instrument. The anesthesiologist peered down the curved part of the instrument in John's throat and immediately recognized the important landmarks. With a few minor adjustments, the vocal cords came into clear view. The clear tube in his other hand was placed in John's mouth and inserted a few inches beyond the vocal cords. The balloon at the end of this tube was filled with air to keep the tube from coming out errantly and to keep any regurgitated stomach contents from going into the lungs.

In rapid sequence, the doctor attached his ambu-bag to the visible end of the tube and breathed for John. With each squeeze of the bag, John's chest rose and then fell. A nurse took over as the doctor pushed one of his large machines over and replaced the ambu-bag with the tubing emanating from the machine. The machine displayed a number of dials, each of which was adjusted to both breathe for John and to give him gaseous anesthetics through the same tube. The tube in John's mouth was secured with a plastic device that went over it and between his lips.

"OK, let's turn him, so you can start the prep."

The nurses rolled John like a log onto his right side and belted him onto the surgical table. They used square scrub brushes impregnated with a dark brown, iodine-based soap to wash his flank in circular movements. The anesthesiologist placed foam pillows under John's head, shoulder, hip, and between his knees and ankles to keep pressure from causing damage to nerves. An electrical grounding pad was placed on his left thigh, and the nurses covered him with an array of sterile drapes. Another large drape was placed at his shoulders, so that his head and neck were all that was visible on one side of the drape, with the rest of his body on the other. Two large trays full of surgical instruments on tall stands were moved up to the patient.

The technician returned and placed an x-ray film on a view box on the wall before exiting briskly. Even a layperson could recognize two bright objects, one on each side, high in the abdomen. Small tubes led away from each to the bladder sitting in the pelvis.

"That ought to make the surgeons happy," said the anesthesiologist. "Two big kidneys, normal ureters."

One of the nurses left momentarily and returned, followed by two masked surgeons, who held their washed, dripping arms upright in front of their bodies. A full ten-minute scrub to eliminate all germs from the skin was undertaken to avoid contamination from accidental glove damage. Another nurse handed them each a sterile towel that they used to dry their extremities, starting from the hands and moving towards the elbows. They were then each handed a sterile surgical gown, which they deftly put on. Then they turned so a nurse could tie the gowns in the back. Each was then handed sterile gloves that they adroitly pulled onto their hands without contaminating the outsides. During this process, they had managed to read the x-ray hanging on the view box. Now, facing the patient, each approached on a different side and stepped up on step stools. The primary surgeon felt through the drapes for four key landmarks: the bottom left rib, the bony crest of the left pelvic brim, the stomach, and the back.

"Scalpel."

He was handed the enduring and essential surgical instrument. A long incision was made in a semihorseshoe shape over the flank, extending further onto the back than the stomach. The expectant bleeding in the skin was completely arrested by hot electrical cautery. The patient did not flinch.

The incision was deepened layer by layer with fastidious attention and expertise. Finally, a special layer of recognizable tissue was reached. It identified the organ of desire that lay just below it.

The next part of the surgery would be the most complex. A major artery, a major vein, and another muscular, tubular structure would need to be transected, and the organ plucked out rapidly and placed in an organ-sustaining bath, all within a few moments.

The anesthesiologist continued to monitor the vital body functions of heart rate, blood pressure, breathing, oxygen content in the blood, and temperature, as well as depth of unconsciousness.

The surgeons visualized the large vessels running in and out of the kidney. The primary surgeon palpated the artery and placed a clamp.

"Prepare the bath," one said.

The extraction commenced when everything was perfect. "Voila!" said the primary surgeon as he held up the organ away from the surgical field and admired it for a fleeting moment. It was a beautiful and vital organ, perfectly shaped and healthy. He placed it in the bath and immediately connected tubes to two of the three large vessels coursing from the middle of the kidney. The assistant surgeon began to work on his own to close up the gaping wound in John's side. John was now officially minus a kidney.

Although the anesthesiologist pretended not to watch, something unusual transpired. Typically, an icebox would await the organ. The organ would be cooled down quickly and placed into the box. The box would then be taken to a "runner," who would deliver the organ immediately to any of a zillion destinations around the globe. Today, however, the organ was not removed from the bath, and not cooled down. Instead, the bath was unplugged and rolled, on auxiliary power, to the door, where the awaiting personnel continued the transit to somewhere beyond the closed doors. He knew much better than to ask questions.

The bath was rolled to the door of another operating room nearby and stopped. One of the guards bowed his head and knocked demurely. The two doors swung open, and several weapon-laden security guards exited and surrounded this group. This operating room was different than the other one with respect to its adornments. There were several religious relics on the walls and a quiet chanting from within. There was another patient on an operating table, similarly draped, with machines running. A whole new Caucasian crew and anesthesiologist were present. This patient was lying on his back, and all that was visible was a gaping lower abdominal incision. Despite the surgical shrouding, the recipient appeared substantially shorter than the donor. One surgeon stood at his side. There was a small amount of blood on his gloves and robe.

Both the assistant and the main surgeon had little tolerance for the rituals taking place. Since both wanted to live longer and certainly prosper, neither let his feelings be known, in any form, to his employers.

The primary surgeon walked toward the door. A man in religious garb was blessing the newly removed kidney. The surgeon waited patiently, and when the parishioner finished, he received the bath, which flushed the sacred organ with its bubbly solution. He looked back to the other surgeon and nodded in approval.

"Good-sized afferents and efferents," he said in a British accent. He paused for a moment and then continued, "Excellent specimen. Excellent."

He was most careful not to touch anything but the inside of the bath, lest he violate his sterility and potentially risk the entire surgery due to infection. There just was no room for error on this particular transplantation.

He disconnected the kidney from the two tubes and carefully carried it in both hands over to the operating field.

"Start the clock now."

He quickly laid the organ on the drape above the incision and changed his gloves, just to be safe. Three clamped vessels were visible in the field below. They corresponded to the three vessels of the donor kidney. The donor and recipient's vessels' caliber was not quite the same, but it did not matter.

"Let's connect the artery first," the surgeon said, bringing John's kidney closer to the incision. "Microscope, please."

A sterile microscope on a large arm was brought into the surgical field. It had two sets of binoculars, so that both surgeons could work together to hook the kidney up to it's new owner.

"OK, let's take down the clamps and fire her up."

The clamps were removed, and the kidney changed quickly from its oxygen-starved bluish shade to a nice, rich, healthy pink.

"No bleeding from the surgical sites," the surgeon said. "Give the second dose of the anti-rejection medication IV, and let's close up."

Layer by layer, the abdominal wall was sutured tightly as the anti-rejection drugs took action. These drugs have made transplantations possible since their initial synthesis back in the 1980's. Although these medications did not offer a 100 percent guarantee, in the predominance of cases, these drugs kept the body from reacting against the transplanted organ. Once rejection of the organ got firmly under way, it was almost impossible to stop the stampede of events that would undo so much work and banish so much hope.

If John's kidney worked as well as it was supposed to in its new home, it would return its recipient to an essentially normal life. It would sever the recipient's umbilical connection to the hemodialysis machine, the use of which previously had been necessary for several hours, several days a week. It would stave off the anemia that accompanies renal failure, as well as the skin changes and gradual wasting away that is seen with chronic kidney failure.

The lead surgeon had been meticulous in his technique. As with the many other similar surgeries, he did not find it hard to imagine why one would desire a successful kidney transplant and would go to almost any extreme to make it happen.

The doctor and nurse sat by themselves in a poorly lit room in the hospital, waiting. They were both exhausted from the intensely vigilant care that they had rendered to their patient while flying the friendly skies. Although they each tried to doze off, neither could. It wasn't the heat or the perspiration.

"How long do we have to wait?"

"We'll be the first to know. Try to get some rest in the meantime," answered the doctor, pretending that she had interrupted his sleep.

"This place gives me the creeps."

The doctor just looked at her without response. Suddenly, the bearded Arab guard walked in the open door. "Let's go," the guard said.

The two health-care providers hopped to their feet like cadets and followed the robed soldier to the elevator. He did not pause to let them pass first. When the doors closed, the aroma of his sweat was almost nauseating. He stared at the opposite wall in a noncommittal fashion.

The doctor fumbled to make conversation. "That was close back there on the airplane on the way in, but I think he'll be just fine. Just fine."

"Yeah, we fixed him up. He'll be just fine," echoed the nurse.

The soldier paid no attention. When the door opened again, he exited without a word and headed toward the ambulance. They followed. The ambulance attendants were smoking and joking until they saw the soldier. At that point, they extinguished their cigarettes and stood at attention.

"You ride back here," he said to the doctor and nurse. "It's time to go." He signaled to the attendants to drive as he opened the rear of the van and stepped back.

As the doctor and nurse climbed in, the guard brandished his silenced automatic weapon and killed them both. If they had managed to look back, they would have seen the smile on his face. He simply closed the doors and walked to the cab.

"Take them to where the camels sleep."

Chapter 6

The next day might as well have been the same day. Cheryl hadn't slept. She had tossed and turned and awakened multiple times. She couldn't stop thinking the most horrible thoughts. Her Johnny would never return to her. What would she do—a single mom with four children, out in the country, with no one to share life's richness with? She would be so empty without him. The practice, the country, the horses ... none of it meant anything without John. She just knew that something horrible had happened to her husband.

She stood in her bathrobe, sipping coffee and looking out the window of the kitchen into the several acres that lay beyond. Marley and Panzer were examining the soil leading up to the stables. Cheryl marveled at how late they had left the night before, and how early they must have started that morning. It gave her some comfort to know they were delving so intently into John's disappearance. She looked at her watch to see exactly how early it was.

"Oh ... the kids!" It was seven fifteen, and she was thirty minutes late in waking them for school. She ran down the hallway to their bedrooms and awoke the three older ones. "Come on, you guys, it's late ... my fault, let's go. No showers, no teeth brushing this morning ... just get dressed and eat. Rise and shine, everybody."

Unlike John, the kids never jumped out of bed immediately and quickly did what needed to be done. So much in her existed in relation to John: How would John do it? How would John see it? She could not live without John, period.

"Oh, Mom! You know I like to wash my hair before I go to school!" exclaimed Eric.

"Well, excuse me, but if it's that important, you have an alarm. Use it." She continued in a nicer tone, having caught her own edge. "Michael, little one … wake up, sleepy head."

As the kindergartner, he was still essentially a baby and required extra care. The hugs he gave in the morning and at bedtime were always special. At that moment, they were especially appreciated.

In the kitchen, she put out bowls and spoons, as well as a multitude of cereal boxes and the milk jug. The waffles went into the toaster as Cheryl poured a second cup of coffee. She reached into her purse and pulled out six dollars, placing two dollar bills on each of their place mats. She did not have the time or inclination to prepare lunch.

When breakfast was complete, the kids grabbed their backpacks and headed outside with their mother's assistance. The bus would pick them up at the end of the drive.

Eric was the last one out. "Mom, who are those guys in the backyard?"

"Oh, you saw them? They're just property inspectors … no big deal."

"Come on, Mom, they've got suits on. And they look like cops."

"Don't be ridiculous. Now, go on, before you're late. I love you."

"You too," he replied, and he was gone.

She reflected on how perceptive he was, even at the tender age of almost twelve. She had averted giving the bad news for a few more hours, but soon she would have to level with the children. How would they handle it? She suspected that the little ones would handle it better than the big ones. Certainly the baby would be the least of Cheryl's problems.

The children had been gone for twenty minutes. Cheryl stood in the kitchen, back to the counter, sipping her coffee and staring off into a dimension beyond the walls. Her trance was interrupted by a knock on the front door.

Marley and Panzer looked through the screen door.

"Gentlemen."

"Mrs. Harris," Marley said, speaking for the duo as always. "Do you mind if we call you that, rather than Doctor? I think you need to be a wife now, not a doctor." She nodded. "Could you accompany us partway down the driveway? You may need to change your shoes first." He glanced at her slippers.

She kicked off her slippers, then slid her feet into a pair of loafers she kept by the door. "What's going on?" she asked.

"We just need to show you something and ask a question. Did you have anything to do with the security system of this house, or was it here before you moved in?"

"No … that was mostly John's department. The system installation was a concession I made so that John could feel safer. You know how those city boys are."

They walked most of the way down the gravel drive and stopped at the edge.

"Do you know what this is?"

"Yeah, it's the infrared sensing device for the drive and front lights. It also chimes a bell in the house. Why?"

"Look closely there, on the side. Did it always have that on it?"

"Gosh, I don't know … I don't remember. What is it?"

On the outside of the sensor was a shiny one-inch cube with a small, antenna like projection from its top. It clearly was not an original part of the weathered sensor.

"I'd bet anything that it's some sort of transmitter," Marley said. "No! Sorry, don't step into the dirt, please."

"And?"

"And, if it is, it might tell someone at a distant location that your drive lights have been triggered."

"Why would anyone want to know that?" The two detectives looked at each other and gave her a minute to sort it out. "Oh, oh … then they'd know when someone left the property, right? Is that what you mean?"

"Mrs. Harris, I'm sorry, but I think that now we're going to have to officially list your husband as missing."

Cheryl had known those words would come; the words didn't surprise her—unlike the tidal wave of emotion that now threatened to bring her to her knees. She broke down and sobbed. Marley held her. When she calmed a little, he asked, "May I use your phone? My battery's low and reception's not too good up here."

They walked back to the house, with Cheryl keeping to herself. Marley let himself into the kitchen and phoned the Larchmont station. He arranged for an upgrade in the status of John Harris III. He also asked for a member of the fingerprinting team and a footprinter to meet him in the drive within the hour.

The children began their trek up the driveway, dancing and frolicking and playing with each other. In the usual fashion, about three-quarters of the way up the drive, the playing abruptly stopped as they all broke into a full sprint, racing to see who would hit the porch first. In theory, that would determine who got to play Nintendo first. The reality was that the oldest, Eric, always got his way, regardless of how he placed in the heat.

They entered the house and immediately sensed a problem. Their loud voices and energy dissipated quickly.

"Hey … what's Grammy doing here? Hi, Grammy," said Eric.

"Grammy!" yelled Michael and Erin as they ran to greet her. She stood there with bloodshot eyes and a bunched-up Kleenex in one hand.

"Kids, after you say hi to Grammy, I need to sit down and talk with you," Cheryl said. "It's important."

Hugs were exchanged, and Michael shared his day with his grandmother. Cheryl gave them all a snack and sat her captive audience down at the kitchen table (with the exception of Nicole, who watched *Beauty and the Beast* in the family room for the thousandth time).

Michael concentrated happily on the sweets, as he always did when sugar was served. Eric and Erin, however, were tentative with theirs, sensing danger.

"We think there's something wrong with Daddy," said Cheryl, her voice cracking and tears welling in her eyes.

They all stopped eating immediately. Gone were any expressions of enjoyment; they had been replaced with grave faces.

"Like what?" asked Eric, speaking for all the children.

Erin started crying; she was always so in touch with her mother's feelings.

"He didn't come home last night. He never made it to work yesterday. No one has seen him. No one knows where he is."

"Mom," said Eric, visibly upset, "maybe he had to go out of town and forgot to tell us."

"I've checked that out. That just isn't true. I wish it were."

"Yes, it is! You just don't know! You're stupid!" Michael retorted tearfully.

Cheryl moved quickly to comfort and hold him. She cried and whispered to him, "I wish it were true, sweetie." She pulled Eric into the hug. She knew he had to be upset, but would have trouble experiencing and verbalizing it at his age. Erin was already at her side. They all hugged. Grammy Eleanor stood by herself in the kitchen, clutching her tissue and crying to herself. She moved toward the group.

"Everything is gonna be all right," she said as she touched Cheryl's shoulder.

The muscles in Cheryl's shoulder and neck tightened. "Mom, you always say shit like that." She paused to understand the flurry of thoughts and emotion that had seemed to come out of nowhere. She continued in a more controlled fashion. "I don't mean to take it out on you, but you have responded to crisis like that as long as I can remember. It just doesn't fit. It's not real. It's not in keeping with the circumstances. How can what has happened possibly be OK, all right, or anything good ... or even acceptable? It just can't. Don't try to smooth things over unless you have a real factual or emotional basis to it. Just be there. It's more real and helpful."

Eleanor joined in the hug and tears. For the longest time, no one wanted to break the group hug.

"Kids, I've got to start dinner," Cheryl finally said. "You're welcome to stay in here with me and help, or just stay here. I'm thinking that if any of you can remember anything interesting or unusual that Daddy may have said or done, let me know, so I can tell the detectives."

"Is that who those men really were this morning?" Eric asked.

"Yes. And I'm sorry for lying. I just didn't want to upset you before school. I hope you'll forgive me. I think it was the best thing to do at the time."

"Oh, no problem, Mom." As the eldest son, Eric had just begun filling in his Dad's footsteps—taking care of Mom.

Dinner was completed, homework was finished, and the children were in bed. Grammy had read Michael a bedtime story and retired into the guest room. When a knock sounded at the front door, Cheryl was the only one to hear it. Her guests had already called her to let them in the front gate.

She opened the front door to see Marley and Panzer. They looked serious, and Cheryl started to cry instinctively.

"Oh, I'm sorry," said Marley. "No, it's not that bad."

She looked back at both of them, alternating from one set of eyes to the other rapidly, and then spoke. "Please come in."

They sat in the living room again.

"We've found his car," Marley said. "It's empty. No blood, no direct signs of foul play."

"Where? And what do you mean by 'no direct signs'?"

"At the old Larchmont Fashion Mall ..."

"Now, what would it be doing there? He would never, ever go there. First of all, he doesn't shop. Second, if he did, he wouldn't go there. It just doesn't make sense—"

"There's something more that I—we—find of concern," Marley said.

"What's that?"

"There are no fingerprints. Not a one."

"So?"

"Not even John's. It's strange. The whole car has been wiped down. All fingerprints are gone. We usually find fingerprints ... the owner's, the wife's, the kids'. None."

"So what are you thinking?"

"Well, one of two possibilities. Either someone ... well, let me put it this way. Either it's very professional, or it's totally amateur. So that doesn't help us, except that we now know it was deliberate. Either your husband wiped down the whole car, or someone else did."

"Look," Cheryl said forcefully, "I know you don't know me or John or anything else. But if you have a sense of me and my sincerity, you'll know it was someone else. I know it's your job to question all angles, but I'd hate to see you waste energy on one path, instead of moving full speed down another. I'm not stupid. I know factually, and I know inside, that every day that passes means that it is less likely that you will find my John."

"We appreciate your honesty, but we wouldn't be doing our jobs if we didn't consider everyone a suspect, even your husband. Have no fear. We will cover every base, turn every single stone. We will find him."

"I wish I felt as confident. Have you anything else to go on?"

"No, not yet."

Chapter 7

Nearly a week had passed when Cheryl went to work for the first time since John's disappearance. The children pretty much acted normally now, although they fought more, unaware that their quibbles were typically over who got more attention. Cheryl had nearly infinite love and attention to give. But who was to give it back to Cheryl? She needed John.

Her sleeping had not improved since the nightmare had begun. She had not been to work. She wished she could do something constructive to help find John, to feel as if she were doing something to dig out of the void, but there was nothing to do but let the police do their jobs. What if they were not great at what they did? She had met plenty of doctors who were mediocre—some worse than mediocre. She could only hope that Marley was truly excellent at what he did. She and John were at the mercy of the Larchmont police.

She was going to give it a little more time. If nothing developed, she might hire a private investigator for her own peace of mind.

She had left a message for John's parents, Mr. and Mrs. John Harris II, early on. It was the first time she had tried to verbally contact them in well over five years. As a parent, she found their lack of response astonishing. Cheryl knew that if she were in their shoes, she would have been on a jet that day. Hell, his parents had so much money, they could have chartered a plane if no flights were available. Why had they not come?

Then again, these were the same people who let their staunch concerns regarding an interracial marriage in the family estrange them from their son and his family for over a decade. Would not the disappearance of their only child supersede all this? Maybe not.

Perhaps they just hadn't gotten the message, she reasoned. Maybe they were out of town … in Europe somewhere.

Everything was confusing to her. She had gone from near-bliss to disaster in the stroke of a single day. She often cried, sometimes out of guilt. The last time she had seen John, he had wanted to make love with her. She had refused. She wished she had not. She might never make love with him again.

Entering her office for the first time in a week, Cheryl anxiously ran her hands over her clothes and hair, instinctively expecting her outside to match the mess inside. But her white coat was spotless and impeccably ironed. As with most pediatricians, she was dressed very nicely under the coat, an almost absurd notion for the doctors who stand the greatest chance of being vomited upon by their patients.

As she stood in the hallway outside the examining room, she plucked the patient chart from the door slot and looked at its content to refresh her memory before entering the room. Her patients must not sense her anguish.

In the room sat a beautiful little girl in her underpants on the examining table, looking at the pictures in a book as her mom read to her. Although the child was distracted by the book, she looked slightly uncomfortable.

Cheryl opened the door, but did not step in. Rather, she paused for a moment, then got down on her hands and knees awkwardly and stuck only her face in. With the biggest, warmest smile she could muster, Cheryl said, "Hmmm. Has anybody seen my favorite little two-year-old patient, Jamie?"

"I right here!"

From that moment on, Jamie was eating out of Dr. Cheryl's hand. The examination proceeded in an orderly and caring manner. With the stethoscope in her ears, Cheryl did not hear her pager go off. Jamie's mother tapped her on the shoulder to let her know.

"Oh, thank you. Please excuse me. I'll be right back."

Cheryl returned to her office, expecting a call from a referring doctor or perhaps a call regarding a pediatric emergency.

"Hello, this is Dr. Harris."

"This is Russ Marley. It's probably a bad time, but do you have a few minutes?"

"Of course. Hold on," she said as she stood up and closed her door. "I'm back. Go ahead."

"Brace yourself." Cheryl began crying immediately. "We've found your husband. He's alive, but in critical condition."

"Oh my God! Where is he? What's wrong? I need to be with him, now."

"He was found by the maids at a chain motel in Kansas. He had his ID and money and credit cards with him in his wallet, but he was unconscious."

"Jesus, what do you mean, unconscious? And what's he doing in Kansas?"

"I don't understand all the medical mumbo-jumbo, but he is effectively in a coma," Marley said carefully.

She gasped for breath and felt nauseated as she braced herself.

"The doctors don't know why he's unconscious," he continued.

"What? Oh my God!"

She looked around, not focusing on anything. Her office was not the place to experience extremes of emotions. She felt panic and relief at the same time.

"Mrs. Harris, are you OK?"

"No, not really. Tell me everything you know."

"Well, I don't have a lot more to tell you."

"Can I go see him now?"

"Yes. He's in Kansas City, Kansas, in the Sutterfield General Hospital. I'm told that it's an excellent hospital … a trauma center, whatever the hell that is. Now, I've checked the airlines. There's a flight out in two hours. You can probably make it. May I go with you?"

She walked back into the examining room in a daze, her eyes and nose red and swollen.

"Doctor cry, Mommy. Crying."

Chapter 8

A number of people shared the large waiting room. Despite her preoccupation with her husband, Cheryl felt distinctly out of place. She had been in a waiting room many times over the years ... but never as the family member.

She sat with her head against the wall behind her seat, resting and dreaming. Detective Marley stared into the waiting-room abyss and twiddled his thumbs.

"Dr. Harris?" asked a middle-aged nurse who seemed to materialize from nowhere.

"Yes, I'm Dr. Harris." She stood up.

"Dr. Siegel has asked if you would join him in the ICU."

"Of course."

There was familiar buzz in the ICU, but for once her life, Cheryl did not find that energy exhilarating. Personnel were everywhere, all in scrubs of various prints and pastel colors; they reminded her of ants on food. The rooms were small and situated around a large central station, like spokes around a hub. John was in cubicle number five.

Cheryl hesitated and squinted at the doorway, expecting the worst. Then she went directly to John's bed and touched him.

He lay on his back, a clear breathing tube coming out of his mouth and connecting via blue accordion tubes to a sophisticated machine of dials and gauges. Both wrists were restrained with some soft material—a good sign, thought Cheryl. It meant he was moving both arms, and the staff did not want him pulling out his breathing tube or IV.

"Is he triggering the respirator on his own?"

The respiratory therapist paused before answering, unaccustomed to family members asking clinically adroit questions. "Yes. Yes he is. About fourteen a minute." He left.

"Johnny ... it's Cheryl. I'm here. I love you," she muttered through her tears, not knowing whether he could hear her. She thought he moaned—but then, she knew all family members thought that about their comatose loved ones. He looked gaunt, as though he had lost some weight. She peered at his heart monitor mounted on the wall and noted a regular and normal-looking rhythm, as far as she could remember from seeing adults in medical school. His blood pressure was 117/92—also good.

"Hello, Dr. Harris. I'm Dr. Siegel ... Dan Siegel," said the doctor, approaching her at bedside. "I am an internist and critical-care specialist. What is your specialty?"

"I'm a pediatrician," she answered softly.

"I would like to describe to you what we have here in technical terms. If I'm too far out of your specialty, just let me know." He offered her some tissue. "Your husband is in critical condition, but it's not quite as bad as it sounds. When he was found, he was unconscious. This has improved somewhat over the hours in that he is much more responsive to painful stimuli. He had no signs of head trauma. The sharp emergency-room doctor put in the breathing tube to protect his airway and make sure he didn't aspirate any vomit. The chest x-ray and brain scan are normal. And he has brain activity on a preliminary EEG."

"What about a toxicology screen?"

"It's positive for benzodiazepines only; however, flumazenil or romazicon did not reverse his condition. And as you know, the rapid urine test can only identify the presence of a handful of common drugs."

"So what is your impression of what's going on?"

The specialist paused before answering. "As you well know, doctors are hesitant to guess about a patient in your husband's condition. But, if I were a betting man, I'd put my bank account on him still being drugged. Most drugs are eventually detoxified by the body."

Cheryl felt numb. She was not sure if she should feel relief or despair.

"So, as you sit here right now," she asked, "can you put percentages on his chances for a full or partial recovery?"

"Oh, how we doctors love percentages, don't we? I wouldn't even hazard a guess until he is at least forty-eight hours into observation here in the ICU. Realistically, I've never seen a patient *not* recover when the tox screen is negative. Now, Dr. Harris … there's something else that I must tell you. I'm afraid it will be more shocking than what I've already told you."

"What?" she said, with a look of horror.

"When he was brought to the ER, we found something strange. He had a fresh, but healing, left nephrectomy incision site."

"What? How did he get that? You mean, he had kidney surgery?"

"Yes. Please sit down here. The plain x-ray taken of his abdomen after he received the dye for his brain CT scan revealed that he had only one kidney, that being the one on the right …"

"Wait a minute, just wait a minute," said Cheryl, trying to catch her breath.

"He had metallic surgical clips in the area where his left kidney should have been. Ultrasound has confirmed that the kidney is gone."

"No. Oh, no," she said in partial disbelief, searching his expressionless face for some sort of sign that she had not heard what she had just heard. "Are you saying that before he came to this hospital, someone removed one of his kidneys? Oh, my God. Show me. Show me right now. Please!"

Signaling for the nurse to help, Dr. Siegel and the attending nurse gently rotated John. The doctor held his patient in position as the nurse slowly took down the covers to reveal a bandage on John's left flank. The large bandage was removed to display a huge incision with glistening steel surgical staples along its entire length.

Cheryl recoiled and then slowly moved her hand toward the surgical wound. Before making contact, she passed out.

Chapter 9

At 5:00 AM, Cheryl Harris met Detective Marley and a Kansas City detective at the doors to the ICU. She pressed a button, and a voice came on the intercom.

"Hello, this is Dr. Cheryl Harris. I was called here by Dr. Siegel to see my husband, Mr. John Harris." It was unusual for her to refer to herself as 'doctor' when she was not doing direct patient care. Right now she just needed to make the distinction.

"Oh, hello, Doctor. Dr. Siegel will be out in a second to bring you back. Hold on."

Dr. Siegel came out and asked them to follow him. He began his updates en route.

"Well, John had a good night ... a very good night. In fact, I called you because he is awake and following commands. I'm just waiting for his blood gas. The respiratory therapist is checking his negative inspiratory force and all those types of things and, if they're normal, I'll be extubating him real soon."

"What is 'extubating'?" asked Marley.

"Taking out the breathing tube," Cheryl answered.

"So then he'll be able to talk?"

"Well, yes. At a minimum, he'll be hoarse. He may also be exceedingly tired and breathless for a while."

Cheryl desperately walked away from the conversation and went straight for John's bedside. As she eagerly entered the room, he turned toward her and made clear eye contact. Cheryl began to cry and ran over, dodging the various tubes, to hug and kiss him. His hands were free, and as he hugged her back, the nurse scrambled to keep the various tubes from disconnecting.

The Harrises' car was sandwiched by two black-and-white police vehicles escorting them home to their ranch in the mountains outside of Larchmont. Detective Marley rode shotgun in the lead car, with Detective Panzer sitting in the back.

The familiar aroma and sights along the highway brought tears to John's eyes. At one point just a few days earlier, he had been sure he was dead, experiencing the things that he imagined dead people did. Now he felt so relieved, so happy, and so fortunate, despite the pain in his flank.

Cheryl squeezed his left hand intermittently along the journey home. The message was clear: she could not imagine a deeper sense of joy.

On a midmountain stretch of curved highway, John suddenly felt queasy. He moved about, unable to find a position of comfort.

"Johnny, you OK, honey?"

"Yeah ... I don't know. I'm a little sick to my stomach."

"Could be postsurgical. Could be the road."

"I've never gotten sick on the drive before."

"And you've never had a kidney removed either. I'll roll down the window anyway."

As they continued along the road, the sickness quickly passed. Near the end of Highway 18, John sat up. He saw the small sign for Mulberry Lane. In the blur as it flicked by, he thought he saw some fresh flowers on top of it.

As Cheryl turned the car onto their driveway, the full enthusiasm of his welcome was more than apparent. John's attention was immediately caught by a huge, multicolored balloon ornament arched across the entrance. Numerous newspeople were also visible, wielding cameras and microphones. Cheryl honked her horn for them to move away and rolled up the windows. Just before the glass slid shut, John thought he heard a comment so inane that he discounted it immediately: "John, how does it feel to have only one kidney?"

Cheryl just shook her head in amazement. A police officer kept the horde from following them down the drive.

Along the drive, numerous small yellow ribbons hung from an increasing number of tree branches. The pièce de résistance hung over the length of the front porch. A computer-printed banner proclaimed, We Love You, Daddy. Tears flowed freely from John's eyes and down his face onto his collar. His nose ran like a faucet as he smiled with shameless joy. As John opened his door, Cheryl came around to assist him. He grabbed her arm as he slipped out of the cab and stabilized himself on the ground.

"Whoa," he whispered to Cheryl, as he laughed and cried.

At that moment, the front screen door flew open, and four children and two dogs came running out the door. The combined momentum of the oldest three children was too much. They made contact with their dad and kept going. All four ended up in the dirt of the drive on top of their dad as Cheryl could only watch and scream.

"Be careful!"

Nicole slowly descended the few stairs, ran to the group, and just jumped on top.

When the dust had settled, Cheryl quickly assessed the damage.

"All right, kids, shouldn't we let him sleep *in* the house tonight, instead of in the driveway?"

John managed to extricate and extend his right arm out to Cheryl. Instead of helping him up, he helped her to the ground, whereupon the laughter and happiness continued.

"Oh, John!"

In the tumult, John's shirt was pushed upward. When the kids peeled off him one by one, they quieted as they noticed the large bandage. They stepped back and stared.

"What?" asked John, unaware.

Nicole gently put her hand on the dressing.

"It's OK," he reassured them. "It doesn't hurt much. I'm OK." Then, to Cheryl: "You told them about the surgery, right?"

"Of course, but it's one thing to talk about it and another to see it."

"Hey, it's OK, you guys."

When they all walked into the house, covered in dirt, more prizes awaited John. A house full of crepe streamers, family, and friends opened up to receive him. It did not matter much to the well-wishers that John was a little thinner now, or that he had a long scar on his torso, or that he was covered with dirt.

As John looked up and received hugs and kisses, he saw the jubilant faces of all those who were important to him. The satisfaction was overwhelming. He had not thought he had any tears left. He was wrong. He looked around for a second take. He wondered where his mother and father were. He had thought of them often in the past, typically in anger, but never really needed them. All told, he reckoned after all these years that their absence was not surprising.

John scanned the room, then took a seat, emotionally overwhelmed and weaker than he had been at the start of the day.

Toward the end of the evening, a neighbor who worked as a forest ranger dropped by.

"Wow, John! How the hell are you?" he asked, hugging John awkwardly.

Although John seemed overwhelmed by his visitor, the fact was that he experienced slight nausea again, this time brought on by the green uniform before him. He was not sure why.

"Well, I'm here, aren't I?" John muttered, trying to sort out the internal machinations that resulted in a rolling stomach.

"Amen to that," his neighbor said. "You look fine ... a little skinnier, but just fine. Welcome home."

Cheryl noticed John's baffled state and asked, "What's the matter, honey?"

"Oh, nothing. Thanks for coming by," he told the ranger, waiting for the unwelcomed feeling to subside.

"I stopped by while you were gone to keep an eye on things, you know," he said. "You know, make sure Cheryl and the kids were all right."

"Mighty obliged. Anything new around here besides me?"

"Oh, John. Not very funny," said Cheryl.

"Nah. Same old, same old. Oh ... the Houstons had a foal while you were gone."

"Gosh, I almost forgot they were expecting."

"And someone stole one of our trucks. Nothing else exciting around here ... other than you, that is!"

This piqued Marley's interest. "Someone stole a Forest Service truck? For what? How do you hide a pukey green—sorry, a ranger pickup truck?"

"Got me," the ranger said. "Never found it. We thought originally that some kids took it for a joyride or somethin', but no. Just disappeared. Hey, listen, I'm on duty all night, and I gotta go. I'll see ya soon, John. Good to have you back home, and if you need anything, just give a holler."

Detective Marley walked out with the ranger to get more information. He returned a few minutes later and said good night to the Harrises. This time, John and Cheryl walked him outside.

"So, what comes next?" asked John.

"I presume Cheryl has told you that we have very little to go on."

"Has anything like this happened before?"

"Not around here, but apparently others have had the same misfortune ... and I presume still others were not as lucky as you. If you know what I mean."

"No, what do you mean?"

"Oh. Apparently there are isolated reports, here and there, of similar organ rip-offs, if you will. Most of them have been fatal—vagabonds and the like. I haven't seen any actual reports yet, personally. You should also know that the

FBI will be involved with your case soon, since it is an interstate crime. They will likely have more information on similar cases, if they truly exist. I've requested this information, and I'll be happy to share it with you when I get it."

"Yes, I'd like that, I think."

"Whatever happened with that transmitter thing?" asked Cheryl.

"What transmitter thing?" responded John.

"You know, that device found on the driveway motion detector. Remember?"

"Oh, OK."

"I got the information today," said Marley. "It's a German device, available on the open market and found in many countries, including this one. So, not much help. No fingerprints either, for that matter."

"Just like with the Range Rover," said John. "What about serial numbers and that kind of stuff?"

"Excellent question. Scratched off."

"Professional," said John.

"Everything about your case is professional," Marley said wryly. "Now let me ask you one thing before I go, if you don't mind."

"Shoot."

"When that ranger friend of yours came in, it shook you up a little, or so it seemed. Was there something that struck you?"

"Actually, I felt sick, but I don't know why. Something about his uniform … the colors, I think. God, I wish I could be more specific."

"Listen, let me know of anything that comes to you that seems related, no matter how insignificant. Alright?"

"You got it."

When he entered the master bedroom that night, John made a brief, yet sufficient analysis that most men can make, regardless of their disabilities. Cheryl looked nervous, slightly straddling one corner of the end of the bed. She never sat empty-handed anywhere on the bed; she never wore lipstick to bed. His favorite teddy was on under her gown. She wanted him.

As John walked past Cheryl en route to the bathroom, he became intensely aroused. He would pretend, for the time being, that he had not noticed anything.

In the bathroom, he could not think of a plan, with the exception that he wanted to touch every inch of her body. Not commonly predisposed to this type of thought process in the bedroom, he wanted tonight to be extra special.

It felt strange but wonderful to be in the bedroom with his wife again. He was amused at his own giddiness and walked out of the bathroom completely naked.

They lay there, motionless, fulfilled, and fully spent. There was a flicker of life as one of them moved slightly.

"No! Don't move!"

"You either!"

Every single nerve ending in both of their bodies was raw and hypersensitive. They could not help but burst out in laughter. John hugged her as if his life depended on it and kissed her upper back passionately.

After another several moments of longed-for closeness, Cheryl whispered into his ear.

"Well … no problems down there, huh, John Harris III?"

"I love you, Dr. Harris. So much about what happened to me is hazy, but there were times that I thought for sure that I was dead, and that I'd never see you or the kids again. I love you so much, and I'm so happy right now … so very happy."

"Me too, Johnny. Me too."

Chapter 10

The sun shone like a welder's arc; the heat was dry, but debilitating. The same bearded man who had led John's kidnapping sat in the back of a black limousine with his loose white garment, turban, gold jewelry, and black attaché case.

The limo was allowed to pass by heavily armed guards at the palace's gates. Behind the building sat an Olympic pool, manicured gardens that would rival Hampton Court, basketball and tennis courts, and a large helicopter resting on a helipad. The youths played basketball in common athletic sports gear and turbans. Large garages harbored limousines and a legion of exotic sports cars. The grounds crawled with soldiers.

The limousine coursed uphill on a serpentine road around the palace and through verdant grounds with lush vegetation that contrasted sharply with the topography outside the walls.

Two waiting servants opened the rear door of the estate as the limo pulled to a stop. Inside the palace, the bearded man greeted others with hugs and bows of subservience and friendship. Guards responded with only minimal acknowledgment. He was not the least bit fazed by the small children who giggled as they rode the marble floors in $11,000, electric child-sized toy replicas of Rolls Royce cars. One of them, who looked small for his age and oddly proportioned, received a bow from the visitor, however.

Up an elevator and down a few more hallways, he encountered even tighter security. The visitor was ushered into an antechamber and asked to wait. Before long, he was brought into the royal chamber, where he assumed the most subservient posture. Once salutations were out of the way, he started to open his briefcase. The click of the latch brought ominous-looking weapons out of guard's robes. He froze, and with his head bowed, he offered the brief-case to an aide, who opened it and removed a DVD.

On a far wall in this room, but directly in front of the sheikh, stood a twenty-foot projection screen. The lights dimmed as the DVD's contents were displayed. Dozens of American reporters surrounded and followed Cheryl Harris and Detective Marley into the Sutterfield General Hospital in Kansas as a news reporter narrated. The sheikh and his closest advisers leaned forward in their seats to read the program's Arabic subtitles. The man who delivered the DVD was not offered a seat.

After a short black gap in the DVD, the newscaster continued his report, showing a sickly John Harris exiting the hospital with his wife. The reporter closed with, "Urban legend has suddenly become a reality as Mr. John Harris leaves Sutterfield General Hospital, minus one kidney: a victim donor. This is Matt Hurley, special report for CNN."

The screen went blank.

Visibly angry, the sheikh simply turned toward one of his advisers and asked, "How widely viewed was this show?"

"CNN … could be millions in the U.S., many others in Europe."

"What?" he shouted. Turning to the visitor, he continued. "And whose idea was Kansas?"

"Mine."

"What have you learned?"

"I'm sorry, Your Excellency. I do not understand."

"Get me a map of the United States."

An aide scurried out of the chamber, returning immediately with a laptop with a map of United States on the desktop and handed it to the sheikh.

"Here is the donor's Utah, and here is Kansas. Have you never heard of the FBI?" This required no answer. The visitor began to visibly perspire. "Farzak, tell him," the sheikh commanded.

"Once a crime is committed across state lines, the FBI automatically becomes involved," said the aide.

"And?" asked the sheikh, now standing and beginning to pace.

"Once the FBI is involved … well, they have powers … resources … and reach far beyond the borders of the U.S., sire."

The sheikh stopped and turned to glare at the man, who immediately fell to his knees. He knew no explanation would change his likely fate. The sheikh made a hand signal that the man did not see. A guard drew a silenced pistol and pumped bullets into the man. He slumped, stone dead, as the sheikh returned to his throne and spoke as though nothing had transpired.

"He must be watched closely. Allah willing, all will be well. Have him watched, but discreetly. Treat his life as your own."

Chapter 11

Cheryl awoke at 4:00 AM on John's first day back to work.

"Honey, don't be ridiculous," John said. "I appreciate it, but it's just not necessary. Come on, go back to sleep."

"I'm not working today. So while you're showering, I'm gonna make you a special breakfast. You need lots of energy for today."

Although it was time to get back to work, John wasn't looking forward to seeing his boss. The relationship would be more intense, for Harvey Mankin had taken over John's work during his brief hiatus. Harvey was not the type of guy to let something like this easily pass, kidney rip-off or not. John toyed with the notion that dealing with Harvey might be more distasteful than actually losing a kidney. He realized that this was, of course, silly. He would give anything to have not lost his kidney, to have not had his whole existence thrown into such chaos. His tinge of bitterness over the experience had shortened his fuse, and he hoped he had the willpower to curb his mounting anger in front of his boss.

John joined Cheryl in the kitchen for his favorite breakfast: thick French toast with nutmeg and cinnamon.

"Hurry up and eat. You don't want to be late."

"Jeez, thanks. Smells wonderful."

"Worried about work?"

"Let's not talk about it, OK? Let's talk about your work instead. How's it been going for you?"

"OK. Hmm ... I haven't worked for a few days. Let me think. Well, I did see this little girl the other day. Sydley was her name. Anyway, she's almost three. Beautiful, mind of her own, great big eyes ... a little like Nicole. When I go into the examining room, she's sitting up on the table, patiently waiting for me. Me. And she's in this cute party dress. This is a first. Anyway, she looked adorable. And she kinda blushed as she stuck her tongue into her cheek, with her head hung down. Her mother asked if she had something to show me. And she lit up and looked at me and grabbed her dress and presented it to me as she said: 'Pretty! Pretty!' Johnny, if you could have seen her face. I was almost speechless! She wanted me to see her most special dress. I've never had a patient do that."

"What did you do?"

"Well, I hugged her, of course, and told her it was beautiful and thanked her for sharing with me. I told her that she makes me smile, just like my own kids, and that the whole day I would have this smile on my face ... maybe even all week. Then I went and looked at her chart, and I'll be damned if she wasn't late for one of her vaccinations."

"No! Not a shot?"

"I said, 'Sydley, I have some bad news. I don't want to spoil your day, but we're gonna have to give you a shot, and it's gonna hurt. You're gonna cry, and your arm's gonna get big and swollen like a balloon, and you're going to get sick to your stomach ... maybe even puke.'"

John stopped midbite and stared at Cheryl, who had turned away and was walking to the sink to rinse dishes. "No," he said. "Come on. You couldn't have!"

Before she reached the sink, Cheryl dissolved into uncontrollable laughter.

"Sheesh. I can't believe I fell for that!" said John, before bursting into laughter at his own gullibility. "You really got me. Good one. You'd take advantage of a sick man, eh? So what did you really do?"

"I lied, kind of. I pulled her mom aside and told her I didn't have the heart to give her the shot she needed. We rescheduled her for next week."

"Now that's more like it. That's the Cheryl I married. Well, I'd better go. Can't delay it any longer."

He kissed Cheryl good-bye and was out of his driveway by 4:45. Easing into the curves, he found himself becoming increasingly anxious again for no apparent reason. As anxiety deepened into nausea, he took deep, deliberate breaths until it passed. He turned up the stereo, reclined his seat a bit, and settled in for the drive to town.

There was no greeting party at his office at that ungodly hour, but his reserved parking space still bore his name, and that was good enough. He walked into the main lobby alone, briefcase in hand and took the elevator up.

Everything about his office was familiar: the look, the smell, even the peculiar dull noise the elevator made on its ascent. John was the one who felt unfamiliar. His three-piece suit felt loose.

The brokers and understudies present had already logged on to their computers and were studying the market trends of the New York Stock and NASDAQ exchanges and preparing to join in. Lost in their important work, they did not seem to notice John—which didn't bother him in the slightest. Right then, anonymity felt just fine.

His office was dark, as were a number of others. Most of the action that morning was taking place on the floor, per usual. Maybe he'd just sit in the dark for a moment and take a few deep breaths.

As he switched on the light, loud voices screamed "Surprise!" in unison. It scared the daylights out of John, and he dropped his briefcase. Quite a few people had packed themselves into the small space, along with plenty of streamers and banners.

John struggled to focus as the throng of well-dressed coworkers surrounded him, hugged him, poked at him, and talked at him.

As the witching hour was rapidly approaching, the ceremony died quickly, and everyone returned to his or her workstation ... except for Harvey Mankin, who lingered a little too long for John's liking.

"Welcome back, John."

"Why, thank you."

"We've got some catching up to do. I think I've kept up with your accounts and kept your customers satisfied," said Harvey, clearly waiting for a show of gratitude.

"Hey," John said, "I can't thank you enough for covering for me. But ... nothing personal, but I'll need a little while to get situated here. I believe I'm up on the market, no doubt about that. Just got to get my stuff in order here. Why don't we meet a little before the AM roundtable, OK?"

"Sure, buddy," said Harvey, mercifully leaving John alone.

The first half of the day went surprisingly well. Lois stayed by John's side and helped him immensely. John and Harvey caught up on business together without incident, the roundtable went smoothly, and John was scheduled to meet with his own team after lunch.

During his lunch hour, John pulled into the parking lot of the Larchmont police station. He had not heard from Detective Marley for over a week, and he felt compelled to get an update.

The visitor parking lot was segregated from the officers' area. In fact, there was no way for a vehicle to pull close to the building. Reasonably, the concept of community outreach for a metropolitan area of nearly two million stopped here. The fortress had to be protected.

The front of the station was white, clean, and well manicured in an effort to bolster its public image. The walls were deceptively thick, and bulletproofed against large-caliber gunfire, as were the glass doors leading into the building. The reception window was also composed of incredibly thick glass. The desk sergeant did not open the window, electing to communicate via the intercom.

"What brings you out this afternoon, sir?"

"My name is John Harris, and I'm looking for Detective Marley. He knows me."

"You the guy in the paper recently?"

"The one and only."

The window slid open, and a hand was extended.

"How the hell are you, sir? You look good. Welcome home."

The greeting caught John off guard.

"Thank you. Is Detective Russ Marley in, by any chance?"

"I don't know for sure. You never know with these detectives. Let's ring him up." The sergeant dialed an extension. "Sir, there's a Mr. John Harris here to see you. Send him up? Sure. Will do…. Mr. Harris, I'll buzz you in over there. Go down the hall halfway and take the elevator to the third floor. And good luck."

When the elevator opened on the third floor, Detective Marley greeted John in the hall and showed him to his private office.

"This is a surprise visit," Marley commented. "What brings you by?"

"I was in the area, and I felt this hankering to get an update."

"Is that right. A hankering?"

"Yep."

"Well, I'm glad this is all sort of friendly, because I'm afraid that I don't have a lot to share. I was half hoping that maybe you had recalled something that might be of value. No such luck, I take it?"

John shook his head.

"I'll tell you where we stand. Aside from the telemetry device on your driveway entrance, which was a blind alley, we have nothing. Essentially, you disappeared without a trace, and then you reappeared without a trace. Without a single fucking trace. It's unbelievable. We'd have had better luck if you were a meteor—no offense. I'm very frustrated, and the same goes for my FBI contacts."

"I'm frustrated too."

"We don't have a single lead in Kansas, either. I went down there personally again and surveyed the scene with their people. No one saw or heard a thing. Nothing. Nada. How do you get someone your size into a hotel without anyone seeing a thing?"

"How about that stolen ranger truck?"

"The theft predated your kidnapping by a day … but other than that, who knows? It vaporized. We've put the word out on the street—chop shops, you name it. So far, it's as if that vehicle never existed. But we've got to give it a little more time."

"What now?"

"Well, all of this painful dialogue we've been having does provide us with a clue or two of sorts. What happened to you was extremely organized. Major point: experts were involved, and it cost a lot of money to pull this off. My gut tells me that the solution lies in understanding the organ rip-off industry … if there is such a thing."

"What's your plan, then?"

"We need more help from the Feds. No way around that. When they've come up with a strategy, if their game plan doesn't include my hunch, I'll spring it on them and somehow make them think it was all their idea."

"Why all the tap dancing?"

"The Feds don't like being told what to do or how to do it. I've been in this position before. If I'm patient and gracious, I'll get exactly what I need."

"Have they at least provided you with a list of victims of similar crimes?"

"Not as of yet. Patience. Patience."

"Well, I gotta tell you, Russ, I'm starting to get antsy. Actually, 'antsy' downplays how I'm really feeling."

"I'm not surprised, after all you've been through. I'll keep you posted, I promise. That's the best I can do."

"Well, I guess we can't ask for more than that."

The mood shifted to one of resigned finality. Both men stood, and John headed for the door. "Say hello to Dr. Harris, will you? … Oh, and John? What's happening with that sickness you had?"

"I'm not sure exactly what you're referring to."

"You mentioned that you felt sick on a certain stretch of Highway 18."

"Well, it's still there. In fact, it was the worst today."

"I don't think we can ignore that. Tell you what I'd like to do."

"What's that?"

"I think you and I need to take a drive together up Highway 18. Soon. Let's look at our calendars now and set up a date."

Chapter 12

The president rarely used his White House private quarters for meetings, but this urgent late-night conference justified an exception.

Outside the single door stood a secret-service agent. Inside sat four nervous men: the president, his chief adviser, and the directors of the CIA and the FBI.

"Mr. President, with all due respect, this has 'backfire' written all over it," the chief adviser said. "I could not be in stronger opposition."

"Divorce yourself, if you can, from the White House for one moment," responded the president. "OK? Now, what would you say?"

"Well sir, I'd be slightly less pessimistic, but not much. If word of this were ever to get out, the outrage of our citizens would be exponentially greater than that of Watergate."

"What are the chances for failure?" asked the president, directing his question to the other two in the room.

"Obviously, nothing is foolproof," said the CIA director, "but we've run this thing up one side and down the other … dissected it, computer analyzed it, the whole gamut. We would have zero tolerance for failure on this particular project, and we believe we can attain nearly those odds."

"And I might add that the benefits would be unparalleled for generations to come," said the FBI director. "You, sir, would never be able to claim the credit for the success, I'm afraid. But that's been the plight of many great men.

"On the other hand, were the unimaginable to happen, you would never be linked to any of this. You are sterile. For the White House, there is only benefit … no risk."

"Let's not lose sight of the humanitarian aspects of this," said the chief of staff.

"Humanitarian aspects? With all due respect, that's what this is all about: humanity. The humanity of the collective American people."

"Bullshit," interjected the chief adviser. "Mr. President, I must advise you against it. I do so without hesitation."

As the president stood, so did the others in the room. The FBI and CIA directors had anticipated opposition to their plan.

"Gentlemen, thank you for your time, input, and consideration," said the president. "This meeting never happened."

The president walked behind his chief of staff, leading him out the door first, while massaging his shoulders. As the other two passed him on the way out, the president made eye contact with the pair and nodded his approval.

Chapter 13

The children played loudly in the family room, with the TV off as the result of misbehavior. Cheryl and John sat in the kitchen, she entrenched in a book and he reading the Sunday paper.

"Eric!" yelled Erin. "You get out of here. You're cheating. I'm telling Mom, you jerk. Mommmmy!"

"OK, OK," said Eric, attempting to whisper. "I won't buy it then."

"Yeah, you won't buy it. What about moving back one space? That's my property, and you owe me rent."

"I'm sorry!" said Eric sarcastically.

"That's bullshit, Eric! You are not sorry!" yelled John from the kitchen, so loudly that Cheryl dropped her book.

Using profanity in front of the children was distinctly unusual for John, although he was prone to it when out of their earshot. Cheryl recovered quickly and pretended to read again as she waited to see what developed. John had been increasingly edgy since he had come home from Kansas ... but even taking that into consideration, what he had just done was out of character.

The children quieted immediately. In a situation where she would normally go for the jugular in making her case against her brother, Erin did not push it.

After a few minutes, more heated whispering came from the family room. John put down his newspaper.

"Johnny, forget about it. Let them work it out, honey."

John dismissed her with a wave and continued listening, his head cocked slightly.

"John, why is this so important to you?" Cheryl asked. "Kids argue. Our kids argue all the time. Let's let them work it out. OK?"

"Eric!" the whispering continued. "You can't do that. Pay me. Pay me now."

"I'm bankrupt, you idiot. I can't pay."

"Then mortgage something … or quit, and I win."

"I can't do that."

"Then I win! You quit!"

"Nuh-uh, you don't win. I have more property, so I automatically win. You lose. I win."

"I'm telling—"

"Jesus!" said John as he strode into the family room. "No!" he shouted at Eric. "You lose. You are no longer allowed to play. Get in your room … now."

Without waiting, John gave Eric an unnecessary push toward his room. He raised his hand again, and it looked as if he were going to hit his son. The other children watched in terror, including Nicole. John just stood there, looking around, hand frozen in the air, seething. No one, including John, knew exactly would come next.

"John! Come outside with me. Now!" Cheryl caught him off guard and broke his trance.

Headed out to the backyard, she did not need to glance back to see if John were following. She heard his heavy footsteps.

"John, you are out of control. Can you feel it?"

"Yes. I. Feel. It." John enunciated every syllable. "But I can't stop it."

"You've been tense, but this is way out of line. You don't talk about it with me, but I presume … I hope … you're discussing it with your counselor." She waited for a response, but none was forthcoming. "Well, what is it? What the hell is it?"

"I don't know. I don't quite understand it myself, Cheryl. It obviously has to do with the kidney thing. I've been feeling more and more upset and angry. Even at work. I'm so angry and unhappy."

"What about your family?"

"I love you all. I don't know what I'd do if it weren't for you—I can express myself here."

"Yes, but there's got to be a better way to express yourself. You're going to drive us all away with these outbursts. John, it looked like you were going to hurt Eric. The punishment didn't fit the crime."

"I wasn't aware of it happening until it was too late."

"Have you felt this way before?"

"Yes, but I was by myself."

"Have you discussed it with your counselor or not?"

"We've touched on it a bit."

"Well, since you're in it now, maybe you and I can start with what you were thinking about in the kitchen while I was reading?"

"All I think about every day is catching the bastards who did this. Nothing more, nothing less. And the police have nothing. It seems like the FBI is being evasive, if you ask me."

"And you're being paranoid."

"But I've thought about it. Take away my anger. Give me one piece of anything we've gotten from them, other than the fucking transmitter in the driveway, which is a dead end.

"What happened to me is unbelievable, unacceptable. Cheryl, they took me away from you and the kids. They kidnapped me, then performed major surgery on me. It's worse than rape. And then they let me go. Why? And who's next? Why doesn't anybody seem to care about who's next?"

"I don't know," she said, caught off guard by the last question.

"Is this the decline of society or what? Because it doesn't seem as though there's any lower place to go. Hell, this organ-stealing business may even be worse than genocide in a way. You drop chemicals or a bomb and kill several people—maybe hundreds or thousands—and it's in the name of something, no matter how pathetic the cause: culture or religion or economics, whatever. With genocide, you at least have a bullshit reason for doing what you do ... some conviction. And you have a connection to your victims. Key words, Cheryl: conviction and connection. With what happened to me, there's no issue or cause at all ... and certainly no connection or conviction. Right?"

"Yes, I see what you're saying. Presumably none."

"I mean, I'm clean. Have you thought about that? I'm squeaky-clean. *We* are squeaky-clean. What they have done, whoever they are, is say, 'I want that, so I'm going to take it. It belongs to another living, breathing, human being, but we're just going to take it.' Why? Because they can. Because they want to. They don't know me or hate me. I don't represent anything to them. I'm no threat. I just had something they wanted."

"I know, honey." Her eyes pleaded with him. "It's the worst form of assault and robbery. It's beyond comprehension."

"No, Cheryl. It's far, far worse than that. Look. You're a physician. Do you realize that a doctor, a surgeon, performed this surgery on me? Fuck the Hippocratic oath here. A *doctor* did this, Cheryl. Someone like you. They did it with precision—and, I would surmise, pride of workmanship. Nice incision, no infection. I didn't get sick. And it seems as though they didn't want to lose their patient. Again, I ask: Why?"

"I don't know."

"They could have just wasted me, but they didn't. It would've been a whole lot easier and safer for them. No?"

"You're right."

John paused, seemingly spent and thoughtful. Cheryl glanced toward the house. John did not notice the kids by the window, watching him standing and lecturing and waving his arms vigorously at their mommy sitting in a lawn chair.

"You're onto something," Cheryl said. "You answer those questions, and we're a whole lot closer to finding who did this. So why would they pick *you*? There are a lot of easier targets. Much easier."

"I don't know. We need to know that piece of the puzzle, all right, but we have to start with the corner pieces and then the border pieces, know what I mean? Those pieces are the easiest to put together."

Cheryl was into the hunt now. "You're right ... but which parts of this puzzle make up that border?" She thought a moment. "Wait, before you answer that, let me put a totally different spin on the issue. OK?"

John nodded for her to continue.

"Could anything really resolve what happened to you? Will you ever be satisfied? Is it an eye for an eye, tooth for a tooth? Will busting these people really help you? And what if it takes a long time to find them? Are you going to be angry for a year or two or five? Is that an acceptable risk to take with your family? Because, don't think it won't take a toll on your family. It will. And if we all are the most important thing to you right now, and I think we are, can you take that risk?"

"What do you suggest?"

She paused to think of the honest answer, then searched her brain for other possible answers. "Honestly?"

John nodded.

"OK, this is *not* going to sound fair. I realize that right now. But let's start with how I feel ... perhaps the irrational side of me. Ready? OK, here we go. I want you to forget about it all." She held up a hand to fend off his urge to interrupt. "I want you to forget about it like it never happened. I want our old lives back again. I want to move on like nothing's changed."

John just looked at her in disbelief.

"I know, I know. I didn't say it was rational or reasonable, remember? And I'll give you this: It doesn't help you deal with your feelings over the whole thing, does it? If I pretend it never happened. Actually, quite the opposite. I understand that. So maybe that's the irrational side of it, the unreasonable side."

"Maybe?"

"Look, honey, I love you, and I want to help. I realize that what I just said could never happen. So now I am going to be totally rational. How can I help you?"

"I don't know. Let me think about it."

"How about right now?"

"I'm doing my best, Cheryl. Don't push me."

"No, I mean how can I help you right now, this moment?"

"I don't know … I just don't know." John shook his head.

"Well, let me ask you this: What is it you would want from the police or FBI now, short of the identity of the kidnappers?"

"Well, first I'd like that fucking list of those others who have had the same experience as me, if it really exists."

"Why?"

"Why?"

"Yeah, why?"

"Well … I'd have a better handle on the magnitude of the problem."

"And?" Cheryl waited.

"Oh, I don't know. Maybe I'd have someone else to talk to who knows exactly how I feel. There's comfort in that, you know? Maybe we'd turn up new clues if we compared our experiences, and if it's the same people doing all this—if you want to call them people."

"You've spoken directly with Marley, right?" John nodded. "Have you spoken directly with the FBI?"

"No. I've just relied on what Marley tells me."

"Well, I think with something this important, you need to hear what's going on from the horse's mouth, even if it's not the news you want to hear."

"Yeah, I suppose you're right." John looked more at ease now. "But Marley says that's definitely not the way to go."

"So, we take an indirect route. Maybe we can search the Web for articles on people who have had their organs stolen. Maybe they even have their own Web sites. Jeez, Johnny, why didn't we think of this sooner?"

"Guess that's what trying *not* to think about something'll do."

"Well, another reason we haven't done this together is that you've not discussed any of this with me. Another reason is that I've avoided discussing it with you. And for that, I'm sorry."

Cheryl stood and hugged him long and hard. She looked at the children over his shoulder as she held him tightly. The children showed relief from their window position.

"Are you less angry?" she asked softly.

"Yes, I am."

"Well, take note. It's because you've talked about what's on your mind. We need to do this more often and I think you need to bring it up to your counselor more often. Wouldn't you agree?"

John nodded.

"Now, before we hop on the computer, you're going to have to go in there and eat some major crow with Eric. He's got to know he's not responsible for your behavior, that he's done nothing wrong, and that he's not the source of your wrath. At his tender age, if you don't do something, you're going to put a gap between the two of you so big that he'll never get over it."

Arm in arm, they headed back into the house. The three older children turned away from the window and dispersed in an attempt to conceal their surveillance.

"See?" whispered Cheryl.

John woke Cheryl after midnight with a small sheaf of paper in his hand.

"What did you find?" she asked between yawns.

"Well, a lot … and nothing. I had to use a ton of different search terms to get the little I got."

"Like what?"

John looked at the papers in his hand. "Like organ donation, organ stealing, stealing organs, robbing organs, organ theft, organ trafficking, and stolen organs. Some of these titles had articles listed, the vast majority having absolutely nothing to do with the forced donation of one's organs."

"How frustrating. So what's the bottom line?"

"Bottom line is this: In the U.S., there are all kinds of urban legends about crimes like this. These have been researched and found to be totally bogus. You know, someone wakes up butt-naked in a bathtub filled with ice, and there's a note that says 'Call 911.' When he stands, he has two fresh incisions on his back … and so on. These tales have been shown to be 100 percent fabricated … hence the term 'urban legend.' On the other hand, there seems to be a black market that deals in stolen organs—or bought organs, for that matter. This market seems to operate entirely overseas ... in particular, in China and India. In China, organs from executed criminals are sold on the open market. In India, there's a different twist: poor people are actually selling their kidneys for money to live on. They can get a year or two's wages for a single kidney."

"Whoa," Cheryl muttered, now wide awake. "That's nauseating. What's this world coming to?"

"There are also reports in these countries of people being abducted and later found dead, their organs missing."

"So, you haven't found anyone online with your circumstances?"

"I've got more work to do, maybe tomorrow, but it sure looks like they don't exist."

"So where does that leave you ... us?"

"Well, clearly I represent something new and different. That makes it tough. I may be wrong, but I think we need to learn as much about every aspect of organ transplantation as we can. I'm gonna need your medical expertise."

"You got it."

Chapter 14

The intercom chimed in Detective Marley's office.

"Yeah?"

"Sir, Detective Panzer called and said he's running late, but thinks he'll be back in time to meet you for lunch."

Over the next few hours, Marley tackled administrative paperwork at his desk, hoping that Detective Panzer would return with news on a lead in the Harris case.

Panzer showed up just before noon. He was animated and talkative—for Panzer, anyway.

"You know that kid they caught the other day trying to heist that Chevy? I had a little talk with him, and he's been kind enough to furnish us with the location of a chop shop here in Larchmont that we weren't familiar with. I'd like to get a search warrant and check it out. We have probable cause, wouldn't you agree?"

"I think so. Let's go see if the DA agrees."

The inconspicuous large, white building was indistinguishable from its neighbors in the industrial park. The front and rear entrances were closed. The only windows were located high on each side, just below the eaves. The midafternoon bustle of business did not stop to notice the two unmarked vans approaching the structure. The first van pulled up alongside the building, near the front, while the other moved quickly to the rear.

At a synchronized moment, the back and side doors of each van flew open, and several heavily armed police officers swiftly and deftly assumed positions at each end of the building. As they all stood awaiting the command from

Detective Marley, the vague sounds of heavy machinery could be heard from within the building.

The order was given, and the seizure began. Locked doors were encountered by both groups of officers. Attempts to pick the door locks were successful; however, locking devices on the other side still held the doors tightly shut. The snafu was not unpredicted, and Marley quickly radioed the officers from inside the van command post.

Around the block, a battering-ram vehicle had already backed down a ramp from a flatbed truck and was headed toward Marley's location. Meanwhile, half of the officers in the rear ran to join those positioned in the front.

With their weapons trained on the front of the building, the officers separated into halves and made room for the battering ram. The potential for casualties was high in surprise circumstances such as these, so the officers were poised for action. The vehicle rolled over the curb and struck the heavy metal door dead center. The structural integrity of the door and its jamb proved to be greater than that of the cinderblocks surrounding it; the door heaved only a bit before a number of the cinderblocks around the periphery of the door broke out. The entire door fell inward, with the surrounding cinderblock intact. The battering ram quickly backed up to allow the officers to enter and do their job.

Inside the shop lay a vast open space cluttered with a number of vehicles in various stages of deconstruction. Orders had been placed for certain parts of certain cars, and a number of workers had obviously been laboring diligently to fill those orders. Judging from the chaos, the workers had been caught off guard when the front of their workplace imploded. In the time it took most of them to assimilate what had happened, numerous police officers with large weapons had infiltrated their space. The officers fanned out and shouted orders for the criminals to lay spread-eagled on the ground.

Marley and Panzer filed in behind the rest of them, their handguns drawn and ready for the sort of action that they hoped not to encounter.

A few moments after the police burst into the chop shop, Marley noticed movement in the corner of his eye. It took Marley a split second to focus on a man with a gun perched in the rafters above. The gun appeared to be an automatic weapon, trained on the officers in front of Marley. Without hesitation, Marley shot the man twice. Both bullets struck the target in the upper torso, causing the man to fall thirty feet to the pavement below.

The loud gunshots disoriented to the rest of the police officers. They immediately pivoted toward the source of the noises. Once they were convinced that all appeared to be OK, the majority went about cuffing the criminals and securing the rest of the building.

At the far end of the structure were an office and a short hallway leading to the rear exit. During the short burst of gunfire, the individual in the office quietly made his way to the rear door, unlatched several dead bolts, and slid out the door. To his surprise, he was met by the jet-black barrels of a number of weapons. Without hesitation, he dropped his bag of cash and held his arms well above his head. He was quickly brought down to the ground and cuffed as the officers entered the building from the rear, shouting "Larchmont police!" as they made their way to the others.

The building was secured. In all, seven men were arrested. The one casualty was unfortunate, but not unexpected. Had Marley not seen him, the death toll could have been a lot higher.

Naturally, all the vehicles in the chop shop proved to be stolen. Not one of them was a pickup truck, much less a green vehicle of the ranger variety.

After all the criminals had been read their rights, Marley and Panzer moved quickly to interrogate the gentleman who had tried to escape out the back. It seemed as if he would be the one with the most information. They used his office and he did not object.

Marley asked the first question while Panzer set up a recorder.

"Mr.… uh, your license says Thomas. Is that right? Thomas?" asked Marley, looking at the man's driver's license. Thumbing through the wallet as he talked, Marley found pictures of small children and a number of bills in large denominations.

The man did not answer. He was clearly angry, although he did not seem frightened.

"Mr. Thomas—if it is Mr. Thomas—you've got a real serious problem here. All those vehicles in there? They're stolen. That's pretty bad, whether or not you've got priors. You'll do time, no question. And then there's this little problem with the guy in the rafters. Attempted murder. And you are all accomplices. Bare minimum, you'll miss seeing your kids in grade school and middle school."

"Yeah, you might be let out just in time to figure out how you're going to pay for college," said Panzer.

"Fuck you!"

"Hey, hey!" said Panzer, smacking Mr. Thomas on the side of his head.

"Fuck you," the man repeated. "I want my lawyer. I got nothing to say to you two."

As the interrogation continued, those handcuffed in the main part of the shop were searched again, and their belongings checked for identification. The rest of the officers searched for any incriminating items throughout the building, including up on the rafters.

"Mr. Thomas, I'll be honest with you," Marley said. "I'm not interested in all those cars in there. Nor am I interested in that guy I shot. What I am interested in is a green Forest Service pickup truck that seems to have disappeared off the face of the earth recently. In fact, I am so interested in it that I may be willing to work a deal."

"I don't know shit about no ranger truck. Now get me my lawyer."

"My guess is that you'll be changing your mind real soon. I'm going to tuck my card in your pocket. Ask for me when you're ready." Marley turned. "Now get him out of here. I'm sick of looking at him."

As they all stood, a smiling policeman walked in and dropped a large, heavy, black duffel bag down on the ground in front of them. Metal from within made a telltale clanking sound.

"Whatcha got in there?" asked Panzer.

The officer unzipped the bag and everyone, including Mr. Thomas, shifted to see what lay within.

"Well, Mr. Thomas," Marley said, "looks like one of your people has been collecting license plates."

"License plates?"

"I could be wrong, but from the looks of it, we've got enough here to link you to an incredible number of thefts. Enough to lock your ass up for a very long time. Want me to make that lawyer call for you, Mr. Thomas?"

The man was temporarily speechless.

"Get him out of here."

As Mr. Thomas was taken out and shackled with the rest of his cohorts, Marley donned a pair of surgical gloves and thumbed through the license plates.

Marley emerged from the office a few minutes later and signaled to one of the officers, who walked over.

"Bring Mr. Thomas into the office, will you?"

Mr. Thomas was returned to his office and placed back in the chair. This time, he wore wrist and ankle cuffs, which were interconnected by a series of chains. He looked at Detective Marley to see what was coming next.

"Mr. Thomas, do you know what this is?" asked Marley, holding up a white license plate with a capital *E* followed by a few numbers.

"No, I don't know what that is," scoffed Mr. Thomas, overenunciating each word.

"It's the license plate of a government vehicle. Federal."

Marley drove quite some distance from Larchmont to the major steel mill for the district. The plant and yards covered roughly thirty acres of land.

Marley had just reached a tentative plea bargain with Mr. Thomas based on a statement that read,

> The Forest Service truck was brought into the shop by some Arab dude. He handed me lots of cash and asked me to have it destroyed that day. I just removed all the electrical equipment, sanded off all the insignias, destroyed the ID numbers, primed the whole motherfucker gray, and sent it off to the crusher.

Marley walked across the parking lot toward a narrow, towering building. On this trek, a huge building was visible to his left. Through its large, open doors, the glowing furnaces and splatter of molten metal shone against the dark backdrop. To his right stood piles upon piles of metal in all different shapes and sizes, most of which were tarnished and rusted by the elements.

Marley entered the tall structure and took the single, small elevator to the top. When the elevator door opened, he stepped into an office of about one thousand square feet. Glass surrounded the entire floor, giving a 360-degree panoramic view of the mill. A receptionist asked Marley his name, then pointed toward a burly, red-headed man.

"Well, Detective, like I said on the phone, I don't think we're going to be of much help to you."

"Be that as it may, I've got to follow up every lead to personal satisfaction. Know what I mean?"

The man nodded. "Now, it seems to me that you wanted to try to locate either cars to be scrapped, or the scrapped cars we would have received from Larchmont and surrounding areas—hopefully before they've been melted down. Bear in mind that we process a car shipment in two steps. First, the cars are weighed and stripped down. Then they're put in the compactor and crushed into large metal boxes. Eventually, they're melted down."

"Have you been able to locate my vehicle?"

"Well, I don't know. In the last few weeks, we've gotten a few pickup trucks, and we've compacted a few. I have no way of knowing if any of them are yours. Why don't I show you what we've got? OK?"

They made their way down to the parking lot and hopped in the supervisor's pickup, where Marley's host handed him a hard hat. The men headed to the vast area behind the large building Marley had noticed earlier. The structure was a football field in length. Beyond it were fields of metal and two large magnet cranes. The pickup came to a stop, and the two men were joined by another.

"Detective, this is Todd. He's in charge of all the inventory waiting to be melted down. Let's go with him first."

Marley and Todd shook hands, and Todd walked them all over to his forklift.

"I want each of you to stand on the back," Todd directed. "Detective, he'll show you exactly where. I'll drive. It's the only way to maneuver in there." He pointed to a wall of five-feet cubes that had obviously once been cars.

About halfway down a long row of piled squares, Todd stopped the forklift and killed the engine. Marley looked around in amazement. He was surrounded by stacked towers of perfectly crushed cars. The stacked aisle went on in each direction for a great distance and rose far above his head.

"It could be somewhere in there, sir."

"I get the point. Show me the pickups that haven't been compacted."

They drove to a large clearing. Here a number of vehicles were lined up, waiting to be compressed prior to the final process of melting down. A huge crane with a magnetic plate moved toward the compactor in the process of crushing a vehicle.

"Don't worry. I told them not to crunch any trucks until we checked out the merchandise," said the foreman. "Besides, these vehicles still have more processing to be done."

"What do you mean?"

"A number of vendors pay us for the privilege of coming in to remove whatever is left on these cars—upholstery, tires, engine, you know—before we crunch."

Marley surveyed the thirty or so vehicles in front of him. Four of them were pickups. Without speaking a word, he briskly walked over to the first of the two pickup trucks, each of which were primed in gray. He donned surgical gloves, peered into the cabin, removed a medium-sized knife from his rear pocket, and scraped off the primer in several random spots. The underlying color was black. He moved to the second vehicle and did the same. Pay dirt. The underlying paint shone green. Opening the cab door, Marley eyed a metal bracket under the dash that likely had housed a two-way radio at some time. The small hole in the roof of the cab, with empty wires that likely had connected to emergency lights, clinched it.

"Well, sir. Today's a good day. A very good day. I'm afraid I'm going to have to impound this vehicle."

An hour later, the stolen pickup was being loaded onto a flatbed truck while Marley and Panzer looked on.

"Soon as this gets back to impound, I want the print team all over it like a fat chick on a Twinkie."

"Yessir," Panzer responded. "Fat chick. Twinkie."

Marley and Panzer followed their payload slowly out of the steel mill. As the flatbed approached the exit, an unmarked cop car with flashing red lights on the dashboard screeched to a stop in front of it. Two suited men sporting sunglasses jumped out, holding up their badges.

"What the hell?" was all Marley could say.

Panzer was not far behind him. "What's going on?"

"I am Agent Moreno," said the lead man, handing Marley his card. He removed his sunglasses. The handsome Latino man in his early forties had perfectly coiffed graying hair. He came off as direct and professional, but not overbearing. "We talked on the phone last week. I'm sorry, but we'll have to impound this vehicle ourselves at this time."

"What? This vehicle is vital to our investigation. Under what jurisdiction do you think you can take it?"

"You know as well as I do, sir, that the crime was interstate. You have no jurisdiction in interstate crime. And, I might point out, this is likely a government vehicle. With all due respect, I must ask you to relinquish the vehicle to us."

"I do see what you're saying, but can't we work together on this? I mean, I've got the print people standing by right now."

"Honestly, Detective, I can imagine your frustration, and I apologize. I've got my orders. I'm sure you understand. I'll do everything to get the prints and any other data to you as soon as we have it."

"When will they print it?"

"Quickly," Moreno said. "I assure you."

Chapter 15

The University of Utah was a long drive from the Harris ranch. John and Cheryl set out early, without the children. They had both scheduled a day off work. As Cheryl drove at a safe speed through the curving downgrade of Highway 18, the familiar uneasiness crept into John's consciousness. Each time, he would perspire and feel nauseated and anxious—even claustrophobic. The left side of his neck now mysteriously ached.

The Utah University Medical Center was the mecca for medical care for the entire state. It was also an organ-transplant center. The Harrises had an appointment with Dr. Alfred Ginsberg, a renowned transplant surgeon who specialized in the transplantation of kidneys.

"Well, you seem to be in a very good mood this morning," Cheryl commented as they made their way to Dr. Ginsberg's office. "That's good to see."

"Yep. You're right."

"Any way we can bottle it and take it out anytime we need it?"

"I wish."

"So what's up?"

"I guess it's just because we're getting somewhere. We've got one green, well-used ranger truck that was involved in a horrible crime."

"You mean, the FBI has it."

"Could be worse. And we're on our way to learning more about my surgery. You're damn right—I feel great."

The waiting room was small, and two frosted sliding-glass windows shielded whomever or whatever needed shielding inside. They could make out the vague silhouette of a woman behind the glass. Every so often, she moved. She was not talking on the phone or to another patient. She certainly had to have heard or felt the door to the waiting room opening and closing. The lowly courtesy of a bell was even missing from the counter before them.

John knocked on one of the frosted windows. A sharp-faced, elderly woman threw open the window, but managed to keep it from smashing against the jamb. She said nothing.

"Hello. I'm Dr. Harris," Cheryl said, ignoring the woman's dour expression. "My husband and I have an appointment with Dr. Ginsberg."

The woman handed them a clipboard with a three-page health questionnaire. She closed the window without a word.

"Bitch," whispered Cheryl as she took a seat.

"Customer's always right," whispered John into Cheryl's ear, actually making tongue-to-ear contact purposely. Cheryl laughed.

Despite the guard dog skulking behind the frosted glass, John and Cheryl were determined to speak with Dr. Ginsberg. As a resident in pediatrics, Cheryl had rotated through Utah University Medical Center many years ago, which saw a good deal of pediatric surgical cases. She had validated firsthand Dr. Ginsberg's reputation of being a total bastard to those under his tutelage. She was convinced there was not a chance he would remember her. She had also come to learn he was the best at what he did in the intermountain West. It seemed a contradiction, but it didn't matter. The Harrises had important business to conduct, and it was merely that: business.

Eventually they were shown to the doctor's suite. Across the room, looking out a large picture window, stood a white-coated, massive body.

"Just didn't have the rain last year that we should have, and the way this winter's going, this year looks like a repeat," said the doctor without changing his position. "Things are a-changing. See the oleander down there in the garden? All the other years, the branches would be touching and interweaving. During the spring and summer, they'd form a hedge so thick, you couldn't see through them. Now, the infrastructure is sparse, so come spring, there won't be much of a hedge."

"Weather's been changing for at least the last eight years, sir," said John, hoping to engage the physician. "I've noticed it, and I don't like it. I'm John Harris, and this is my wife, Cheryl," said John, extending his hand. "She's a doctor too."

The portly doctor shook each of their hands and signaled his guests to the two chairs in front of his desk. The furniture in the room was nice, but the suite lacked warmth.

"What can I do for you?"

Cheryl cleared her voice and took the helm as John took out a notepad and pen. "Our reason for being here is simple. My husband, you may have read, was kidnapped recently, and one of his kidneys was removed. We'd like to ask you to look at his surgical scar and tell us one way or another, if you can, whether the approach taken is common or perhaps particular to a certain center ... if that's possible."

"Hold on just a minute," the doctor said. "I do remember hearing about you. Over the years, I've heard a few similar stories but have never seen any proof. Are you for real?"

Without answering, John verified that the office door was closed, then unbuttoned and slipped off his shirt. He stood and turned so Dr. Ginsberg could get a direct look.

"Would you mind coming around to this side of the desk in the light? I want a closer look."

In the natural light, the wound appeared angry and purplish, but that was part of the healing process. John and Cheryl waited for the doctor's appraisal.

The doctor examined the incision closely, turning John from side to side slowly. To John's surprise, the doctor touched the wound and traced its path.

"You can go ahead and put your shirt back on while I fetch one of my textbooks, if you don't mind." The surgeon moved to his bookcase and removed a large book. "Ah, here we go. Look at this." He turned the book toward them. "Your incision represents the classic retroperitoneal approach, as performed most often here and in Europe. This is the same approach I use. Your surgical incision is relatively small, indicating both a skilled and possibly caring surgeon. If the latter were possible in your circumstance."

"Europe and the U.S.?" John muttered, not bothering to write it down. "Is that all you can tell?"

"I'm sorry I can't be of more help. The technique is quite effective and quite common. Might I suggest you stop by the ROPA department on the floor below before you leave? They might be able to give you some more useful information."

"Ropa?" asked John.

"Regional Organ Procurement Agency," said Cheryl.

An elevator ride, a few hallways, and a large door with a brass placard reading "ROPA" later, the Harrises entered a large office with files and computers. An attempt to brighten the environment with plants was just that: an attempt. An older woman sat alone working at the closest desk.

"Hello," said John.

"Hello."

"We're the Harrises. This is Dr. Harris. I'm John."

"Did you have an appointment?"

"No, unfortunately. We just met with Dr. Ginsberg, and he suggested we come down to this office."

"Oh, that's just like him, that oaf. I'm afraid that I'm quite busy now and for the rest of the day. Have a couple of transplants waiting … and that's a real emergency, you know. Gotta drop everything when it happens. And, as you can see, I've got some staff out sick. What were you looking for?"

"We needed to learn about transplants. We have some questions," said Cheryl.

"I'm so sorry. I'm Mrs. Dennison. I sort of run this place. Here's my card. Call and we can schedule an appointment. That's the best I can do for you right now, under the circumstances."

John and Cheryl left Mrs. Dennison's office wondering what they had gained that day. By the time they walked out of the medical plaza, they were holding hands and feeling better. In the final analysis, the day had been far from a total loss. John's surgery could be pinned to a surgeon who had at least trained in the United States or Europe. That might be a significant piece of information one day. More importantly, they had made a connection that was critical. They would be calling ROPA soon to schedule a meeting.

In the parking lot, a well-groomed, bespectacled, suited Caucasian man sat in an unmarked late-model American car, watching the Harrises climb into their car through high-powered binoculars.

The busy Lyndon Drive ran parallel to the parking lot. The short hedges lining Lyndon were low enough to afford a view from the sidewalk. There, another man, casually dressed and of Middle Eastern descent, also watched the Harrises from a bus-stop bench.

On the drive home, a thought occurred to John. "What is the alternative to kidney transplantation?"

"Hemodialysis. You know, through a machine," answered Cheryl.

"Why does someone get a kidney transplant then? I mean, what's wrong with hemodialysis?"

"Hemodialysis is a pain in the ass. It takes three to four hours or more, at least three times a week. You're stuck lying there. That's a major disruption in what could otherwise be a fairly normal life with transplantation. Transplants are much more effective in clearing toxins than hemodialysis and I'm sure people probably live a whole lot longer with transplantation too."

"Hmm," said John. "But there's got to be more to it than that. Can we call Walter Harriman and put the same question to him?"

"We can try. It's a workday. Look in my purse for my PDA and look up his office phone number."

John dialed and hit the SEND button on his cell phone, then enabled the speakerphone setting.

"Dr. Harriman's office. Good morning, Laurel speaking. How may I help you?"

Cheryl whispered to John, "Compare that to Dr. Ginsberg's secretary."

"Uh, hi," Cheryl said more loudly. "This is Dr. Harris. Is Walter in and available?"

"Yes, he is, and I don't think he's with a patient. Let me check. Hold on."

There was a pause, and then a man spoke.

"Cheryl?"

"Hi, Walter. John and I are on our way home. We just met with Dr. Ginsberg."

"How is that fat old goose?"

"About as you'd imagine."

"Hell of a guy. Real dynamic!" yelled John.

"Listen, we have a few questions stimulated by our day at the university. Do you have a moment, or do you want to link up later?"

"Sure, I've got a break right now. Shoot."

"What are the advantages of a kidney transplant over hemodialysis?"

"Well, there are a ton of good reasons, and only a few downsides. OK, reasons. With hemodialysis, you are umbilicated to a machine for about four hours, three to four times a week, fifty-two weeks a year, every year. Now, that's no small matter. Think about it: planning vacations is a nightmare. Planning your everyday life around it is a headache to begin with! And if that weren't bad enough, you still have to be on a lousy-tasting diet: low sodium, low potassium, and limited fluid. With a transplant, patients have no dietary restrictions, no dialysis treatments. We're talking a normal lifestyle, folks, or damn near. Now, if you talk to patients on dialysis, like I do once in a while, they'll tell you how they always feel sick and lack energy. This malaise is especially pronounced right after the treatment. That's why many adults prefer to schedule hemodialysis in the evening, so they can go to sleep afterward. Imagine how that would interfere with marriage and your family life. And have you seen people on hemodialysis? They all look sickly. They're anemic, so their skin has a chronically ill, pasty look to it. You rarely see that in transplanted patients."

"So what are the downsides?"

"One other thing first. This one is pertinent to women."

"In women, when your kidney function or blood creatinine hits values of 3.4 to 3.5—which is all the time on hemodialysis—you become infertile. Bottom line. Women can't get pregnant on hemodialysis. With transplants, depending on their underlying disease, they at least have a chance. Now, downsides. They have to be on medications to keep their body from rejecting the transplant—immunosuppressives. The risk of infection in transplant patients on these drugs is far, far greater than that of hemodialysis patients. The higher the dose of suppressive medication they are on, the more risk they undertake. Other downsides: There's the risk of rejection. The antirejection drugs themselves have a very narrow therapeutic window. This means that the dose difference between what keeps them from rejecting their kidney and what makes them sick is very small. Some patients will get sick on the drug that is vitally important to them. So overall, transplanted patients do live better—and, you should know, they live longer too. But only if the transplant is a total success."

"So if you had your choice, what would it be?" asked John.

"Give me a transplant any day. Hands down. Most patients make the same choice, by the way. It's just a matter of finding the right kidney. That takes a while, maybe forever, and there are no guarantees."

"So, Walter, can you tell John what factors determine the right kidney?" Cheryl asked.

"This is complicated, but to summarize, there are six locations, called loci, that the scientists have found on the chromosomes. The more that match between the recipient and donor, the better and longer lasting the transplant. The less likely rejection. Hey, John, that reminds me of something."

"Yes?"

"When are you going to come and see me?"

"Actually, doc, you're in luck. I have an appointment in the next few days."

"Oh, I feel so lucky."

They all laughed, although John resented that the visit was necessary on medical grounds.

Chapter 16

The plan seemed sound. Since John always reacted badly on the same stretch of Highway 18, John and Marley had made a morning weekend date to take a little drive.

It was dawn, the sun just beginning to peek above the horizon. Daylight was not far away. Detective Marley stood outside his vehicle, leaning against the front fender, savoring the brisk temperature, the ranch scents, and his favorite pipe. He had lost track of the exact time. It did not matter; he was in no rush. It was Saturday morning, and he was free from real work—that was, unless a major crime was perpetrated somewhere. On the hood of the car sat an insulated cup of home-brewed coffee. At his feet was a light backpack.

Marley saw the light go on in the kitchen. A few minutes later, John stumbled bleary-eyed out of the front door. He dragged himself out of the house and into the cold with his steaming cup of coffee. Both men were dressed warmly.

"Marley, you're something else. My only chance to sleep in is on Saturday morning. Monday through Friday suck big, and Sunday morning is mass."

"Would you mind if we took your car?" Marley asked, ignoring John's whining.

"Sure. Why?"

"Well, I figure we've got one chance here, so let's give it our best shot. Let's do it right: you drive."

John noticed a long two-by-four piece of lumber sticking out of the side window of the detective's car, with the typical red flag on its end. He walked up and fingered the flag as he turned to Marley.

"By the book, eh, Marley?"

"Always."

"What's it for? Building something?"

"So to speak. You'll see." The lumber was transferred to the back of John's Range Rover; it stuck out the rear open window. Marley's pack went in back as well.

"Oh," Marley said. "Would you mind zeroing the trip odometer before we leave?"

"No problem."

They headed down Highway 18, punctuating small talk with some serious talk.

"So what's new from the Feds?"

"Nothing. I would've called you immediately. I keep calling them ... but nothing. All zeros. Are we getting close to where this feeling comes on?"

"Pretty soon. The truck?"

"They said it was clean. No fingerprints at all. Just like your Range Rover. John, what I'd like you to do is read off the trip odometer the moment you start to feel sick. OK?"

"Sure. Hey Marley? Is this what is feels like to be a dick?"

"If you are referring to the folklore use of 'dick' to reference the respectable and often underpaid art of sleuthing for the state government, then yes, this is what it sometimes feels like to be a dick."

John laughed.

Marley became serious. "Now, how does it go? Does it get bad and stay bad, or does it start out mild and peak at some point? Or something else?"

"Well, I feel fine until an exact moment around one of the bends, and then I feel more and more sick and anxious for a variable amount of time after that. Lately I sometimes get a weird sensation in the left side of my neck too."

"Like what?"

"I don't know. Sometimes a tingling, other times some mild, deep pain."

"Well, then, that settles that. Let me know exactly when any of it starts. If no one is behind us, I'd like to ask you to pull off the road at that point if it is safe ... or as soon after as is possible."

"You mean stop?"

"Don't worry. Just follow my instructions. And don't forget to call out the mileage. By the way, do you get that feeling traveling in both directions, or just one way?"

"Mostly heading toward the city. Occasionally the other direction, but barely noticeable. Oh, here comes the bend." John gripped the wheel tightly; he didn't look well. "Nine and three-tenths miles."

Marley wrote it down as John slowed.

"OK, pull over."

"I don't know …"

"What do you mean, you don't know? This is no time to play around. Just pull over. Come on. It's important. We've got work to do."

John pulled the car to a stop and began to shiver.

"Are you OK? Are you OK?" Marley repeated, tapping John's shoulder.

Sweat began to pour down John's face. Before Marley could get another word out, John floored the gas pedal, and the Range Rover took off, throwing both men back in their seats. The car careened downhill, screeching around the next turn.

"John! John! Slow down! It's OK!"

Instinctively, Marley grabbed the center console stick and put it into sport mode, downshifting rapidly. The effect was to slow the car down considerably. Marley did not know what he would do next, but he did continue to yell out John's name.

John slowed on his own accord. When the vehicle came to a stop, he seemed to close his eyes, shaking and breathing rapidly.

Marley reached out, and John caught his arm midway without turning his head. "I'm OK now."

Marley looked behind them and still saw no one.

"John, pull over there on the right, will you? Let me drive."

John did as he was told. Marley opened his door and walked around to the driver's side as John climbed over the console to the passenger seat.

"You sure you're OK?"

"Positive."

"That ever happen to you before?"

"Never. But I've never stopped before either. I would only drive quickly past it. I just came loose, didn't I? Whoa. I was just outside of myself … out of control."

Marley peered at the odometer, then noted the good visibility in front of him. He subtracted the initial mileage John had called to him from the current mileage.

"I'm going to turn around and go back to the spot. If you feel at all bad, at all out of control, tell me, and we go straight home. Otherwise I want to stop for a moment."

"Jeez, I'm sorry ..."

"No. Nothing to be sorry about. My fault," Marley said brusquely. "If I knew it would have this effect on you, I would have never suggested it. I'm sorry. Now let me know if you feel bad at all. I'm not kidding. I can come back here by myself, no problem. You sure you're all right?"

"Sure. Go for it."

Marley stopped at the exact spot of John's apparent abrupt break with reality, but in the opposite direction. He turned to John, who appeared fine—certainly not crazed.

"No problems?"

"None."

"You feel fine?"

"Yes, fine."

"Then look at me."

He did, and Marley was convinced.

"I'm going to turn off the engine. I'm going to get out and take a look. I want you to remain in the car, put your seat back, take some slow breaths, and relax. You got that?"

"Ten-four. Aye-aye, captain," said John, plainly irritated at being treated like a child, and certainly unaware of the peril he had placed both of them in a few moments ago.

Marley took the car keys with him. He looked at the road first. There were some gouges in the pavement perpendicular to the road. He stooped down and touched them. They had no particular meaning to him. He next examined the soft shoulder. Nothing looked out of order. He looked over toward John, who was resting, reclined, with his eyes closed. Marley carefully moved to the edge of the dirt, where the shoulder became mountainside. He peered over the edge even more carefully. Below him was a decline that seemed to go down forever. The dense forest vegetation below was obscured by the darkness of the hour.

After a moment, Marley moved away from the edge and returned to the car. He removed the lumber and carried it to the mountain edge. John elevated his seat and watched with interest. Marley collected large rocks and placed them next to the two-by-four. He then swung the red flag end over the cliff and piled the rocks on the rear, so that the wood would not fall over the edge.

Marley walked back to the car and got in.

"Have any more time, or do you need to get back?" he asked John.

"Are you kidding? You've got me too interested now. What's up?"

Near the bottom of the mountain, Marley took turned left, rather than continuing toward Larchmont. The road abruptly switched back in the opposite direction. After about a quarter of a mile, the paved road ended. Sometimes at a snail's pace, Marley followed the bumpy dirt road for another half mile before it too ended. An open area void of vegetation and other cars served as a forest parking lot.

The two men exited the car, stretched, yawned, and took in the surroundings for a moment. The dawn had illuminated the environment considerably. The profound silence was broken by the calls of a large bird circling overhead. Two hundred and seventy degrees of the clearing edge was level, forested area. The remaining portion of the circle was rocky mountainside, roughly one mile from where they currently stood. The road they had just descended was not visible. The majestic mountainside rose almost a few thousand feet and was densely forested only in the lower hundred feet.

Marley opened the rear hatch of John's SUV and removed his gear. He opened the pack, placed binoculars around his neck, and slung the pack over his shoulders.

"So tell me, what's with the binoculars?"

"Just to see what's ahead of us, in there," said Marley, pointing to the woods in front of them.

"And the pack?"

"Will you just trust me here? Food, some odds and ends."

"Come on. Can't you just tell me what we're doing here, for God's sake—in God's country?"

"I don't know exactly, to be honest. Just a hunch, related to what throws you into a frenzy on the small stretch of road up there. Follow me."

They headed into the forest. It was forty-five degrees in the shade and remarkably beautiful. The dense and moist compost under their feet, mostly made of fallen leaves, crunched softly with each step. An immense quiet was notable between steps. Towering trees formed dense vegetation over occasional fallen logs and numerous seedlings. Algae and fungi grew in sparse areas on the fallen trunks. The whitish-brown fungi formed thick, fan-like projections that resembled wall sconces. Neither man could figure out the position of these primitive plants in the chain of life.

Occasionally a blue jay darted above their heads, making absolutely no noise as its wings sliced through the still air. The aroma was reminiscent of the Harris ranch, only more intense.

Marley stood on a downed tree and caught his balance. He then removed his glasses and placed the binoculars up to his face. He scanned in all directions as John stood on the ground below him. They moved on. About a half mile in, the rush of water could be heard faintly from the distance.

"Wow, do you hear that? That must be the Stanbury River, right?"

"Yep," Marley said. "Courses all the way down from way above your house."

"Were you intending to go to the river?"

"Well, yes, and cross it."

Marley took the lead once again. As they continued, the sound of the river intensified. Within several yards of the river, they encountered the carcass of a raccoon. Actually, the head was the only recognizable part of the animal, whose internal organs and extremities had been efficiently removed, essentially leaving a bloody pelt.

"Hmm," pondered Marley. "What do you think? Coyote? Fox?"

"I guess so. You … you don't think it could be … no, never mind."

"Mountain lion? I don't think so. I haven't seen any reports of any, have you? I mean, usually they're at higher elevations. Any reports near you?"

"None that I'm aware of."

"Well, I doubt it then. But just in case, let's keep our eyes open. Judging by the condition, I'd say this is more than a couple of days old anyway."

They continued their trek to the riverbank, where the twenty-feet-wide river roared by. Numerous large boulders formed the base and sides of the waterway. Rock projections from within splintered the water into different paths, which united again farther downstream—until the next projection. The water was cold and clean, having traveled many miles from its icy origin high atop mountains far above.

"She's kind of low. Not a lot of rain the past year," said Marley.

"You been here before?"

"On occasion over the years. Living as close as you do, you've never been?"

"Well, no."

"God's country at your back porch, and down here too—you're a lucky man, you know? We need to find a place to cross the river. Let's go upstream until we find a decent spot to cross. I'm not interested in getting wet. Trench foot can just ruin your day. Know what I mean?"

"I hear ya," John answered.

Marley paused and surveyed the terrain. The forest on the other side of the river was much more sparse as rock formations began to dominate the landscape. By the time the men reached the mountainside, they would be navigating almost pure rock. Marley climbed up on a flat-topped rock and lifted the binoculars to his eyes again. He did not scan behind him. Rather, he looked at the terrain in front of him and then began looking toward the top of the mountain. He was looking for a tiny wooden projection with a red flag on the end of it. It was barely visible far off in the distance. Marley reckoned that they had to proceed upstream at least a mile in order to be in line with the flag.

"See anything?" asked John.

"Nope. All right, let's keep moving then."

It was beginning to warm up. Moving along the bank, they encountered a fallen tree that spanned the width of the river.

"What do you think? asked John.

"Well, number one, I'm getting a little hungry," answered Marley, scratching his head. "And, two, I say we consider this spot and go up farther to see if there's something better. If not, we come back here. Crossing here would be risky. You agree?"

John surveyed the terrain. The fallen tree was at least four or five feet above the river. It looked quite slippery—in fact, so slippery that it would be difficult to hold on, even scooting across on one's bottom. "I agree."

"Let's give ourselves another half hour. We stop then. If we've found no place to cross by then, we'll come back here and take our chances."

"Sounds like a plan."

The territory upstream continued at a modest climb as they proceeded along the river. The roar of the river seemed louder ahead of them; they soon encountered a moderate waterfall. The mouth of the river leading to the fall was wide and flat. Near the edge sat several stones that one could imagine stepping across to the other side. As the men aligned themselves at the level of the fall, they both pondered the possibility.

"Well, then, what will it be?" asked Marley. "Cross here, or on that slimy log downstream?"

"Since you put it that way, let's take our chances here."

"Saddle up."

They both moved to the dry land at the edge of the fall.

"Well, looking at it isn't going to help us," Marley observed. "Those rocks look large enough to be stable, but we're not going to know until we actually make contact."

"Well, if they were loose, there's certainly enough water running by them to sweep them away, don't you think?"

"Here I go. Let me go all the way across first before you go. No sense in two people getting wet. If I go down, meet me downstream. With this low a river, I won't go too far … that is, if I fall."

Marley stepped carefully from stone to stone, holding his arms out at his sides like a scarecrow for balance. Most of the stones were solidly based and stable. Those few rocks that wobbled were easy enough to navigate. He made it to the other side unscathed and signaled for John to cross.

John had made note of the potential pitfalls and began crossing. Taking extra care to not look over the fall's edge, he alternated his gaze between the rocks in front of him and the side where Marley stood. John ventured out and traversed the first several stones and then stopped for a breath. The next stone he encountered was loose and he maintained equal footing and weight between the loose rock and the one before it. Cautiously, he put more weight on the forward stone. It felt stable, and he stepped all the way onto it. At that point, the rock wobbled, and John compensated by moving his arms and butt in opposite directions, above his bent knees. Just when it seemed that he was balanced enough to move forward again, the rock shifted, and John nearly went over the edge. He caught his balance and scampered all the way across.

"Holy moly, you scared the bejesus out of me," Marley said.

John continued up the steep grade, over occasional tree roots and around rocks and bushes, with Marley taking up the rear. Another half mile went by in an hour.

John stopped suddenly in his tracks and yelled and waved for Marley to join him with haste. Marley broke into a full run. He stopped, eclipsing John, and both just stared. They were close to the base of the mountain.

In front of them lay the carcass of a crushed and flattened automobile. For the most part, the vehicle was destroyed. Marley pulled a small camera out of one of his pack pockets and snapped a few pictures of the car and its surroundings, signaling John to stay put. Then he approached the car methodically, as he would at the scene of any crime, studying the ground. Once at the vehicle, he got down on all fours and looked into an eight-to-ten-inch space of cabin that was visible below the nearly collapsed roof. Within, Marley could make out what appeared to be at least two badly decomposed humans and a black automatic weapon. Looking through open spaces as he circled the car, Marley saw more human remains and weapons.

"Hey, Marley. What's going on here?"

"I'm not sure," said Marley as he walked over to John. "Here, take these binoculars and look up about as far up to the top of the mountain as is visible, directly in line with where we are now, and tell me what you see."

John took the binoculars and began to scan.

"What?" he asked, staring through the lenses.

"Anything red?"

"No … wait a minute. Yeah, I see it. What the hell is it?"

"It marks the exact spot where you have the anxiety attacks on 18."

"Are you shitting me?"

"Nope."

"Come on, Marley. What's it all mean?"

"Hell if I know. But, clearly, there must be a relationship between this vehicle and its contents—highly suspicious contents, I might add—and what happened to you. If you ask me, it is the first solid lead we've had since you returned home from Kansas. That simple. That amazing."

"What do you mean, highly suspicious contents?"

"There's dead people in there."

John tried to take little glimpses around Marley, who stood directly between him and the wreck.

"Marley. Tell me this. Are they wearing khaki ranger uniforms?"

"From what I can see, yes. Why?"

"I'm not sure."

The homicide, search and rescue, and criminalist teams reached the site of the crunched vehicle a few hours after being summoned over Marley's two-way radio. Numerous men and women combed the area, with the car as the epicenter. Human fragments, weapons, and other debris not indigenous to the surroundings were logged. John sat in the shade and watched the activity. It was just like on TV, only there were no squad cars or unmarked police cars—or commercials.

He could overhear the chief criminalist's comments to Marley: "Humans, at least three different people. The scavenger animals carried some remains outside. They usually don't go beyond our perimeter, so we should recover a lot of those carried away. Of course, the smaller parts may have been pulled underground or into a hidden animal den. Those are gone. The real challenge, as you might imagine, will be to uncrunch the car and get to all the evidence inside. There should be quite a bit in there. Anyway, we're done here."

Marley walked to a clearing with a funny-looking weapon in his hand. It looked like a harpoon gun without a harpoon. Marley spoke into his two-way, then aimed the gun above his head and fired. A green, smoking flare ignited in the air and rose several hundred feet.

Within a few minutes, the distant thunder of a helicopter was heard. An unusually large, double-bladed helicopter quickly materialized overhead. Two men slid to the ground on cables. They walked over with their respective cables and examined the situation. One radioed to the helicopter. Someone pushed a large package out of the aircraft's huge open door. Slowed by a third cable, the package was lowered to the ground.

The package was a large, thick tarp. The original two cables were connected to the wrecked auto. The helicopter's engines whined louder, and the car started to rise from the ground. When it was about three feet from the ground, the helicopter pilot paused and allowed the team to place the tarp under and then around the car. Once the tarp was fastened in place, the car was lifted high into the air and flown toward the dirt lot where Marley and John had parked.

"Well, I guess you'll be calling the FBI, then?" asked John.

Marley blinked at him. "What? I don't see how this has any relationship to John Harris, do you?"

Chapter 17

The sheikh and his son sat next to one another, watching *The Lion King* on the large screen. Behind them sat women whose faces were partially obscured by their garb. Off to one side was an abandoned electric Rolls-Royce replica. The sheikh turned and stared at the boy affectionately in the dark.

The child was particularly handsome, but odd-looking—disproportion-ately small. One of his little hands lay on top of the sheikh's. As they watched, an adviser entered the room and approached the sheikh. Before the visitor could speak, the sheikh raised his free hand, signaling him to be quiet during the scene where the lion king risked his life to save his lion son. When the sheikh dropped his hand, the adviser whispered into his ear.

The sheikh paused the movie; lights came on in the room. The child jumped up, but then demurely bowed his head and waited.

"Please give me a moment, and we will start again," the sheikh said.

With that, the child and the women disappeared without a word.

"I am sorry, sire. There have been new developments that you should be aware of."

The sheikh waited.

"I'm afraid it has to do with the donor."

Suddenly quite concerned, the sheikh stood and turned sharply toward the adviser, who bowed his head and cowered.

"Tell me what it is that you have to say."

"It seems as though the donor is pursuing his own investigation."

"How? In what way?"

"He searches online for information about kidney thefts. He has visited a world-renowned transplant surgeon not far from his home."

The sheikh's face gave nothing away. "Anything else?"

"Yes."

"Well, what?"

"It involves more than the donor, sire."

"The FBI?"

"No. They have been surprisingly quiet."

"Tell me—now."

"A local policeman has worked with the donor. They have somehow uncovered the bodies sacrificed during the operation."

The sheikh slowly sat, absorbed in thought. "Is there any possible way to link those sacrificed directly to us?"

"No. I am sure of that. And the drugs used were to have obliterated any memory of the abduction."

The sheikh looked him directly in the eyes to verify what he just heard. "Then a message must be sent to the donor … and quickly."

Chapter 18

"Hey, Marley, I know you wanted me to come see you tonight, but you're not going to believe this. I just went out to the car, and it's dead. The engine won't turn over ... no lights ... nothing. I'm stuck at the office. Unbelievable timing, huh?"

"Car trouble. Hmm. Let me see what I can work out. I wanted to go over some of the preliminaries on the car in the forest."

It was past quitting time when Panzer, sitting in his unmarked car, received the call from Marley.

"Yeah?"

"Are you anywhere near the business district?"

"Not too far. Why?"

"I was supposed to meet with John Harris tonight, but he's having some car problems. It would save a lot of time if you could pick him up at his office on your way back to the station."

"I'm on it."

John was nearly alone in the building. The twenty-four-hour roadside service could not pinpoint the problem and had to tow his car to Range Rover of Larchmont. He got a little extra paperwork done before he descended in the elevator to meet Panzer. The elevator stopped only once before reaching the parking garage. A single, well-dressed Middle Eastern man entered the elevator.

Initially John paid no attention to him. Then, out of the corner of his eye, he noticed something odd. He looked more closely; the man wore a black suit and black gloves. It seemed out of place. When John took in the man's facial profile, something seemed painfully familiar about it. The panic hit quickly. He was not sure why, but he wanted off the elevator ... now! He told himself to relax and looked the other way.

The man stared straight ahead, as most passengers tended to do, until the elevator door closed. The man sunk a pronged key into a slot in the elevator panel and lifted up, avoiding the emergency alarm. The elevator abruptly came to a stop.

On instinct, John threw a punch at the man, but the man caught John's fist nearly at the end of its trajectory, midair. There was no time to be stunned. John kicked the man in the shin and received a swift jab to the abdomen in return. John's legs gave out, and he fell to the floor—but not before the man caught John's face with his fist. The combination of face moving downward and fist moving upward broke John's nose and split his upper lip, rattling his teeth. John lay stunned, speechless and in pain, bleeding on the elevator floor. He curled up, struggling to catch his breath.

The man kicked John's arms in retaliation for the shin kick that John had given him. He knelt and pulled an exceptionally long-barreled gun from inside his coat and pressed it into the side of John's skull.

"What do you want?" John managed to get out. "Take my money. It's inside my coat."

"You need to stop talking about your kidney. To anyone," the man said clearly, despite his Arabic accent.

"Why?"

The silenced end of the weapon was pushed harder against John's skull.

"If I come back again, I will not be so nice."

John felt the pressure on his head ease as the man started to rise to his feet. Before he did so, the man punched John's exposed left flank. John moaned at the square hit on his surgical site. The attacker stood, replaced the weapon in its hidden holster and brushed off his clothes. He fished for the key in his pocket and nonchalantly shoved it into the brass plate in front of him. As the elevator finished its descent, John lay paralyzed by the pain in his flank and face—pain he had not experienced even just after the forced surgery.

As the doors opened, one person stood ready to get on.

"John! My God, what happened?" said Panzer, taking a few seconds to assimilate. He stepped back and reached for his weapon.

The man asked John, "Is this your friend?"

Not waiting for an answer, he shot Panzer in the forehead with a silenced bullet. Panzer was thrown back and began seizing on the ground.

"Remember what I said," were the man's final words as he walked away from the elevator.

"No!" screamed John as he crawled to the elevator's brass plate and pulled the alarm. He opened the telephone box, dialed 911, and then collapsed to the floor again. He knew there was nothing more he could do.

"This is Detective Marley with Larchmont PD, calling for Dr. Harris. Could I speak to her please?"

"She's in the examining room with a patient. Should I disturb her, or could she call you back?"

"I'm sorry. Yes. I need to speak to her now."

A moment passed before Cheryl came to the phone.

"Marley?"

"Yes. I'm sorry to bother you at work."

"This is my only late day."

"Listen, John's OK ... but he's been injured."

"What? What do you mean?" asked Cheryl, not noticing the strain in his voice.

"He was apparently mugged on his way out of the building tonight."

"Is he all right?"

"He's hurting. His nose looks broken, his lip is split. Other than that, I think he's OK. The doctor is with him now. I heard him say something about an x-ray."

"Which hospital are you at?"

"We're in the ER at Bayer Memorial."

"OK, listen ... you have a pencil? I'd prefer that a plastic surgeon or ENT specialist suture his lip, if it's not done already. If Mark Levin is on staff there, he would be my preference. Did you get that? Mark Levin?"

"L-e-v-i-n, right?"

"Right. I just can't believe this."

"I'll see your there. Drive safely."

Cheryl parked in the doctor's parking lot outside the ER. On occasion, she had seen a patient in the ER or admitted one to the pediatric floor. Once every six weeks, she took calls for the ER. She knew the hospital well.

Cheryl took her hospital ID out of her purse and attached it to her lapel. She did not want any barriers between her and the facts. As she entered through the automatic doors of the ambulance entrance, she passed familiar staffers.

The clerk took Cheryl's arm and showed her to a large room with several stalls separated by curtains, each with an unusually bright overhead lamp. Mark Levin was at work on John.

"Hi, Cheryl."

"Hi. Is he OK?"

"He'll be alright. Just cosmetic injuries and that's my forte."

John couldn't speak. His upper lip was being repaired; only his mouth was visible through the three-inch oval hole in the sterile towel lying over his face. The lip was split through and through, fat and swollen. As a physician, this did not faze Cheryl. As a spouse, it upset her quite a bit.

"How are the teeth?"

"Just fine," Dr. Levin answered. "The lip took the brunt of it. The nose did too. It's fractured, but I've straightened it out." He returned to his work. "I've closed the orbicularis oris muscle, and I'm working on the subcutaneous layer. After that, I'll line up the vermilion border, and we're home free. Thank you for asking for me."

"Don't be silly, Mark. Thank you for coming to see him." Cheryl fought to think of the best thing for her to do next. As she saw it, there were a few choices: She could go find Marley, or she could seek out the ER physician. She chose option three, moving over to John's right side and holding his hand. "Do you mind if I stand here?"

"You mean sit?" said the clerk as she brought over a chair.

"No, not at all," Dr. Levin said. "But I tend to get real quiet when I'm concentrating. So, don't take it personally."

"Oh, no. You just do your thing. I'm here for Johnny." She looked around a bit, but every aspect of John was covered either with a blanket or a surgical drape.

About twenty minutes later, the doctor announced that he was done. He followed this with a warning: "Cheryl, before I take off the surgical field … I know you're a doctor, but you need to anticipate what you will see. This is not a patient. It's your husband. I have not splinted his nose yet. I'll do that in a second. However, his nose is very swollen. His face, especially under both eyes, is ecchymotic. As a matter of fact, he looks like all my nose-job patients. I haven't seen his face for a while, but I suspect his eyelids will be pretty swollen too. This will all go away. I promise. OK?"

"OK." Cheryl stood and took a deep breath.

Dr. Levin removed the towel. She saw little below his brows that did not look like raw hamburger. She selected a clear area on his forehead and planted a soft kiss there.

"He'll be OK."

"I know. It just looks like it hurts so much," she replied through tears. "John, would you mind if I touch base with the ER doctor and see what else, if anything, is up? Then I'll come back and fill you in?"

"Cheryl ... they killed Panzer," John said through swollen lips.

"What? Who are 'they'? What are you talking about?" asked Cheryl. She tried to assimilate the gravity of what she was being told by someone who sounded very much like her husband, but did not look a thing like him.

"I don't know who 'they' are."

"I thought Marley said someone just tried to rob you? Honey, let me go speak with Marley and the ER doctor and see if I can get you out of here. We've got to get the hell out of here."

As she walked away she had a sobering thought. What if this were somehow related to the kidney incident? She passed that thought off as ridiculous.

As she exited the room, she saw Dr. George Carver at the clerk station, writing away on one of his charts. *Good*, she thought to herself. The doctor, who was named after the famous botanist and chemist from the turn of the century, looked up briefly as she headed his direction.

"Dr. Harris," he acknowledged her. "Come into my office for a moment." He led her to the cubicle where the night doctors were occasionally lucky enough to get a little shut-eye. He sat her on the bed, took a chair, and continued. "John will be fine. I heard you saw his face and spoke to Mark Levin about that aspect. He feels your husband will do well. His neck is fine; his cervical spine and chest x-ray are normal. He has no other significant injury other than his face. Although he was punched in the abdomen, I've checked it several times, and it's not very tender. His urine is void of blood. His kidney function is normal." Her eyebrows arched, and Dr. Carver realized she wasn't in the know. "Oh, he was punched on the site of the surgery. I've spoken with the urologist—you know Steve Schleger—and he tells me that since there's no kidney there and it's this far out from the surgery, there's nothing to worry about. All in all, he's bruised up badly but not too severely. Neurologically, he's fine. Didn't have any head injury other than his face. Unless Mark Levin says differently, home he goes. And he wants to go home." He reached over and hugged Cheryl. "I know this is a lot. Any questions?"

"Are you sure he's ready to come home?"

"Any problems, I'm here all night. Just call or bring him back. OK?"

"Have the police been here?"

"Oh, yes. Come and gone. I'm sorry. He gave me his card ... Matley, something like that. He had a few words with your husband and left. He said he'd be by the house tonight. He was in a hurry. Apparently someone was killed in this same incident."

Cheryl just looked at him in disbelief. It was true.

They sat in the living room, the three of them, very solemn. John had a large bag of ice on his face; he rested his head on the back of the couch. Cheryl was beside him. Marley sat a chair, facing them both.

"John, may I see your scalp where he put the gun? Where was that?" Marley asked.

"Sure," said John, pointing to the left side of his head.

"I'm gonna move the hair out of the way, OK?"

Marley stood over John and, using both hands, rapidly separated hairs into groups, looking for damage to the underlying scalp. "Cheryl, can you hold my flashlight right here, please?"

"No problem."

Detective Marley separated the hairs around a red, circular area measuring an inch and a half in diameter. There was a central clear area about the size of a .38-caliber bullet.

"Thanks," he said as he let John's hair fall as it would. "Could I borrow your phone? Reception."

"Yep. You remember where it is?"

Marley went into the kitchen. Flipping open his small pocket notebook, he pulled a business card from it. In the center of the card were thirteen gold stars and the unmistakable letters: FBI. An agent's name and number appeared in opposite corners. Marley dialed the number and reached an operator.

"My name is Detective Marley of the Larchmont Police Department. I would like to speak to Agent Moreno, please." He spoke quietly, so as not to be heard by the Harrises. After a pause, he continued. "No, this is not an emergency, but I need to speak with him now. He'll have to make that decision. Tell him who I am, and let him decide."

He returned to the living room to find Cheryl curled up next to John. Both appeared to be sleeping.

Marley whispered, "John, you awake?"

"We're both awake," said Cheryl.

Both opened their eyes and came to attention, visually begging for him to continue.

"It is my opinion, based on what you've told me, John, that this person is out of your hair as long as you keep quiet regarding the kidney or related issues. But there's no way to know for sure. As a result, I think we need to place someone at your house for protection."

"I'm really scared," Cheryl said. "This guy was dead serious. But, if I take a moment to be rational, it seems to me that if he wanted to kill John, he would have done it right then and there."

"I agree. But I'm still going to post someone for a while, for peace of mind."

"Hey, Russ," John said. "Before you go, answer me this. What were you looking for on my head?"

"The size of the gun barrel pressed into your scalp. It left a circular impression."

"So?"

"Probably a .38-caliber gun."

"And?"

"Not meaningful in itself. But, John, what you described indicates that the shooter used a silencer. Only very organized professionals use silencers—Mafia, spies, crap like that. Even your most advanced criminals never use silencers. Throw in the accent, and we're not dealing with anyone from around here. No common criminal types."

John leaned forward and let the ice bag hit the floor. "We figured that long ago. I can't quite place the accent." He paused. "Hey, Marley?"

"Yeah."

"We're so sorry about Detective Panzer. If there's anything we can do …"

"I agree," added Cheryl.

"I have to see his family right now," the detective answered grimly. "I wish you could go in my place."

Chapter 19

Despite the late hour, three limousines idled in front of the palace. Their drivers huddled together, smoking and talking. The palace itself would have been silent, were it not for the sheikh raging in his private quarters behind a guarded door.

He stopped, turned, and pointed toward the military men. Even without his power and authority, the scowl on his face would make most men cower.

"Who killed the police officer? Who was that stupid?"

"He was in plain clothes. He went for his weapon. It was unavoidable," responded the senior officer.

"Allah will not be as lenient as I have been. There is no other choice. It has to be done, and it has to be done immediately. We will need outside help."

A typically long workday over, John began to unwind as he guided the Range Rover homeward. Isolated patches of snow dotted the roadside. As he approached the spot on 18 that had disturbed him in the past, he slowed to a stop and put down his window. He felt nothing. He raised the window, and a smile broke across his face as he drove the final stretch home.

On impulse, he dialed home on his cell.

"Hello," came the pithy response.

"Michael?"

"Yes."

"How are you doing?"

"Fine."

"Watching TV?" John already knew the answer.

"Yes."

"How much do I have to pay for more than one syllable?"

"What?"

"I'll be home soon. I miss you."

"Me too, Dad."

Michael hung up without further response. At six years old, most kids were terse like that, especially if they were watching TV. Actually, John felt fortunate that someone had bothered to answer the phone during a TV program. He smiled to himself at how Michael had changed over the last two years. He had gone from child to boy during that period of time. Innocence had not yet been lost, but he was now a team player with the rest of the kids. He played games with them, stood up for his rights, and had his own friends. And what a beautiful boy he was. John wished he could freeze the entire family the way it was now, at least for a while. Better yet, if he could only have frozen everything the way it was before he was kidnapped and violated.

As John drove up to the circle-H entrance to the ranch, the patrol car met him and acknowledged that it was safe to pass. John and Cheryl had recently discussed with Marley whether the need for such protection was fading along with the swelling of John's face. John's car triggered the outside lights, but there was no greeting party as John rolled up the long driveway and parked next to Cheryl's car and the family minivan.

He realized everyone must be busy watching the tube. But did dogs watch TV too? He walked into the house, set his briefcase down in the kitchen, then walked into the family room. There they were. All but Nicole had their eyes glued to the screen. Nicole was tired, but smiled and held her arms out for her daddy. Quietly, he picked her up, trying not to disturb the rest of them. The last scene played out, Cheryl and the two older kids laughed, and the TV went dark.

"Daddy!" yelled the other two middle children in unison, running to his legs and giving him a big hug. Eric sat, tired, daydreaming.

"Hi, guys. Hi, Mommy. Hey, where're the dogs?"

"They were out chasing something about a half hour ago. Must be on the scent of something."

"Yeah, probably the Murdocks' female dog," Cheryl added.

That caught Eric's interest. A knowing smile spread across his face. Despite his brief eleven years on the planet, anything even vaguely sexual seemed to catch his interest as of late. John reckoned there might be a connection between this and the acne that had recently erupted on Eric's face.

John walked out the back door of the house, kids in tow, and listened for the dogs. Then he gave a loud whistle. Nothing.

"Oh, well. They'll be back. It's bedtime. What do you say we get ready and read a bit?"

"No!" they responded in unison, as they did every night.

"What is this aversion you guys have to sleep?"

Cheryl chimed in, exhausted at the end of a long day: "Simple. Because they are kids. That's what kids do, since the beginning of time."

"Thank you, Dr. Spock."

Endless teeth were brushed and flossed with Dad's help. Eric and Erin were self-sufficient in this area, although spot checks were necessary from time to time to keep them honest. Eric and Erin put themselves to bed, while the parents prepared the two younger ones, read them stories, and lay with them for a while. The two older kids often said they did not mind the attention showered on the younger ones; however, Cheryl knew better and felt bad about the necessary circumstances. Somehow, she would make it up to them.

John checked on Eric after the two little ones were well on their way toward REM sleep. True to form, he was deep asleep. It would take an earthquake to wake him up now. Erin, on the other hand, was wide awake. That child never went to sleep early. In fact, she had given up her naps far earlier than any of the others.

"Hi, sweetie," whispered John.

"Hi, Daddy," she said, holding her arms straight out for a hug. She was certainly her sweetest and softest at night. During the day, right up to bedtime, she could turn at any moment and become a beast. She was the moody child. "Daddy, why do you have to work so much?"

"Remember that Beatles song Mom and I used to play for you? 'To get you money, to buy you things' …" he answered, singing the last sentence.

"I know. But do you think you could take me ice skating again soon?"

"We can try. It's not just my work; you and your brothers and sister have so many things going on these days, including on the weekends, that it's hard to find a time when we're both available."

"Daddy?"

"Yes, honey bunny."

"Does your scar hurt you anymore?"

"No. Neither does my face. Why? Do I act like I'm in pain?"

"No."

He said nothing.

"I guess I'm wondering if you think about what happened to you very much."

"I bet *you* think about it a lot, don't you?"

"I don't like it, Daddy."

"Me either. Hardly a day goes by when I don't think about it. I do think that I'm thankful it's over. But I bet I know why you don't like it. I think it's because Daddy protects you and keeps you safe, and maybe you wonder who's gonna keep you safe if they can hurt your Daddy."

Erin was quiet, preferring simply to hug. He was right on the money.

"Well, let me tell you this," John continued. "Mommy and Daddy will always protect you and keep you safe. So you don't need to worry about that stuff. Promise. OK?"

"OK."

"Goodnight, sweetie."

"Night, Dad. Love you."

"Love you too. See you tomorrow. Sweet dreams."

Moody and serious, sensitive, occasionally worried, John thought to himself. *But not troubled.*

John went to his bedroom, where he expected to find Cheryl. She was not there. He checked the kid's rooms, one by one, and could not find her. Returning to the family room, he found Cheryl sleeping on the couch, in a sitting position. Her hair flowed over the back of the couch as her head lay to one side. She breathed easily. Her white, long-sleeved cotton blouse was unbuttoned to mid-cleavage. A chenille vest covered her ample breasts, although it was unbuttoned. Below was a rich snakeskin belt, with a large silver buckle, that wove through the loops of her light blue jeans. Her legs were slightly parted. He faced a familiar dilemma: let her rest, or gently jump her bones? For the moment, he just looked at her. She was beautiful, and he loved her so much.

John went into the kitchen to grab a bite to eat, and think. There he heard the single chime as the outdoor lights went on. He walked into the living room. Looking out the window, he saw no cars pulling up.

Another deer, he thought. He smiled at how the sudden lighting must have scared the crap out the poor deer.

Moving back to the family room, he gently sat down next to Cheryl after grabbing the remote control. Without waking, she turned and coiled up in a fetal position, against his side and under his arm. John flicked on the ten o'clock news, which had already started.

John awoke with a start. Perhaps, he reasoned, it was the musical introduction to the eleven o'clock news that had awakened him. But he felt anxious and was not sure why. As he stood, Cheryl woke up as well.

"What?" she asked softly. "Oh, I must have fallen asleep. I'm sorry." As she focused on John and became more alert, she could see that something was wrong.

"John?"

"Shhh!" He held his hand toward her to be quiet.

"What?"

"I'm not sure."

At that moment, a man stepped out from the shadows. It was the man who had killed Detective Panzer!

John reacted without thinking and reached for a heavy metal urn on the coffee table.

The man responded quickly by leveling a gun at John.

"I would not do that," he said, then shifted his gun toward Cheryl. "I will kill her."

"Why? Why are you here? I haven't said anything to anyone."

"It is not yours to question. Both of you are coming with me."

"I have spoken to no one, just as you told me."

"My God, what do you want from him?" Cheryl begged. "You already have his kidney!"

"Quiet, bitch!" He gestured to follow with his gun.

John did not know what to do next. The man had moved within ten feet of John when Michael walked into the family room, holding his Teddy bear and squinting. He could not see the stranger, who now turned his attention and weapon in the direction of the child. John lunged at the man with one hand, pushing the man's arm and weapon to the ceiling. John's other fist crashed into the man's jaw. The silenced weapon fired into plaster of the wall near the ceiling as the man was knocked off his feet. Cheryl grabbed Michael and carried him down the hallway as she ran, closing and locking doors behind her.

John maintained his grip on the man's arm as the two hit the floor. The man moaned as John landed on top of him. John was screaming, the visceral response of a primate fighting for his life. He dropped his other hand to the man's throat and squeezed. The man brought his knee up into John's backside. As John lurched forward, the man butted him in the head with his own forehead.

John moaned, but then gave it right back to the man even harder with his own forehead. The man let go of the gun in the moment it took to recover from the blow. With his sheer strength, the man threw John off him and into the wall, then reached toward the gun. John recovered and kicked the gun down the foyer, several feet away. He recoiled his leg and kicked again, this time catching the intruder's foot, causing him to trip and fall to his knees. They both stood and faced off. A smile crept onto the man's face; John was clearly no match. John threw a few punches, only to be blocked and punched back, once on the side of the face and once in the abdomen. John was left with no options as he frantically glanced around for any sort of weapon. He found none. Desperate, he flung himself in a football tackle. The man shifted and deflected John into the wall, then made for the weapon.

As he began to turn with it toward John, a voice rang out from the kitchen.

"Larchmont police. Put the gun down now, or I'll shoot."

The man continued his arc in the direction of the voice.

Blam! Blam! Blam! Blam! Blam! Blam! Blam! Seven shots rang out in rapid succession, each hitting their mark. The assailant sunk to the floor, a bleeding hulk.

Detective Marley changed clips without altering his aim or concentration while John checked for a pulse and shook his head.

Outside, amid police cars with flashing red lights and an ambulance at the entrance of the driveway, a police officer hunched over his steering wheel, a bleeding bullet hole in the back of his skull. Overhead, a helicopter roared in circles, its searchlight illuminating the Harris ranch for the K-9 units looking for further threats.

Inside, a medic tended to John. A bruised and slightly swollen forehead complemented his recently injured yellow, bruised nose and cheeks. The only other injuries were scraped knuckles and sore ribs.

Under the watchful eye of Detective Marley, Cheryl and the children huddled on the family-room couch. All of the children but Eric had fallen back asleep. Cheryl eased herself away from the slumbering lot and went into the kitchen. She borrowed the medic's stethoscope and listened to John's lungs. His abdomen was not tender, and his thought processes seemed fine.

"Go ahead, Bravo Seven," said Marley into his two-way.

"Two dead Irish setters out by the road and down apiece. Both shot in the head."

"Ten-four. Rope 'em off."

Cheryl and John heard the transmission.

"What are we going to tell the kids?" she asked.

"That we're fucking lucky to be alive. Hey, Russ, you got a minute?"

"A minute, and only until I'm needed again."

"How did you get here so fast? Cheryl didn't call 911 until she had rounded up the kids and herded them into our room."

"The officer out front didn't check in. It was a hunch at that point. I came over, you know, just to be sure. Remember that telemetry device on that sensor out in the front?"

"Yeah?"

"Well, I had one of my own installed on your driveway sensor. This way I would know all the times of arrival and departure. It struck me most unusual that it should go off at around 10:15 PM on a weeknight, after two earlier transmissions—yours and Cheryl's. So it went off, and with no response from the officer outside, I just put the pedal to the metal."

The Harris family relocated to the Larchmont Police Department in the early hours and relegated to a large break room with old, vinyl couches. No further chances would be taken.

John stood looking out one of the barred windows at the freedom below, wondering if it might ever be safe to return home again. What if Marley hadn't saved them? He began to shake as he turned to look at his sleeping family, spread out and sleeping awkwardly on the couches in the cold room. He wondered why the intruder had not shot him or Cheryl while he had the chance.

Marley had advised the Harrises the night before that the FBI was joining the scene and would meet with them this morning. John wondered what the Feds could possibly have in mind. They hadn't been any help thus far. They had yet to finish their analysis of the ranger truck and Panzer's death. On the other hand, perhaps John was being too critical. It turns out the shooter had disabled the surveillance cameras in the parking lot prior to Panzer's death making their job that much more difficult.

As the children and Cheryl stirred in the first rays of morning sunlight, John still stood, watching the beginnings of normal life outside. He looked at his watch. He would have been at work for two hours already. For once, he actually missed waking up early and going to work.

The hours John had spent awake and standing did not yield him any useful information. He had no ideas, no plans. He and his family were at the mercy of law enforcement.

After eight, Marley came in with several McDonald's breakfasts for his guests. "Good morning, all. There's plenty here for everyone. John and Cheryl, maybe once you have them situated, we could talk over there." Marley pointed to a corner of the room.

"So, what's up?" asked John.

"No new information on that guy at your house last night. We haven't found evidence of any accomplices yet. The FBI will be joining us momentarily."

"What did they have to say?"

"Well, I guess I just want to prepare you. They're talking about enrolling you all—now, just for a short while—in a federal witness-protection program."

"What!" said Cheryl, trying to whisper. "You've got to be kidding!"

"I know, but try to be logical. Number one, it's not witness protection, but functions the same way. Number two, it would be temporary. Number three, two police officers are dead. Number four, you could still be in danger, right? In fact, everything points to that possibility. You need to be protected until this whole thing is sorted out. Now listen—look at me—the final decision is yours. But it looks like the right thing to do. I personally see no other options. Just think about it. That's all I ask. OK? You told us that the man in your house was the same one who shot Panzer. We have every reason to believe that he was not acting alone. We're talking a professional outfit here. At least in all likelihood." His eyes, with lines of age and worry radiating from their corners, pleaded with John and Cheryl.

"You don't even trust the FBI, Marley," said John.

"I don't trust their politics, but I have no doubt in their resources and abilities."

At that moment, a serious-looking man with salt-and-pepper hair walked into the room.

"John and Dr. Harris, this is Agent Moreno of the FBI."

Both shook his strong hand reluctantly. He turned and pointed to more suited agents in the doorway. "I'm Special Agent Moreno. Until we nail the people behind these attacks, these fine men and women are going to be your new family."

Chapter 20

It took almost three weeks to get to Los Angeles, and the adjustment was going to be more difficult than anticipated. For one thing, the Harrises were back in the city—and not just any city, but one of the largest in the free world. It embodied the exact opposite of Cheryl and John's hopes for their family life and everything they had done to change their circumstances. For adults, this was tolerable when the threat of death was the alternative. For the children, change was not welcome. With the exception of their parents, they had lost all that was familiar and comforting to them. They felt little security. The possibility of new friends and a different life held absolutely zero appeal. The whole family felt miserable and frightened upon arrival. The crowds at Los Angeles International Airport made Larchmont look like a ghost town, even during rush hour.

Special Agent Evert was a serious, attractive, unmarried woman in her thirties. She assured the Harrises that the crowds provided an edge of safety, strategically speaking. Under heavy sensory overload, the Harrises found themselves herded like cattle from the arrival gate to a van waiting at the sidewalk. They purposely hadn't checked any bags.

John heard Evert speak into her transmitter: "The bounty has arrived." Silently John objected to being referred to as bounty, but he was in no position to argue.

Moreno had arrived ahead of time with John to be sure all arrangements were adequate and secure. He awaited the party at their hotel destination while John and agent Toliver went to the airport to pick them up.

The heavy traffic didn't seem to bother agent Evert. It was different for the driver of the van, who occasionally cursed under his breath. John figured the cursing must represent some concern other than traffic—perhaps personal problems, or maybe just lack of sleep. The agent, an older, pudgy fellow, certainly had nowhere else to be and nothing else to do at the moment. Compared to other "clients" the agents must have had to protect, John mused, didn't this seem low-risk—almost like a vacation?

The van was different from most passenger vans in that it had no windows in the passenger areas and no back window. In the rear sat John, Cheryl, Michael, and Erin. Nicole nestled on Cheryl's lap. In the middle seat, Agent Sarah Evert sat by the sliding door, with Eric next to her.

The van pulled into traffic and headed for the nearby freeway ramp. "Moreno, en route, freeway, traffic," Evert said into the microphone on her lapel, answering the inquiry that only she and her fellow agents could hear in their earpieces.

The young tank-topped driver of a flatbed truck hung partway out of his window, waving his hand, appealing to the van driver to let him in as he edged in front of them. Music blared from the truck, although the two other men in the cab were not moving to the music at this early hour. Huge panes of glass were mounted on both sides of the truck from about mid-tire level to above the cab, angled slightly inward. Numerous smaller pieces were piled in between, on the flatbed part. An early start for a day's worth of work. What different lives people led.

The van driver honked. "Asshole," he whispered under his breath. The hand-waving appeal from the other vehicle was a formality. They clearly had no intention of taking no for an answer.

The traffic continued its crawl with frequent stops. The haze was starting to burn away, portending a reasonable California winter day.

"Hey, Toliver?" asked Eric, hoping to confuse the driver. "Would you please put on some hip-hop?" Eric bent over, opened his backpack (which was sitting on the floor), and fished around. He briefly pulled out a fake plastic foot with a pant leg attached to it as he searched for something else.

Agent Evert saw this and smiled.

"Not that rap crap," the driver said. "You've got to be kidding."

"OK, how about something like … you know … rock and roll?" asked Erin.

"My God. They haven't heard any rock and roll for several hours, poor things," joked Cheryl.

"I left my MP3 player at home, Mom."

Agent Toliver chose to ignore the little monsters as the van again came to a full stop. The sun's glare limited his visibility out the windshield.

With the glass truck in front, the occupants of a cab two car lengths behind the van seized upon the opportunity. The driver and passenger, both in gray camouflage, put on masks and quickly exited the cab, submachine guns drawn. They moved to a position directly behind the van and went unnoticed by Agent Toliver, who was honking at the truck and dealing with the glare.

One man helped the other gently to the roof of the van.

A soft thud came on the roof of the van. The van rocked ever so softly.

"What was that?" asked Erin.

"Could be anything." Agent Evert instinctively removed her weapon and placed a finger over her lips, turning her head back and forth for everyone to see. "John, get the kids down on the floor, and stay there," she continued in a whisper. "Get us out of here, Toliver."

Toliver pulled his weapon and put the van in reverse. He hit the car behind him, which started to honk. "I can't. I'm wedged between the truck in front and cars behind." Both agents strained to listen for abnormal sounds as Toliver searched the rearview mirrors and gazed out through the windshield.

An unintelligible, soft rubbing sound came from the direction of the roof. Toliver cranked the electric mirrors skyward as far as they would go. He saw nothing. Redirecting the mirrors downward, he saw a cab, empty, with its doors wide open, in the middle of the freeway.

"What the—"

Suddenly a man's face appeared in the windshield, upside-down. He held a gun.

Eric, who had a view from the floor in the middle seat, screamed and pointed.

Toliver raised his pistol and shot the man through the glass.

The children screamed at the deafening detonation. Toliver raised his gun farther toward the roof in the imaginary trajectory of where the body attached to that head would be and fired again, rapidly.

Bang! Bang! Bang! Bang! Bang! Bang! His weapon emptied in a few seconds. He ejected the clip and replaced it with a fresh supply of bullets in even less time.

"Code red on the freeway close to Jefferson on-ramp!" screamed Agent Evert into her lapel.

The children and Cheryl began to cry. John held them close as Agent Evert yelled for everyone to be quiet.

The driver of the truck in front of them opened his door and brandished a weapon as he slid out of the cab. He quickly moved half the length of his vehicle, sliding with his back crouched against the glass.

Agent Toliver had several choices, but only a split second to react. He could get out and attract gunfire and do his best, but there were too many unknowns out there, and he might be jeopardizing his passengers' safety. He fired two shots through the windshield in rapid succession into the panes of glass on the left side of the truck, at an angle that would endanger no one else. The glass exploded. The shards of glass cut the perpetrator like fresh scalpels. He sunk to the asphalt, rapidly approaching death.

"Get on the floor, and stay quiet," said Evert to the Harrises as she unlocked and partially opened the side sliding door. "Anything behind me on the right?"

"Nope! Clear!" yelled Toliver.

She opened the door all the way and squatted. Before she stuck her head out beyond her vehicle, she scanned the 180 degrees in front of her. Her head and weapon tracked together. She could see the look of terror on the faces of those too frozen or stupid to hit the deck of their own cars.

Without leaving the van, she slowly elevated herself with her back against the doorjamb to a position where she could peer briefly over the roof.

"Anything?" asked Toliver.

"Nothing!"

She returned to her squatting position. "Got to be more still out there, but I can't see 'em. How many did you see in the truck in front of us?"

"Damn, just not sure. One more, but could be two."

"I still like these odds better."

John could not believe how cool Agent Evert remained. Just another day at the office?

She looked out the side door again and caught the attention of the driver of the car next to them, who kept peering over the edge of his door and then pulling back his head. She flashed her FBI badge and mouthed "Where?" to him and motioned the same quandary with her hands.

He looked at her and motioned to the ground, under the van, with his head and eyes, then disappeared below his door.

Evert turned to Toliver and quietly motioned the same, as her mind searched for another plan.

"Eric, Eric. Give me that foot out of your backpack, now," she whispered. "Quickly. John, give me one of your shoes." She shoved the shoe onto the fake foot and tied the laces tight. "Tolilver, when I put this foot down on the pavement," she continued to whisper, "get out your door quietly, roll under, and nail him."

He flashed her the A-OK sign.

Evert lowered the fake leg slowly toward the ground, with the toe of the shoe facing toward the van.

Agent Toliver quietly and gently opened his door just wide enough to fit through. He fell to the pavement, landing on his right side, gun extended in front of him. He fired intuitively before he could actually focus. He continued to fire, emptying his load into the single body under the van.

From his position, Agent Toliver scanned beneath all the immediate cars. He then cautiously stood and reloaded his gun as he ran to the back of the van and, aiming around its corner, saw no further perpetrators. Evert moved to the rear right of the van.

There was precious little room between the van and the car behind. The driver of the car could not be seen from Toliver's position. A siren sounded in the far distance.

Both agents moved forward on each side of the van, in parallel, toward the front of the van, fanning back and forth with their weapons.

Agent Toliver entered the van first and prepared to attempt to push the vehicle in front of them forward, and then, hopefully, maneuver into the emergency lane and get away. They still had not cleared the glass truck in front of them, and until they did, driving past it would be dangerous. The single siren approached.

As Agent Evert prepared to hop into her side of the van, two more perpetrators exited the cab of the vehicle in front of them, one on each side. Each had drawn an Uzi. In her motion to enter the van, Evert had her free hand on the top of the door jamb, her left foot just inside the doorway, and her right hand draped at her side with her cocked revolver. She caught the motion from the corner of her right eye. She gripped the van tightly as she stopped her forward motion and pulled her right leg up. She then arched her body backward in tripod fashion from the van, elevating her right arm straight out from her side.

She fired simultaneously with the man in front of her. She had him directly in her sights and nailed him in the chest, neck, and cheek. He managed to pull his trigger fractions of a second before he died, his weapon spraying bullets into the space between the cars as Agent Evert intuitively jackknifed her body and pulled herself into the van with all her might. She could hear and feel bullets pass. She began to smile in relief, then felt a sharp, hot, deep pain in her right buttock. She yelped involuntarily as she closed the van door behind her and locked it.

"I'm hit! Oh, shit, it hurts," said Evert, clutching her backside.

"Let me look!" said Cheryl, who leaned across the floor.

Without hesitation or embarrassment, Evert pulled down her pants so Cheryl could examine her right cheek. "Can you see an entrance *and* an exit?"

"Yes. Not bleeding too bad, either," said Cheryl. "Fairly superficial."

The children were still crying. "Is anybody else injured?" asked Evert.

"Not me," said John. "Kids, are you guys hurt?"

Three sobbing "no"s were heard.

Agent Toliver did not divert his attention from the situation before him. His weapon was leveled on another perpetrator through the clear portions of windshield between the spidered glass. In the rearview mirror, he could see the red lights of the incoming Highway Patrol vehicle, its siren now deafening. The gunman pointed his gun alternately at the windshield of the van and at the windshield of the approaching police car.

The Highway Patrol vehicle roared up the emergency lane and kept driving. It rammed the gun-wielding man as a spray of bullets hit its windshield and the light rack on the roof of the car. The man flew through the air, his legs and pelvis already shattered from the impact of the black-and-white. He hit the street and did not move.

The police vehicle skidded to a stop, and the officer slammed it in reverse amid the smoke and smell of burning rubber. The tires spun as he backed up next to the van.

"CHP is here. Let's get out, now," said Toliver. "Can you make it, Evert?"

"No problem, according to the doctor. Right?"

"Right," said Cheryl.

Toliver exited the van first, producing his FBI badge and holding it in plain view of the officer.

"FBI. Here's my ID. Don't shoot." Toliver placed both hands above his head.

"What the hell is going on here?" said the officer.

"There's one more agent inside and a family that we are transporting under federal protection. The agent is injured. You need to get us the hell out of here, now."

The Harrises exited in front of Evert and, with hands above their heads, stopped at the CHP vehicle. The officer was hesitant.

"Sir," Evert said, wincing from the pain movement caused, "we've got to get in, and you've got to get us the hell out of here—now!"

"What about the other motorists? There could be civilians hurt."

"Get us moving, and radio for help. Help will be here soon ... probably on its way now. You know that. Let's move it!"

As the Harrises and the two agents left, crammed in the CHP vehicle, John looked out the rear window at the battle scene and then at the weary agents. He wondered why anyone would go to such extremes to keep him from talking about his abduction. Exhaustion turned to panic as he asked himself the real question: How had they found him so quickly?

Chapter 21

The mere mention of the San Juan Islands usually brought to mind relaxation, solace, and the ultimate vacation. Nothing could have been further from the thoughts of John and his family.

The San Juan Islands were roughly equidistant from the land masses of Washington state and Vancouver Island, Canada.

Tourists weren't just drawn by the islands' beauty; the climate was exceptional. The San Juans received less than half the amount of rain that fell on Seattle or other Puget Sound areas, owing to its geographical position between two different mountain ranges.

Lopez Island was the least mountainous of the three largest San Juan Islands. Its proximity to Anacortes on the mainland and ample flat areas would make a quick escape possible. For these reasons—and because it was the off-season—the Harris family was moved to Lopez Island.

The Harrises' van sat in the front third of one of a series of long, numbered lines of automobiles awaiting ferry transport in Anacortes. Each number corresponded to a different ferry destination. The actual packing of cars onto the ferry was both a science and an art. Not only did maximum numbers mean maximum profits, but the vehicles also had to be able to exit at the proper destination along the way.

Most drivers and passengers stood outside their cars, enjoying the respite from the frequent drizzles. The Harrises sat inside the van with the doors and windows open. Directly in front and behind them were Jeeps whose passengers had relocated to the four corners of the Harrises' van. Each agent scanned his or her 270-degree visual fields, trained to trust their instincts regarding the most subtle, unusual observations. Despite their casual attire, these people belonged to the bodyguard ilk. A close look would reveal that each had an earpiece. A wire ran just behind the strong muscles of their necks and disappeared under their shirts and over their bulletproof vests, inserted into a hidden transmitter. With the agents so close to each other, it was not obvious to John why they needed transmitters.

Each agent looked to be in excellent physical shape, including Agent Evert. Her minor wound was healing well. Each agent wore a small black fanny pack below the fronts of their vests. Some were made of leather, others of a synthetic canvas material. To the casual observer, the packs did not draw any special attention. To those in the know, like John, the packs meant quick access to a handgun and extra ammunition. Each had a holstered gun in the napes of their lower backs. Some wore an additional weapon in an ankle holster as well. These instruments of destruction were small potatoes compared to the arsenals they had hidden in the rear of the two Jeeps.

Whereas all the cars in the lot were tightly packed, with the assistance of ferry personnel, bumper to bumper, the Jeep in front of the Harrises' car had left an extra space. An aerial view of the lot would reveal similar spaces in each of the several lines of cars, so that the Harris van could be driven out of the large lot at a moment's notice. The agents had made a decision to "shroud" themselves amid the others, rather than sit in the open in the front of the line or somewhere else by themselves. Although this made for a better strategy, John could not forget that the morning traffic on the Los Angeles freeway had been a trap, not a deterrent.

A gigantic, white ferry pulled up to the dock, and loading took only minutes before the ferry was mobile again.

When the ferry reached Lopez Island, the base of the island appeared to be a large wall of rock, as far as John could see. Tree growth began immediately from the edge of the rock and seemed to advance back over the visible portions of the island. They took a two-lane road up a significant grade until the island leveled out. The three-vehicle convoy that included the Harris van passed through a series of green and amber fields.

A beautiful, red schoolhouse was passed on the left; children played in its yard. A series of turns onto different roads brought the convoy to a road that paralleled the southern coast of Lopez Island. Mailboxes appeared on the right side of the road for the properties on the left, which were spaced far apart. The lead vehicle reached the end of the road, then made a U-turn and went back down the same tree-lined, shaded road. All vehicles followed to about half the distance back and turned right onto a property.

The dirt road to the new Harris home twisted slightly back and forth. The land was surrounded on each side by untouched forest. The fallen trees and branches, as well as years of falling leaves, looked undisturbed, except where an occasional camouflaged agent waited with a large weapon.

The road opened into a four-acre clearing, upon which a quaint, barnlike home stood alone. There were two parking areas, but no other vehicles. In front of one of those areas, a dinghy leaned against a tree, its mast against the house. After an agent searched the house, the Harrises exited the van as a family and explored their new home.

Once inside, they were more than pleasantly surprised. French doors opened from the rear of the house onto an open field of grass sprinkled with yellow-flowered ground cover. The field was bisected by a long, gravel path. To the left stood a volleyball net and a tetherball; to the right were a picnic table and a large hammock. Beyond these inviting appointments lay perhaps the grandest of all: the Sound, in all its beauty, for all to behold.

As if all this were not enough, on the patio they found a hot tub. All that was missing was a rainbow … and freedom.

A few days into their stay, the kids had not complained of being bored once. That, in and of itself, was extraordinary. The children frolicked endlessly, alternating between sports and hot-tubbing and skipping rocks in the cold waters on the beach. Intermittent drizzle and rain dampened no one's spirits. John and—to a lesser degree—Cheryl were mesmerized by how content the children were and the amount of precious family time they had been afforded—all, ironically, because of the tumult they had been thrown into.

John even caught himself thinking of their danger in the past tense. But what had changed? They were in hiding. How could something be over when no one knew what that something was? What the hell did *they* really want? And, who were *they*? Why hadn't ripping out John's kidney been enough?

Cheryl shared her own worries with John. What would become of her practice? Who was seeing and caring for all her little patients at a moment's notice? When would their own kids get back into their studies? Would they miss too much school and have to start a year over again? Should she get textbooks and start teaching them herself? Should she not just relax and be thankful that they were all alive?

Detective Marley sipped his hot coffee, waiting to fully awaken. Among other pictures on his desk, one framed two young street cops in uniform together. New guys on the beat: Marley and Panzer.

Marley carried his cup of coffee into Panzer's still-vacant office. The sight was disheartening. On the walls hung a number of photos of Panzer with the baseball and soccer teams that he coached, of his children playing on those teams, and of Panzer showing off prize catches after a day of fishing. Marley remembered well the huge fish Panzer had caught.

Piles of paper cluttered the desk, like on every detective's desk, but appeared to have some sort of organization. The recent picture of Panzer, along with his wife and children, at his daughter's wedding … all the unfinished work. It nearly made Marley choke.

The chief, Gordon Weeks, walked into the office with a pile of papers.

Marley tried to switch gears from maudlin to chipper. "What you got there, Chief?"

"The forensics from the car. Just came in."

"Let's take a look." He didn't have to fake his pleasure at having the report at last.

"Here, I'll give you half of them."

The chief sat at Panzer's old desk, and the two studied the documents, then switched piles.

"Interesting," Weeks mused. "Very interesting. Three illegal automatic weapons, all manufactured in Russia and unavailable in the U.S. What do you think, Marley?"

"I think the situation stinks," Marley said. "The Feds put the Harrises in protective custody, yet they are downplaying everything else: Panzer, the remote device and the dead Middle Eastern guy at the Harris ranch. Acting like nothing whacked is going down. Be interesting to see what they'd say if they saw this. But I'm not offering. They've showed me zip from their end of the investigation. I smell a rat, and I don't like it."

"Look here," said the chief. "The remains of four males were found. Dental characteristics match no criminal in our databases. At least two of them were killed by the same automatic weapon."

"Well, I guess they didn't die from a car crash … surprise, surprise."

"What the fuck is going on here? John Harris sure as hell didn't shoot them."

"Maybe something went wrong. A double-cross or something. I don't know. If something did go wrong, that, of course, creates a larger margin of error and increases the chances of us finding leads."

"Two skulls, and I quote, 'may represent males of Middle Eastern decent.' So, now the guy belly-up at the Harrises' was an Arab and here's two more. You do realize that we're in over our heads here, right?"

Marley did not make eye contact.

"Marley, right?"

"Yes and no, sir. Yes and no."

"Explain."

"Like I said, we've gotten diddly from the FBI. If we work with them or without them, it's a one-way street. We get nothing. And to be honest, I can't be sure that anything we share with the Feds won't end up hurting the Harrises somehow."

"Marley, we're on shaky legal ground here."

"What tangible evidence links this crash to John, or Panzer, or anything else, for that matter?"

"Well …"

"Nothing tangible," Marley concluded. "Not a damn thing. I suggest … I'm asking you, give me more time before we turn this data over."

"Look, I know Panzer's dead," the chief said. "I knew him too, and I know how tight you two were. I just don't want to make the wrong decision based on emotions. Do me a favor. Call the FBI now, on speakerphone, and get and update on the Panzer crime scene. Let's see how it feels."

They went to Marley's office. He dialed.

A woman's voice answered. "FBI."

"I'd like to speak to Agent Moreno. I'm Detective Marley with the Larchmont Police Department, Utah, ma'am."

"Please hold."

A minute passed. "Hello, Detective Marley? This is Martin Breslow, Agent Moreno's superior."

"I'm the chief of homicide, Detective Marley, here with the chief of police."

"Hello," the chief chimed in. "I'm Gordon Weeks."

"Hello, gentlemen. As you can imagine, Moreno's in the field with the Harrises. So what do you have?"

"Uh, we were calling to see what you all have, sir," Marley said. "We're anxious to close the Panzer homicide. Panzer was one of ours."

"One of our best," added the chief.

"Quite honestly, I've got nothing back yet from the criminalists from the scene evaluation. As you know, the field agents came up with zilch. There was no other eyewitness besides John Harris. Believe me, I'll call you the second we get anything. We're sensitive to your situation, officers."

Both men winced at the tag.

Marley mouthed a rhetorical question: "Officers?"

"And the Harrises?" asked the chief.

"Don't worry, boys. We've got it covered."

The chief looked at Marley and made a sign like a knife cutting his own throat.

"Well, then, thank you," said the chief.

"Good day," said Marley, hanging up.

"Well?"

The chief stood and turned to leave. Without turning to look at Marley, he said, "Take your time, Russ. Check in with me. Let's get these bastards. For Panzer."

Chapter 22

The FBI patrolled the grounds and occupied the second floor of the home on Lopez Island. The second floor had its own separate exit and entrance, although it was accessible from a beautiful center stairwell within the home as well. The second floor did not look as it had in the house's original plan; in addition to reflecting design changes, the rooms stored a large number of electronic devices and a small arsenal of weapons and ammunition. A sizable gun, with its large infrared scope, hung suspended from the opened skylight window on the steeply sloping roof. It pointed in the direction of the Sound like the turret gun of a World War II plane.

The family had become accustomed to living with "guests" during their stay on Lopez Island—more than a week now—and that night was no different.

While Cheryl cooked dinner, John played the Egyptian Ratscrew card game with the kids. Nicole was content just holding her own deck of cards and watching the others.

After dinner, they all decided to watch a video movie before they called it a night. Their choices were not plentiful, nor that current. The children chose *Monsters, Inc.* and won by sheer number in the democratic vote.

Later that night, John checked on the children before retiring himself. Eric and Erin slept on the fold-out couch in the living room, Michael on the floor in a sleeping bag in line with the older two, and Nicole in a port-a-crib by the stairs.

As John and Cheryl stood in the doorway of their room, wrapped around each other, they studied their little ones. They did not need to express the mutual love they felt. However, they could not help but reflect on the future as they put themselves to bed.

"I can't believe I've put you all through this," said John.

"As if you somehow engineered it all."

"Where do you think we'll go next? Or if we stay here, what becomes of your practice? My work? Their schooling?"

"Well, no matter where we go, there's always a need for a doctor. And did you see that cute little red schoolhouse on our drive here the first day? Well, the kids could do worse. A lot worse. And, come to think of it, there's nothing that you can't do at home that you do at work, with the help of a computer and modem, now is there? It wasn't as if work was a big turn-on. Maybe you can start working with our savings and parlaying it into millions. How's that sound?"

"Have you thought about who has stayed here before, and what became of them? There had to be someone before us, right?"

"It's been a long day. What do you say we join the kids in la-la land?"

As he drifted off, John wondered how he could feel so weak right now, and Cheryl could be so strong.

John awakened with a start. Agent Moreno placed his hand over John and Cheryl's mouths as he awakened them each in turn, holding a finger to his own mouth. Dressed in black, he carried a large, jet-black weapon, far from the variety with which man hunts an animal. He had black war paint on his face.

"What?" whispered John.

"Listen to me, and do exactly as I say. We need to leave now. Grab the kids, and we go directly to the van. Take nothing else. Be absolutely stone quiet. Try not to awaken Nicole. Keep her in your arms until we hit the main road. Don't turn on any lights. You got that? This is life and death. They are here."

"Who are *they*?"

"Whoever they are. Now let's move quickly."

"What about the vests?" whispered Cheryl.

"They're in the van."

Each exited the bed on his or her own side. John's was closest to the French doors, which allowed him a brief glimpse outside as he rushed toward the children. What he saw in the blink of an eye profoundly disturbed him. In the band of the moon's illumination, below the last branches of the trees down to the ground, were three silhouettes moving cautiously from tree to tree.

Moreno spoke in a low voice into an invisible microphone: "Pick them off now, before they get into the brush on the sides of the property. Use the silencers. Shoot to kill."

Cheryl and John moved with incredible speed to awaken the two older children and gather up the other two into their arms as they continued to sleep. As they did, they could hear the muffled firing of the large-caliber rifle upstairs. The gunfire tempo did not indicate an automatic weapon; each shot was deliberate and, hopefully, decisive. Outside, John saw flashes from silenced weapons as well.

They all quickly gathered in the foyer by the front door. John was the last, since he was carrying the largest load: Michael. In the dark, John got down on his knees, unzipped and opened the sleeping bag, and scooped Michael up, sliding his arms under the child like a forklift and then bringing him close to his own body as he straightened up.

In a heartbeat, an intruder came crashing through the French doors. As wood splintered and glass shattered, he dove and grabbed one of John's ankles.

John fell, wincing and moaning as both of his elbows hit the hard floor of the entry, protecting his valuable cargo. Michael rolled into the legs of the others and began to cry.

Instinctively, John kicked with his free leg. Since their eyes had all adjusted to the dark, he could see that he was kicking some sort of device that sat in front of his assailant's face.

The soldier grunted and stood. Before the attacker reached his full height, Agent Moreno nailed him with three silenced bullets.

An agent from above ran down the stairs. He too had a night-vision device over his face. He yelled to Moreno, "I've got it, I'll take the flank. Cars are running ... plenty of cover."

"Gotcha." Moreno opened the front door and listened. Again he talked into his mike: "Z-1 and Z-2, where are you?" He heard the responses. "Z-3 and Z-4?" Pause. "Here we come. Stay extremely toasty. OK, Harrises, let's move quickly to the van. Stop for nothing."

As they all moved out the front door, the flank agent fired at another incoming perpetrator and silenced him swiftly. Moreno closed the front door and dead bolted it with a key that materialized from his belt line. Later John would marvel at his coolness under fire. It deserved some sort of reward.

They made it to the van unscathed. Nicole still slumbered. The same could not be said for the other three children.

The van, sandwiched again between the two Jeeps, headed down the drive. The cars used only their parking lights. On the journey down the drive, one agent stood on the running board on each side of the van. Roughly halfway down the drive, the agent on the right side of the van fired his weapon. The high-pitched sounds of a silenced automatic weapon now sounded familiar.

At the main road, the lead Jeep turned left, switched on its headlights, and sped away full throttle. The agent on the right running board climbed into the cab. The other agent stepped down from the left running board and joined the Jeep behind the van. The van turned right, and Agent Moreno floored it. The last car turned left.

"Hey, how come they're going the other way?" asked John.

"A decoy," Moreno answered. "Let us do our thing, OK? Stay cool. Now, why don't you all put on the clothes in the bags and then put on your vests."

At that moment, a dark figure materialized on the right side of the road. Before the other agent could get any words out, Moreno had perceived the movement as well. He instinctively turned the car and hit the dark shadow with the right front end of the van with a loud thunk. The man's weapon fired with flashes of light visible only to those in the front seat.

By the time John helped Michael get dressed, the three vehicles converged at a predetermined spot and turned off their lights. It was at the apex of a hill that allowed good visibility below.

"I want all of you to stay in the van. I'll be right back," said Moreno.

As he exited the car, Moreno could still hear the children crying. All things considered, so far, so good. God was with them—again. But it was not over yet, and he knew it.

He brainstormed with the other agents, including Evert and Toliver. This attack had been much more organized than the one in Los Angeles. How had they found them?

"Well, sir, we've got two options as I see it," said Charlie. Because he was the youngest agent and he looked like a surfer, they called him by his first name. "One, we get off this island now. Two, we get off this island yesterday!"

"I absolutely agree. Question is, do we call in a helicopter and draw attention to ourselves, maybe go to that little airport and take a big risk ... or do we hop on the ferry, and take less risk? Besides, if I were these intruders, I think they'd be expecting us to fly out of here."

"Ferry, sir? This time of night?"

"I do believe there is one that runs late. Can't be too crowded either. Let's see … It's almost 2230. I'll be right back." Moreno walked over to the van and opened the front passenger door to retrieve the ferry schedule. He returned to the group. "It leaves at 2320. We can make it with little waiting time. That's good. And we'll call the helicopter anyway, as a decoy. Any questions?"

"How about it if one or two of us returns to the beach house in case the others need our help?" asked Evert.

"That's a negative. First, they would have contacted me. Second, we've got a long way to go before we're safe. We can't jeopardize our ultimate mission. Besides, they don't get much better than the group that stayed back there, now do they? Especially when it comes to night games. Anyone else?"

"Yes, sir. How the fuck did they find us?"

"I wish I knew. We'll worry about that when we get to the next destination. Now, let's move."

Moreno did things by the book, but where the book ended, he could improvise with the best of them. The convoy avoided the most direct route, Center Road, and took the most tortuous route they could after consulting the island road map. When they came to Ferry Road, there were no other routes to take to reach the ferry. As a result, they elected to travel this road at high speed until they reached their destination.

At the port, they took their place at the end of the short line and awaited departure. Two agents checked the vehicles in front of them, then assumed positions at the sides of the parking lot. Moreno and the other agent in the van started to remove their war paint and combat gear.

The ferry docked and unloaded only a few vehicles. Moreno noticed that the first two vehicles to get off were obviously rental cars. They sped away too quickly to identify the number of passengers in each. But both rode unusually low to the ground, suggesting that they were filled to capacity. They could not be FBI, and they certainly were not police. Perhaps the mission had proceeded faster than the perpetrators anticipated.

As the group began to board the ferry, Moreno stopped a ferry official who directed the traffic.

"Say, those cars were going awfully fast. Were they island police?"

"Not hardly. I don't know who they are or what their rush is this time of night. Some people are just jerks. Know what I mean?"

"Sure do. Have a nice one." Moreno moved away and spoke into his mike. "Two Ford sedans twenty minutes away, headed your direction, unknown number of occupants. Take them out."

"Ten-four" crackled in Moreno's ear.

Chapter 23

The Jeeps and van stopped in the rain at a gas station near Seattle's SeaTac airport. This time, just in case, the Harrises were housed in an armored truck on loan from a security company at a moment's notice. While the family used the restrooms in small, guarded groups, Moreno found a dark corner on the station grounds. He was alone, and he was angry.

He called FBI headquarters on a cell phone that operated on an untraceable line that connected via satellite to a number of locations in the United States after routing through Europe. Despite the circuitous route, the transmission was crystal clear.

"Special Agent Z, as in Zebra," said Moreno and dialed in a series of numbers.

"Agent Z?"

"Yes, sir. Fall is a horrible time to express winter's discontent."

"So it is, Agent Z. I've got a preliminary report."

"Well, that's more than I have," said Moreno, barely controlling his tone with his superior. "What is the status from the island?"

"Three agents dead: Z-5, Z-6, and Z-8. Thirteen perpetrators killed. That seems to be all of them. A search is ongoing. Excellent job. Why did you call?"

Agent Moreno was taken by surprise. The reason for the call was obvious, and this was not his immediate superior. He recognized the voice; it was Martin Breslow and it was damn unusual for someone this high up to be involved. And on a protected line, there was no need to refer to the team by their operative designations. Moreno decided to speak formally as well. Perhaps someone else was on the line or in the office.

"Sir, first things first. My bounty is unharmed. But it was too close. They were onto us in a week … highly organized, highly skilled, and damn near successful. There's a leak the size of the Puget Sound here. It has to be from the inside. I know all my people here. It's intolerable, sir."

"I agree. We'll get to work on it immediately. I'll be personally involved. What are you suggesting at this juncture?"

Moreno became more angry over the continued response. He decided to take a different tact.

"Marty, we just lost Painter, Hendrickson, and Liebowitz! Did you hear me? Painter, Hendrickson, Liebowitz. They were all seasoned and dedicated, and you knew them as well as I did. Now they're dead … and over what? A fucking kidney? It just doesn't make sense to me, goddammit! Why are you now involved? And why am I being left in the dark here? This has never happened before."

"Intelligence is starting to come back on the freeway incident. All but one of the perpetrators were of Arabic descent. None were U.S. citizens. My involvement is just between you and me. Major top secret."

"What?" Moreno didn't know where to start.

"We don't know how they got into this country. We're working on finding their connection. I suspect terrorism."

"Terrorism? Jesus, Marty, this just doesn't make sense. I've been with these people night and day. These are normal people. The wife is a doctor, for crying out loud."

"Listen, Moreno … don't trust these people."

"What?"

"Do *not* trust them. Although you are to go to any measure it takes to protect them and keep them from harm, they cannot be trusted."

"What are you saying, Marty?"

"What I am saying is that what meets the eyes is not necessarily so."

"Just what the hell does that mean?"

"I can't say more. Trust me."

"Jesus Christ, Marty, what's happening here? You're leaving us in the cold."

"I have my orders, just like you. Why don't you call the shots? Do what you need to do. What's your pleasure?"

Agent Moreno was thoroughly confused—a novel sensation. He did not like it. The word "pleasure" did not even belong in the conversation. Marty Breslow was not himself, either. This was all out of character for Moreno's superior and the agency.

"I've thought about it, sir. *I* pick the place of relocation—"

"OK."

"—and nobody except me and the other agents with me know where it is. That is, until you all stop the leak. If they find us again, then the leak is at my end, and I take care of it."

"Whoa, kiddo," said Breslow, trying to appeal to Moreno's sense of camaraderie and imagined friendship. "I was talking about the how and where of picking you up. We need to know where you are, or else we can't be of much help."

"You heard my plan, sir."

"You're talking insubordination."

"I've analyzed the situation tactically, just as you taught me. My plan of action is sound and reasonable, and I think you would do the same thing if you were here."

"You sound like you've made up your mind."

"Yes, sir."

"There's one other thing you should know. An agent on the island has identified one of the perpetrators at the beach house as Dominique Sartori."

"You mean the mercenary?"

"You got it."

"Last intelligence was that he was dead. Marty, if this involves international terrorism, then why the hell isn't the CIA involved?"

"We don't know they're not on some other end of the same case."

"I've got to go. I'll be talking to you soon." Moreno cut the line. He couldn't take another second of Marty's doublespeak.

Chapter 24

John stood in his bathrobe, looking out the window. It was early, and the children remained asleep. Frost coated the window, and snow blanketed the rooftops and streets. The skyline was beautiful, but this was no vacation. They had relocated to Manhattan, New York, in an expensive condominium complex that the Feds had confiscated from drug dealers. Agent Moreno had been involved in that bust, and he knew the condo remained unused. He purposely had not told his superiors of their location.

Though John believed Moreno's precautions had finally won them a safe haven, he could not call himself happy. How he missed their freedom, their home, their normal lives. He was no match for the trained soldiers and their associates who kidnapped people at will and stole their organs. By default, John was forced to accept the protection of the FBI. He realized that he should feel more thankful, but, like Detective Marley, he could never fully trust the Feds' motives. Agents Moreno, Evert, Charlie and the others that had joined them had risked their lives. Some had lost their lives in the Sound. He thought he trusted the agents accompanying him and *their* motives, but what if they were all just pawns in a larger scheme? What scheme? Nothing made any sense.

His eyes were bloodshot. He was tired. Behind him, he could see sleeping agents—his extended family. In the bedrooms slumbered Cheryl and the kids. He looked at his watch and decided he would try to join them once again.

The alarm startled John. He had not thought he would fall asleep again. He and Cheryl began the weekday morning ritual that they had adopted since shortly after they arrived in Manhattan. They woke up the three eldest children for school. Eric and Erin would shower. Cheryl and John would prepare breakfast and lunch. The agents would then chauffeur the children to and from school. Cheryl and John would try to occupy themselves and the baby, day in and day out, with difficulty. Neither had thought they would ever see the day when they actually looked forward to doing homework with the kids.

Regardless of the level of planning and preparation, the mornings were always pandemonium. It did not matter what city the Harrises were in. Hair had to be combed, clothing swapped, teeth brushed, zit cream applied, back-packs located, school lunches made. In addition to all this, winter coats, mittens, and hats had to be dealt with. And then, of course, the kids and the drivers had to deal with the drive to and from the private schools in the morning and evening traffic. Kamikaze taxi drivers were not the only forces to be reckoned with. The elements and the pedestrians were also formidable.

Cheryl pulled John aside and whispered, "You know, I've been thinking. I don't want to get you upset. But is it possible that you or someone in your firm pissed somebody off? You know, lost them vast sums of money, and now they're after you?"

John looked at her incredulously. "Let's suppose for argument's sake that I did. I lost someone a billion dollars. Do you really think they'd take my kidney, for God's sake? No, they'd just kill me, maybe all of you too. It doesn't make sense. We don't deal with people like that."

As they looked away from one another, Moreno watched them.

"Sorry, honey," said Cheryl, as she planted a kiss on John's cheek. He pretended to like it.

The underground parking was a godsend; it allowed safety and relative warmth. The agents had accessed an armored black Cadillac stretch limousine with bulletproof windows. Limos, butlers, and bodyguards were not new sights to the residents of the condo building; the Harrises and their entourage fit right in. Cheryl and John, in their robes, helped the kids to the parking garage.

"Michael. Don't forget to turn your homework in. OK?" Cheryl asked. "Oh, Eric. Do you have your homework checklist to turn into Mrs. Mansfield?"

"No. I forgot it."

"OK, you go back with Dad and get it now. Eric, we don't like reminding you. That's your responsibility."

"Sorry."

John headed back with Eric and one of the agents.

"Erin, you've got your gym clothes, right?"

"Duh, Mom."

"OK, Erin, Michael ... hugs."

In a black suit, a tall, no-nonsense agent in his late thirties named Baker stood waiting at the car door. He had replaced Toliver, who went on a long overdue leave. He opened the door as the family arrived. He had already cleared the garage and radioed Moreno. Hugs were exchanged with Cheryl and then Eric came sprinting up, giving his agent a run for his money. The children filed into the car. Agents Evert and Charlie, the agent who looked more like a surfer, joined them.

It was a blistering twelve degrees outside, unseasonably cold for the entire eastern seaboard. As the limo exited, it purposely turned in the opposite direction that it had taken the day before. Moreno stood outside, steam billowing from his nostrils, both arms hidden under a serape-like overcoat, looking about as he alternated from leg to leg, trying to keep warm. What was not visible was the automatic weapon slung over his shoulder, under the overcoat. The balding, middle-aged, affable doorman smiled and waved as the car departed. He, too, was in the employ of the FBI.

Despite the early hour, the children were excited as they cleared condensation from the windows to look outside. As far as they knew, they were inside a gigantic snow globe. They were no less mesmerized by the magnitude of the tall buildings, the tops of which were not visible no matter how hard they cranked their heads, than by the delicate fall of snowflakes.

The limo made its way slowly through the morning traffic. The children sat on opposite sides of the coach, occasionally throwing pieces of paper at each other. Sometimes, they would purposely hit one of the agents. Agents Evert and Charlie actually got a kick out of it. Eric liked to mess with the rear radio, searching for favorite songs. Out of respect for the FBI, he kept the volume at a reasonable level. Despite his relative youth, Baker was no more tolerant of their music than Agent Toliver. He found it distracting. Having been briefed on Los Angeles and Lopez Island, he was not interested in a replay.

Regardless of the ambient temperature, the foot traffic was significant. Unlike in other cities, pedestrians essentially had no rights in New York. It was an unwritten law: cars had the right of way. The Harrises did not need to concern themselves with this. They would not likely be found walking the streets of New York.

Finally, the limo pulled in behind a long line of limos entering the large, circular drive of the Sigmond Oglethorp School. With all the limos and posh private cars, it did not take a rocket scientist to figure out that this was one of the most prestigious, and pretentious, of private lower schools in Manhattan. Annual tuition was nearly thirty grand per child—before contributions. Three doormen with large umbrellas alternated meeting the cars and escorting the young ones to the nearby canopy leading into the school.

To the ire of the doormen, and unlike the other drivers, Baker exited his door and stood until he could see that the kids were inside the building. He kept one hand in his pocket, firmly gripping his handgun. Afterward, he pulled ahead and exited. Out of sight and down the block, he dropped off Evert before continuing with the oldest child and Charlie to the middle school.

It was lunchtime at the Sigmond Oglethorp School when the large, black Rolls-Royce limousine pulled up to the canopy within the circular drive. The snow had stopped, but the freeze continued. The fresh snow was pristine, and the whole city was just beautiful. The driver opened the rear door and helped out the wealthy inhabitants. A tall, middle-aged man in an expensive suit and an even more expensive overcoat exited first. He waited for his wife under the canopy but did not offer her any assistance. She was dressed stunningly and inappropriately for the nature of their visit. When she removed the mink over-coat, cashmere neck muffler, and leather gloves in the building and handed them to the chauffeur, there was no end to the abundance of gold and dia-monds revealed beneath.

Without the assistance of the chauffeur, they followed the signs to "Admin-istration." The busy staff did not break stride when the unexpected visitors arrived. The two just stood quietly until the respect and attention that they commanded and expected was met.

"I'm Mrs. Chenowith, how may we help you?" said a woman from behind the counter as she stood from her squatting work position.

"I am Mohammed Fahd," he said with an accent, pausing for recognition that was not forthcoming.

Advancing the unspoken school motto of "the customer is always right," the woman forced a smile and again asked how she could be of assistance.

"We are here to see the headmaster."

"Is she expecting you?"

"No. We were in the area."

The clerk looked at the clock on the wall. "Let me see if she's available." She picked up the phone. "New parents to see the school. Well, no … no appoint-ment. Yes, yes, standing right here. Fine."

The wife stood there, looking at her nails and jewelry.

"Right this way. Mrs. Montgomery will see you now."

"We have recently come from my country and will be staying for at least the rest of the school year. We have a six-year-old son. His English is good. We would like to see the first-grade classes." And then he said something that turned the headmaster's stomach a bit: "We have an appointment at St. Martin's later." Salt in the wound.

Although St. Martin's was a nondenominational private school in Manhattan, it was Oglethorp's only real competition. In a time of shrinking dollars, enrollment was down, and the competition was keen.

"Lunch will be over soon. I will have Mrs. Chenowith take you to a first-grade class, where you can observe. Please do not interrupt the lessons. Perhaps we can talk again after you've had a chance to observe. If you have any questions now or at that time, I'd be happy to answer them." There was a pause, during which the couple just stared at the headmaster without speaking. "Well then," the headmaster continued brightly. "Let me just ask you one question. Where has your child been in school up to now?"

"In my country, with an American tutor. He is up to standard."

"Excellent. I'll call Mrs. Chenowith. She can show you the grounds and deliver you to a class before it starts," she offered, looking at her watch.

Mrs. Chenowith could not get a sense of whether the couple liked what they were seeing. They were actually more difficult to read than most of the foreign parents—who always seemed, for the most part, expressionless. Facial expressions on the current couple seemed to run only from expressionless to disdain and back again. They asked no questions.

The halls were immaculate, and the original architecture had been well preserved. As anticipated, all the children were indoors. The grounds included an up-to-date gymnasium, which contained an indoor, heated pool. Mrs. Chenowith made it clear that no public or private school could compete with the Oglethorp's resources—academic or otherwise.

"Do you have security?"

"We have no special security here. Actually, there is no need for it. On special occasions, families will provide security for their child if there is a potential for problems."

At the end of the tour, which ended in Mr. Oasay's first-grade class, the final question was asked.

"Does anyone have special security currently?"

"No. None. Now, this is Mr. Oasay's class ... first grade. He is one of the best liked of teachers, by children and parents. I'll set you up with chairs in the back of the room. Class will be entering in the next ten minutes or so. I'll be back in a few minutes to introduce you to Mr. Oasay and his TA—you know, the teaching assistant. Please make yourself as comfortable as you can in these chairs."

The school bell sounded, and quickly thereafter, Mr. Oasay's class lined up outside the classroom door, joining the other classes in the hallway. The teachers exited their private lounge and dispersed to their respective classrooms. Mrs. Chenowith stood at the door, waiting as well. Mr. Oasay discussed the afternoon's educational events with the TA as he approached his students.

"Gertrude," he greeted the headmaster's assistant. "What brings you to this neck of the woods?"

"I put two parents in your class. They dropped by rather unexpectedly and want to see how we work here. I wanted to introduce them to you."

Mr. Oasay lifted his eyebrows before he turned to the students. Despite the noise level in the hallway, he paused at the front of the line to observe his children before unlocking the door. They were quiet, just as he had taught them to be, or there would be consequences. He smiled and opened the door. As they filed in, he touched each one sincerely and said hello. The technique had proven excellent.

The two regal adults sitting in the back of the room did not stand as they were approached by Mrs. Chenowith and Mr. Oasay.

"Mr. and Mrs. Fard," she said, "this is the teacher, Mr. Oasay."

"How do you do." Mr. Oasay extended his hand to both. "That is the TA, Karen, over there. Please make yourselves comfortable and observe."

The TA merely waved, barely acknowledging their presence.

"Fahd," the man corrected, shaking Mr. Oasay's hand with the looseness of someone not accustomed to handshaking.

The bell rang again, and Mr. Oasay clapped his hands twice and spoke to the class. "OK, children, let's sit down and get started. As I promised, we're going to talk about dinosaurs for the next week."

"Please don't disturb the class, and I'll come back and check on you in a little while," whispered Mrs. Chenowith before departing.

The couple at the back observed the class carefully. After only ten minutes, Mr. Fahd whispered to his wife, then abruptly stood up in the middle of Mr. Oasay's exuberant discourse. This disturbed the class, but Mr. Oasay did not miss a beat. Mr. Oasay stared at the TA, prompting her to problem-solve for the obnoxious couple.

"What's the matter?" she whispered to the couple.

"Is there any other first-grade class?"

"Yes, one … Ms. Minohan's."

"Take us there, please."

She did as she was asked, glad to have them out of her face and out of their classroom.

"Please wait here."

She ducked into another classroom and spoke to the teacher apologetically. She returned with Ms. Minohan.

"Hello, and welcome to Oglethorpe. I'm Clara Minohan. Please follow me to the back of the room. There are some chairs set up for you two to observe. The teaching assistant is Ms. Abernathy," she said, pointing.

Ms. Abernathy looked up from her position helping students and waved back.

The children's desks were situated in groups of four; the desks in each group were arranged in facing pairs. The children worked diligently, with their heads down as they scribbled away quietly. The TA sat at one of the table groups and helped those students.

The visitors strained to examine the children, dodging their heads about and leaning forward. At some point ten to fifteen minutes later, they looked at each other, and then the man stood and walked right up to Ms. Minohan, who sat at her desk. From his inside jacket pocket, he pulled out a small leather case, which he flipped open. He showed its contents to the teacher. The bottom half contained a silver badge, not dissimilar to that which a police detective might carry. The top half read "NY Department of Children's Protective Services." It was also officially embossed in the bottom right corner.

"As you can see, I'm with Children's Protective Services," he said softly before being cut off by Ms. Minohan.

"But I thought the other TA said …"

"We did not tell her or the headmaster. We are supposed to conduct some of our investigations without revealing ourselves until the last moment."

The TA strained to listen to the conversation but could not make it out. Most of the children were too absorbed in their work or each other to pay attention.

"What is it that you need?" Ms. Minohan asked.

"I need to talk to a few of the students, one at a time. Is there a private area where this can be done?"

Shaking her head in mild disbelief, Ms. Minohan remarked, "I don't know … this is so unusual."

"I promise you, this will not take long. Is there a place?" he asked firmly.

"I guess over there would be fine," responded Ms. Minohan, pointing to a small area in the very corner of the room where a couch and chairs had been arranged for the students' free time.

"You know what?" the man said. "I think that, although this won't take long, it will be too disruptive over there. Not enough privacy, either. Maybe I could just step out in the hall there for a few minutes with one, then get the next. You'll be able to see us through the glass in the window."

"How about if I or the TA joins you?"

"No. My experience has shown that your presence will not allow us to effectively interview. Trust us. We won't be long."

"OK."

"Could you call Michael up first?"

"Which Michael? We have two: Michael H. and Michael C."

"That one over there."

"Oh, Michael H. Michael H., can you come up here for a minute?"

Some of the students were interested in this activity. The TA just about jerked her head off its axis when she heard Ms. Minohan calling for Michael H. Unbeknownst to the teacher, the TA was Agent Sarah Evert.

Sweet little Michael H. came up to the desk. "Yes?" he said a bit shyly.

"Michael, this official wants to ask you a few questions in private. It's OK. Will you step out into the hall with him, just for a minute? Then he'll bring you back in."

The man walked out into the hall with one hand on Michael's shoulder.

Evert had to make a split-second decision. Should she go and check on Michael and leave her flank potentially open to the woman or take care of the woman first? She stood and walked nonchalantly to the woman in the back of the room.

"Hi, my name is Ms. Abernathy, the teaching assistant," she said in a sweet, engaging manner.

She noticed that the woman held her hand in her open purse.

"What's going on?" the TA asked.

In the hall, the male visitor looked around and saw no one. He reached into his right pocket and grasped a small weapon of sorts. He then bent over to talk to Michael and placed the weapon up to his neck. The sound of high-pressured air could be heard as the man covered Michael's mouth.

"Nothing," the woman answered abruptly. "You can go back to your seat."

"Oh. I'm sorry. I'll just go—" Evert turned, and within one step, turned again, gaining momentum. Her trained right hand struck the woman's solar plexus; her left grabbed the wrist of the woman's partially hidden arm. She twisted the woman's wrist counterclockwise. Two silenced bullets fired from within the purse in the process. One went through the woman's side, the other into some books in a bookcase. The woman managed to raise her right arm in an attempt to strike Evert. Evert rammed the top of her forehead into the woman's chin, breaking off a few of the woman's teeth with her force and changing the trajectory of the arm coming in her direction. Evert guided the woman's momentum and smashed her through the middle two boards of a wooden easel, which crumbled like potato chips. Evert took the weapon from the unconscious woman and tucked it into her belt as she reached inside her own boot and drew her handgun. She pushed the button on a device inside her pocket and turned toward the kids, who sat staring, frozen in fear and disbelief.

Evert clapped her hands together loudly to snap them out of it. "Everyone drop!"

The children nimbly hit the floor and hid under their desks. Ms. Minohan walked toward Evert.

"Stay quiet, kids, and stay where you are," continued Evert. "You are safe."

"I'm so sorry. I had no idea! I didn't know!" said Ms. Minohan almost tearfully, looking toward the door. No one could be seen through the glass.

Baker, Charlie, and Moreno got the code-red beep on their pocket devices. Baker was outside his waiting limousine in the circular drive of the school, talking animatedly with his limo buddies in the cold. Immediately he pulled out his FBI badge and flashed it to them. Replacing it, he drew his weapon and ran into the school, toward Michael's classroom.

At the condo, Moreno told the Harrises to get ready to leave with haste.

"How did they find us?" he asked himself. To the Harrises, he said, "Take nothing. We're leaving here in two minutes. Bundle up. The baby will need to be in that backpack thing on John's back."

Evert edged her way along the wall to the classroom door until she could see obliquely through the glass. She would never forgive herself if approaching the woman instead of following Michael turned out to be the wrong decision. No one was visible in that direction. She quickly crossed the width of the door and looked diagonally in the other direction. Again, nothing.

Evert pushed the door open quickly. No gunshots. She got down on the floor and looked down the hallway to the left. It was empty. She then rolled, somersault fashion, out the door, landing on her back. She rolled onto her stomach and oriented her view down the far end of the hall. The man in the expensive suit walked briskly away with a child slung over his shoulder. There was no way she could get a good shot in. Even shooting one of his legs was too risky. She needed to get closer.

At that moment, she heard running steps from behind her. Rapidly pushing herself to a sitting position, she turned and leveled her weapon at the incoming person as her brain fought to assimilate the next event. She recognized Baker.

"What the fuck is going on?" he whispered loudly, out of breath.

"Large, dark-complected male in a dark blue suit. Tall, dark hair … Middle Eastern. He has Michael. Go get Erin, and take her to the limo. I'll get Michael. If I'm not at the limo in ten minutes, you gotta leave with the girl, and get Charlie with Eric."

"OK," was all he said as he turned and ran off.

Evert ran full speed down the hall. While she did, she tried to review the school's layout, inside and out. She had studied the blueprints and had walked the grounds. She knew the place well. She assumed this would probably give her an advantage. Thank God the school had only one story. In the distance, she heard what sounded like a door closing. It had come from a hallway at the end, to the left. As she approached the corner, she again got down on her stomach and peered around the corner. A muffled bullet struck the plaster above her from about one hundred feet down the hallway. She had two concerns: First, the body of an elderly woman lay lifeless about twenty feet in front of her. Second, the man disappeared behind another door. She did not know if there were other perpetrators, but she did know that the man and his precious cargo were dangerously close to doors leading out from the building. There, a car, and perhaps more criminals, would certainly be waiting. She had to get to them quickly.

She stood and sprinted down the hall, pausing only long enough to see Mrs. Chenowith lying motionless. She did not stop to feel for a pulse. Priorities.

She thought about the layout again. He had gone to the right. There he would find a gymnasium with doors that led outside, but not to any parking lot or vehicles. It would be a trek back to the parking lot that adjoined the circular drive in front of the school. It was not a dead end, but it was a meaningful factor in her favor. However, if he headed outside, there would be an environmental problem of major concern. She was not dressed for the seriously low temperatures outside and, given any windchill factor, hypothermia would quickly set in. There would be very little time to finish an outdoors encounter, were things to play out that way.

Then she heard something that heightened her concerns: music, and the voices of singing children. Good Lord, there was a dance or music class of some sort going on in the gym! As she approached the gymnasium, the music continued, but the voices stopped. She felt nauseated, and her heart palpitated as she looked through a window in the gym door. To each side and directly in front of her, she saw nothing but an old, commercial-grade CD player churning out music from about the middle of the wooden gym floor. A very long extension cord ran into the back of it. She knew she had to enter and knew she was in trouble. And she knew she would quickly lose any advantage that she had fancied herself as having just a minute before.

She edged open the door, looked to her left, and saw more empty space. She waited two seconds, then quickly passed through the door and pivoted to her right. She saw just what she had thought she would.

There stood the man, surrounded by frightened and weepy children about his legs. The children gasped as Evert entered, turning toward them with a gun. Front and center in the group was the bleary-eyed teacher, on her knees, doing everything she could to remain calm and perhaps give the message of hope to her children. Against the torso of the man hung the limp body of Michael Harris. The man was virtually shrouded in children.

His weapon was leveled at Michael's head, not hers.

Her weapon, steadied by her left elbow tucked into her left chest, was leveled at his head.

Although many thoughts raced through her brain, fear did not tinge any of them. She had no time. This was a hostage situation unlike most. The man was sweaty and slightly twitchy. He was not composed at all. He had the weight of a limp body to contend with, his heavy clothes, and he **was** clearly in unknown territory. Was he really at a disadvantage?

"Put down the gun, or I kill the boy," he said with all seriousness, precipitating more sobbing. "Shut up!" he shouted at them all.

She reasoned to herself that if he were going to shoot Michael, he would have already. "I have a better idea. I am with the federal government. Compared to you, I can't just shoot. Especially with all these witnesses. I have to take you prisoner if at all possible. So you put down your weapon and put down the child, and step over here."

"You ridiculous bitch!" he said.

"I believe *that* was the woman with you in the classroom," Evert said calmly.

Without losing concentration, she fired her weapon. The explosion of gunpowder was frightening. However, within fractions of a second, a .40-caliber bullet made its way through his brain after splintering the thick bone of his forehead. He collapsed immediately, falling backward and nearly pinning the children under him. Blood flowed freely. Michael did not move as the rest of the children scattered in all directions, like roaches when a light is turned on.

As Evert ran to Michael, she yelled at the teacher. "Round up the children. Keep them in the gym office until the police arrive. Do it now!"

She picked up Michael, who had some blood on him. Although she initially struggled with his awkward weight, her adrenaline carried both of them at full speed toward the lobby. As she passed by Administration on her way out, employees' heads turned to follow her.

Evert stopped just outside the front doors, under the canopy. Initially, she did not feel the chill. She looked in all directions and could not see a soul. Baker exited the limo and opened the back door, signaling Evert over. She ducked in and Baker closed the door behind her. Erin was sitting in the passenger front seat. Both she and Baker looked at Michael through the privacy window separating the front seat from those in the rear.

"He's bleeding!" said Erin as she began to cry.

"It's not his. He's fine. Don't worry, he's okay." She did not know this for certain and checked under his shirt to be sure.

Moreno led the Harrises out onto the balcony. They had all rehearsed the escape before, but it was unnerving nonetheless.

Below, the doorman stood in his usual position just outside the revolving doors leading into the condos. A car came screeching and sliding up to the front of the building. As the doorman came to help the car's inhabitants out, two men jumped out and pushed him out of their way. The doorman reached into his pocket. Instead of pulling out a gun, he pulled out a remote-control device. When the men began their turn through the revolving door, he depressed the switch at the precise moment. The doors halted and locked in place, trapping the two men in the transition between indoors and outdoors. The rear intruder ran into the front one, who smashed into the thick glass door. They fell, crunched in a very small space. When they surmised what had happened, they looked back at the doorman, who merely held up the little black box between his thumb and forefinger and smiled.

The men yelled in muted voices unintelligible to the outside. The doorman placed a hand to his ear, mocking his inability to hear them. Bulletproof glass gave him that luxury. He would be staying behind to take care of these men and any others yet to come.

They all met at the prearranged rendezvous point in one of the parking structures of the airport. The limousine pulled up next to a rental car, which had arrived only moments before. There were no other cars in pursuit. The limo honked, and the Harrises, Moreno, and the doorman all sat up from their reclined positions.

Evert opened the back door and signaled for Cheryl to come over. Cheryl could see that there was something wrong with Michael. He was limp and pasty. She opened the door and nearly flew between the two cars.

Seeing the blood, she became hysterical. "Oh my God, what happened to Michael?"

"Don't panic," Evert said. "It's not his blood. But they've drugged him with something in an attempt to kidnap him. He seems to be breathing fine and he has a good, strong pulse."

Cheryl immediately calmed back down as she went into doctor mode. She checked his pupils and his eye movements and moved his head side to side. She opened his mouth and smelled his breath. She lifted his shirt, looking for trauma, and placed her hands around his entire tiny rib cage to feel for nonexistent fractures. His abdomen was soft, and there were no abnormal swellings. His penis and buttocks were not damaged. She put her ear to his chest and could make out air movement over both his lungs. Finally she placed one finger over the front of his knees and elbows and tapped them with the other middle finger to check his reflexes. Running her thumbnail across the bottom of his feet, from heel to toe, she watched his big toes curl downward normally.

"He seems to be unharmed, but I don't have the slightest idea what they drugged him with. Could be chloral hydrate, a barbiturate, a benzodiazepine … I don't know." Doctors always felt better when they knew. "We've got to get him to the hospital."

"We can't do that," said Moreno. "Too risky. We have no time. We need to get out of New York as quickly as we can."

"Just what do you mean, too risky? As if you can guarantee his safety."

"I can just about guarantee you'll have no safety whatsoever if we don't get out of here," said Moreno. "Besides, take a second to think here. How long has it been since the incident? Evert?"

Evert looked at her watch. "It's been a little over an hour."

"Doctor, I don't know the answer to this, but what is the likelihood of further deterioration an hour after being doped with anything?" Moreno asked.

Cheryl thought about the question. All eyes were upon her. "That would depend upon the route it was given … how much … what it was."

"They had to inject him with something that would act immediately, probably into a vein. So, statistically speaking, what is the likelihood of further deterioration given the intravenous route?"

"More unlikely than likely."

"Then we take the lower risk and get the hell out of here," Moreno said, as if Cheryl just made the logical decision for them all. "We've got a little time while we work on a plan to get out of here. What medical supplies would you want if we could get a few things from, say, a hospital ER?"

Cheryl had already asked herself that question subconsciously. "A pediatric ambu-bag, a rectal thermometer, a portable pulse oximeter, and the drug Anectine, with a needle and syringe, minimal."

"How do you spell those?" asked Moreno as he took out a small pad and pen.

Cheryl wrote the names. "Oh, and we need warm clothes for Michael. You know, a coat or something would be fine." *Always the mother*, she realized. But it was not clear to her why she had calmed down. *Lord*, she wondered, *could we be getting* used *to this?*

From behind the heavy wooden office door at FBI headquarters, the muffled voices rose and fell, engaged in a heated argument. Present were Martin Breslow and two agents from the Central Intelligence Agency.

"You have got to be kidding. I've got dead agents. I've got some of my best people protecting this family, and their lives are on the line. And you just want us to hand this whole thing over to you? Bring 'em all in, hand over the Harrises, and say good-night?"

"Well, not exactly like that. You would continue to work on the case until it is resolved and the people killing your agents are brought to justice. We would work in concert."

"The people who killed my agents are already dead, thank you."

"You know damn well what I mean."

"To be perfectly honest," Breslow said with sudden satisfaction, "I don't know exactly where they are."

Just then, a side door in the office opened, and in walked Mr. Leonard Freeman, the Director of the FBI. The timing of his surprise appearance left Breslow no doubt that Mr. Freeman had been listening to the conversation from his office.

"Gentleman," said Breslow, "this is Director Freeman."

They needed no introduction.

"Gentlemen, I'm sorry, but the answer is no," said Freeman, extending his hand to the two CIA agents, who stood at this signal. "Good day." Freeman gestured toward the door. He would be calling the CIA director soon.

Chapter 25

Stonington, Connecticut, with its population of 19,000, embodied all that was beautiful and incredible about New England. During the summer and fall, leaves changed from a brilliant green to a collage of browns, reds, purples, and oranges. The air was fresh and clean in all those seaward towns. Saltbox homes, many of them historical, composed the living quarters as well as the store-fronts. In the middle of the town stood a magnificent library; vast, grassy grounds and shade trees surrounding the colonnaded building.

Winter in New England was arguably no less romantic than summer or fall, but tourism was essentially nonexistent. The locals enjoyed the contrast of the winter's solitude. Moreno reasoned that the lull made Stonington an ideal location to protect the Harrises. More importantly, Charlie's family had a home in Stonington that was empty, except in summer. Strategically speaking, Stonington was perfect. They needed a truly safe haven, and Moreno needed some time to sort this all out.

The 130-mile drive to Stonington took two hours during the dry months. In the snow, it took almost twice as long. Moreno said nothing the entire ride. The way he saw it, the whole deal had been nearly blown. The bad guys had actually made flesh contact with a Harris. And only by the grace of God—and, to a lesser degree, the skills of Evert—had Moreno's team prevailed.

Moreno mentally reviewed each incident, step by step, event to event, from beginning to end. For the life of him, and perhaps everyone else, Moreno could not pinpoint the leak. He trusted his team implicitly, but he could not possibly keep everyone in sight at all times. And what the hell had Marty meant when he said not to trust the Harrises? Would the Harrises sabotage their own safety?

Who with children would or could do such a thing? He had met lots of slime-balls out there who would sell their country, their family, their own mother for the right price. But the Harrises seemed like such a wholesome, naive family. Moreno knew he had to do something dramatic to staunch the hemorrhage of leaked information.

Moreno made a pit stop at a fast food drive-through along the way. It was already dark out. The family shuttled in and out. Michael was groggy, but defi-nitely waking up, and Cheryl had stopped her medical treatment. He had wet himself twice and was sorely in need of a change of clothes that they did not yet have.

"Hey, John. Can you join me outside?" asked Moreno. The other agents looked over for a fraction of a second in curiosity, then ushered the other chil-dren back to the van. John followed Moreno dutifully around the side of the building in the cold, to the back, which was empty and dimly lit.

As John turned the corner, Moreno turned, grabbed him, and threw him forcefully against the wall. No one inside or outside could hear the thud. Moreno grabbed the lapels of John's jacket with crossed hands and held him up against the door.

"I want to know everything you know about all this. No more bullshit. Why do these Arabs want you?"

Oddly, John didn't seem frightened. "I've told you everything I know. If I knew something more, I would tell you."

"You're just an innocent victim and nothing more … is that what you want me to believe?"

"Absolutely. Do you really have reason to believe otherwise? Maybe that's what throws you off. Go with your gut, Moreno. Someone's not showing all his cards here, I agree. And it isn't us chickens. It has to be your people."

"Now why would they want to do that?"

"It would have to be something big. You tell me. You know the FBI."

Moreno loosened his grip. "How are they finding us every time?"

"Your people have been with us every second of every day from the begin-ning. Christ, we can't fart without you all knowing it."

"Are you suggesting that Evert did? Toliver? Charlie? Me? Maybe Baker? These people risked their lives for you!" exclaimed Moreno as he retightened his grip.

"First of all, I don't know the others as well as you, Toliver, Charlie, and Evert. They came on after LA. Toliver's on leave, that lucky guy, so he's out.

Baker and the doorman? I don't know … maybe I watch TV too much, but how do you know it really isn't one of the others?"

Moreno didn't answer, just continued to look at John.

"Either way, I'm dead meat without you," John said. "My whole family is dead meat without you. The irony is that you and I are in the same boat. You don't know who to trust, your life is in danger, and I presume you don't know why. Hey …" John's tone turned nasty. "Isn't this the kind of shit that turns you guys on?"

"That's the CIA and spies and all that crap, not the FBI … and not us." Moreno tightened his grip and spoke one last time with his hands near John's neck. "If I find that you're the cause of this, that you have purposely put your family's life on the line, and my agents' lives, I will kill you myself."

At that, Moreno let John go. He had had to rough up John like that … needed to look him in the eyes under duress. "We're going to have to think about putting you under government protection until this whole thing gets figured out."

"You are government protection."

"No, I mean real government protection. Like on an army base somewhere. I don't know."

"Oh, that's just great. That would be a death sentence for sure."

"Why?"

"Because it's your people, the government, we can't trust. That would be putting the lamb in the lion's den."

"I know." Moreno straightened John's collar. "I know. Come on. I'm sorry. Let's go."

"Hate to say it, but we're lost," said Charlie, looking out the window in search of a clue. "It is incredible how different a place can look in the snow."

"What do you suggest?" asked Baker.

"I suggest we go back to that gas station we passed and ask about a nearby street I remember. We won't tip them off to exactly where we're going and, hopefully, I find the summer house."

Moreno just listened and let them solve the problem. He was down—a feeling he'd rarely experienced. After more than four hours on the road thinking, he'd come up with no answers, no ideas. Worse, he was running out of contingencies and time.

As they reached the gas station, nearly everyone was asleep. Charlie started to climb out of the car to get answers to his questions. In that weather, no one was about to come out to the car to answer navigational questions or pump gas.

"Hey, I really gotta use the facilities. I didn't get a chance before. Mind if I go with you?" asked John softly, trying not to wake the others.

Charlie looked to Moreno, who nodded his approval.

Charlie stopped at the door and scoped out the inside of the station before entering. He saw a very small minimart, devoid of patrons, with a lot of junk food piled on the countertop closest to the register. As Charlie and John entered, a pimply teenage girl peered over the register.

"Oh, hi. I need some help with directions … but first, where's the bathroom?" asked Charlie.

The clerk pointed down a narrow hallway at the back of the store.

Charlie and John made their way to the end of the small hallway. There was only one restroom, with one door and no other exit. Charlie signaled for John to wait as he exposed his sidearm, turned on the light switch, and peered into the small bathroom.

"Take your time," said Charlie to John as he headed back toward the clerk.

John closed and locked the door to the latrine. He stepped up to the toilet and unzipped. As he peed, he looked around over his shoulder. His eye caught a black object on the wall that had been hidden by the open door. A payphone … inside a restroom? "Wow, we're certainly not in Manhattan anymore," John muttered to himself.

John zipped up, turned away from the sink, and then lifted the receiver. He heard the dial tone. Immediately he inserted numerous coins from his pocket and dialed from memory. He looked at his watch for the exact time as the phone rang.

"Marley."

"Russ, this is John. Great … you're in the office," he whispered.

"John? John who?"

"John Harris."

"Prove it to me."

"Hiking in the forest for demolished cars. You killed a guy in my home. Panzer."

"Jesus, it is you! They told us that you had all been killed."

"Who told you that?"

"Some guy named Breslow at the FBI."

"When?"

"About a week ago. But it isn't general knowledge. They told me that it was top secret."

The phone line was silent. Why had they told Marley that? Did the FBI plan to kill them? What was their ultimate plan? What the hell was going on? "Top secret. I'll say it is. The fuckers didn't bother telling us about it."

"Where are you?"

"I can't say, except that we are far away. They don't know I'm calling you, obviously. Hey, Marley?"

"Yeah."

"Tell me the results of the forensics on that car pancaked in the gully, and who that guy was that you nailed in my house."

"None of them Americans … not one of them. All males of Middle Eastern descent. None of them had any ID, no passports, nothing. The gentleman in your home has no known domestic or foreign criminal record. Not a single one can be identified."

"Or so the FBI told you." John looked at his watch.

"We ran it ourselves first. Nothing. The only other fact we gleaned was that the weapons they used were Russian in origin, not available in this country."

"So why the fuck do they want me, Marley? I gave them a goddamn kidney. What do they care who I speak to? And if they care so much, why'd they let me go?"

"I'm no closer to that answer than when we raised the question in the beginning."

"Christ, me either. Listen, I gotta go. I'll call you another time."

"Is there anything I can do?"

"Yes. Don't tell them I called. Don't tell them a thing. Deal?"

"Deal."

"I'll get back to you as soon as I can."

Chapter 26

The three older children sat at the kitchen table of their new Connecticut home doing homework while Nicole assumed her usual position on the floor, scribbling on paper.

John looked out a window between the curtains, once again a prisoner in paradise. On an army base somewhere, they'd just be prisoners—no paradise. And no future.

Nicole had recently taken to pointing her finger like a gun and making mock gunshot sounds. This was distinctly unusual behavior for girls as opposed to little boys. Given the circumstances, sadly enough, it was entirely appropriate.

"Elderly white male headed this way," said Baker from his post by the living-room window.

As Charlie headed over to the curtain to take a look, the Harrises retreated into a back room, as they had rehearsed several times.

"Who is he?" asked Moreno.

"Shit, I don't recall his name, but he's the neighbor right across the way. Definitely."

"OK, then you meet him at the door. Evert, you're the wife. Keep your first names, Charlie's last name."

The knock came, and Charlie opened the door with a smile, opening it just enough to sandwich his body between the jamb and the door. "Fred? How are you?"

"What?"

"How are you, Fred?"

"Fine," the man said, looking slightly confused.

"I'm Charlie, Harold and Grace's son."

"Oh, oh, oh. Sure. I'm sorry. You haven't been up here in a few years, have you?"

"Nope. Needed a little getaway."

"I saw the smoke from the chimney and thought, hmm, this is unusual. No one hardly comes up during the winter. Now, summer … that's a different story."

"I'm talking quietly since the baby fell asleep in the living room here, and Nicole's been fussy, so we didn't want to take a chance waking her."

At this point, Evert walked up, opened the door up a bit more, and stood next to Charlie as he put his left arm around her.

"This is my wife, Sarah. Sarah, this is Fred, the next-door neighbor." Evert extended her hand to the visitor. "Well, let me grab my coat and come outside, and we can catch up," continued Charlie, turning to his right as he grabbed the winter coat that Moreno handed him from behind the door.

"Hurry back, honey," said Evert as he stepped outside and she closed the door behind him. "Nice to meet you, Fred," she called before the door clicked in the latch.

The jacket was unusually heavy, thanks to the handguns Moreno had placed in each pocket. As Charlie swung it around to put it on, one of the pockets hit Fred's arm.

"Wow, what ya got in there young man, a gun?" asked Fred jokingly.

"Nah, just a flashlight."

Cloistered in the far bedroom, the Harrises sat quietly with Agent Fournier. He was in his mid-fifties, hand-picked by Moreno to reinforce them after the perils in their previous Manhattan "home".

"Daddy?" whispered Erin.

"Yes, angel."

"Why do we keep going to different places? When can we go back home?"

"We go to different places until Fournier's people can figure out why people want to hurt Daddy. As soon as they figure it out, we go home. It will be soon, angel, I promise."

Even on the lam, John took full advantage of moments of softness like this from Erin. He gave her a hug. He continued to marvel at how quickly her softness could transform, and how Erin could become mean. Each of the children had their own beautiful little personalities. Cheryl always reckoned that Erin was moody because she was the second child and, as a result of that and the particular age spreads of the children, she got the least attention of all the children.

Explanations aside, it had crept into John's mind lately, as it had when he was kidnapped, that he might not live to see Erin and the rest of the kids develop into adults.

That night, the agents congregated in the living room after the Harrises went to sleep. They reviewed their ammunition status before moving on to other subjects. They had been able to purchase bullets at a nearby gun store; however, they lacked nearly all other paraphernalia that would give them an advantage. There were no bulletproof vests, no rifles, no infrared, and no hand grenades. To the younger agents, this was just another challenge that they were up for. It made Moreno and Fournier anxious. Age and experience did have a few downsides.

After the meeting, Moreno stepped outside. Instead of using his cellular phone, he took the van back to the gas station. Although the cellular communicated via satellite, he did not want to take any chances. If programmed appropriately, was it not possible that a satellite would be able to pinpoint the location of anyone on the globe below it? Moreno went to the phone booth and used a long series of numbers that he had committed to memory. The call would be routed, rerouted, and scrambled such that the original location would not be traceable.

"Marty, it's me."

"Jesus, Moreno, where the hell are you?"

"I've been doing my job, trying to protect my precious cargo. What have you found out?"

"I'll tell you what I've found out. This is way over our heads. Do you hear me? Way over our heads! You're to bring in your cargo. I repeat, bring your cargo in. This is an order. Do you understand me?"

"Tell me what you know. Come on, Marty. We're part of the same fucking team!"

"I know. So when I say it's time to bring them in, believe me, it's time."

"You gotta give me something, Marty. Make me feel a little better about what I am about to do, will you?"

"Off the record?"

"Off the record."

"The CIA is in. The case crosses continental boundaries. It's out of our hands once you deliver the goods. Where are you? I'll send out help immediately. Believe me, Moreno: you need help."

"Where's the leak, Marty? How do they keep finding us?"

"Honestly? I have no idea. I've been working on it full time since we last talked."

"Well then, that leaves me no choice."

"Moreno, come on. What are you talking about?"

"I can assure you that if I name our location, the enemy will find us before you. I'll bring them in, but you've got to let me do it. I'll make contact the second I'm ready for assistance. Deal?"

"What choice do I have?"

"Deal?"

"Jesus, Moreno. Deal."

"Marty, believe me. I'm here in the trenches. You're not. That's exactly what it's been like, too: the goddamn trenches. I am doing the right thing. No question. You should be thanking me."

"Then good luck. May God be with you. We're standing by and ready when you are."

The line went dead.

Moreno hung up with both a plan and contingencies. They had never been found in less than three days. They would leave, unexpectedly to all, sometime the next day. No one in Charlie's house would have any foreknowledge. At the same time, Moreno would call and give Marty false coordinates from which to pick them up. He smiled. It was a good plan. No ... it was a great plan.

The sunrise the next day was spectacular as it rose above Rhode Island just moments before it was visible from Stonington. Another several inches of snow had fallen overnight; the driveways would need to be dug out. In the distance, a road-clearing tractor shoveled snow from the road, going back and forth, its characteristic beep sounding from far off every time it shifted into reverse.

The sky brightened at a slow rate that defied the swiftness with which darkness had overtaken Stonington hours before. Everyone still slept with the exception of the night-watch agent. How Baker longed to be snug under his blankets like all the others. With daylight outside and the sound of the tractor very close, he stretched and yawned, knowing full well that he would soon be sleeping.

Pulling the curtain aside just enough to get a view, he looked out the living-room window to the expanse of snow that spread like a white carpet between their home and the one across the way. The serenity of this view was shattered with the crash that followed as the tractor flew down the driveway and slammed into the garage. The garage door ripped apart like construction paper with a terrible sound.

Inside the house, it sounded as if a bomb had gone off. Moreno ran into the living room, yelling at Baker as he attempted to dress, talk, and arm at once. In came Charlie, Evert, and Fournier. In the next room, some of the children cried. The unknown coupled with the chaos was disorienting.

"What the hell was that? Evert, check the Harrises."

"I'd been hearing this snowplow for the last hour or so, getting closer and closer," Baker explained. "Then the bang. Sounds like it crashed."

"Go check it out. And be careful."

Charlie had just put his sneekers, jacket and gloves on and prepared to exit when it happened. Something crashed through the kitchen window and bounced on the floor, releasing smoke.

"Tear gas!" Charlie took a deep breath and dove to pick it up and throw it back out the window. His gloves protected him from otherwise guaranteed serious burns to the hands.

Two human bodies with gas masks over their heads and guns across their chests flew through the picture window of the living room, rolling onto the floor amid shards of glass. Their tumble ended at Moreno's feet. Before they could assimilate their new environment and completely stand, Moreno had delivered stunning blows. Charlie shot them both, firing the two handguns in his coat pockets simultaneously, not taking the precious time to remove them from his jacket. Moreno fired a finishing bullet into each head, but not before removing one of the gas masks. He moved to the picture window and carefully looked outside.

"Evert, you stay with the Harrises," he shouted, seeing no immediate threat outside.

"Got it." Evert struggled to put on her snow gear with John's help. She scanned the room and cursed; she knew full well that each room had windows. It was a vacation home, not a fortress. "OK, all the children in the closet. Cheryl and John too. Now! Lie as flat as possible."

Another gas-masked soldier flew through the bedroom window. Evert nailed him in full flight. Two more entered the uncharted territory of the room from outside. The second met the same demise as the first, but in the process knocked Evert off balance, enabling the third to stand. He might have killed Evert were it not for John, who had taken a cross-country ski from the closet. He swung it like a baseball bat into the right arm of the soldier, who had his back to John.

The soldier and Evert fired simultaneously. Her shot silenced him. She cried out as his bullet tore through the meat of her right shoulder. She quickly transferred the gun to her left hand, which was almost as accurate as her right, and killed the next soldier through the window.

The three older children closed their eyes, covered their ears and protected their heads with their arms as they had learned many times in drop drills in their classrooms. They could not, however, completely silence the loud bangs of the gunfire. Each blast made them flinch and shriek. They were soon reduced to a steady screaming state, hoping to drown out the horrid noises and visions preemptively.

"Go help Evert!" Moreno yelled at Baker. "Charlie and Fournier, outside. Charlie, north. Fournier, south. Circle around and converge on the street. Every bullet is a kill! Show 'em what you got!" He handed Fournier the gas mask on his way out.

Charlie smiled as he exited the front door under Moreno's cover, followed closely by Fournier, who was much grimmer.

Moreno heard noises from the kitchen. He crouched down along the wall between the doorjamb and picture window and aimed toward the kitchen. Another soldier quickly peeked his head around the corner, then retreated. Moreno fired two volleys through the wall. After a second, the soldier stumbled out of the kitchen and fell onto the dining table, deflecting off the edge and falling silently to the ground. Moreno crawled along the floor, looking first around the cabinet juxtaposed to the kitchen wall. No more intruders were seen. He crawled under the kitchen table and finished the soldier off.

Outside, Fournier and Charlie crouched with their bodies pressed against the house and fanned their weapons in 180-degree arcs, waiting for another duck to pop up. None did.

"I'll cover you as you go to the back and around," said Charlie.

Fournier was off, half crouching as he went, moving toward the back of the home. Charlie continued to fan, ready to react without hesitation. Once Fournier reached the back corner of the cabin, he lay belly-down in the snow and peered around the corner. Nothing. He stood, gave Charlie an OK sign, and disappeared.

Charlie saw his neighbor, Fred, looking out his picture window. Charlie signaled for him to take cover. Fred did not seem to notice. Charlie shrugged and devoted his attention to the task at hand. He fanned as he moved to the front of the house with no one to cover him. At the front corner of the house, he could see nothing down the road to the left. To the right, the view was obstructed by a huge tractor with much of its plow on the other side of the punctured garage door. The wheels of the tractor were at least five feet tall and covered with snow chains. The engine had been left idling. Where the hell was the driver?

Making his way around the tractor, checking around the tires and under the elevated chassis, Charlie saw nothing out of order. He had a good view down the road in the other direction. He surmised that the driver had made his way through the garage and into the bathroom, to be nailed by Evert. Charlie climbed up onto the tractor to gain a better view. No action. Where the hell was Fournier? He turned off the tractor and pocketed the key, then retraced his steps. Back at the corner of the house, Charlie could still see Fred in his window. He decided to work his way over there, warn Fred, and survey the view from that vantage point. He could hear intermittent gunfire from either inside the cabin, outside, or both.

He walked, half crouched and fanning, in the snow between the two homes. He had not even noticed that his feet were starting to freeze; when adrenaline pumped, the body felt no pain. About a third of the way across, Charlie found that ground felt different below his leading foot. He paused to make sense of it, but it was too late. A soldier clad in white fatigues jumped up from his camouflaged den beneath the snow. Before Charlie could react, his gun was kicked from his right hand. It flew a few feet and disappeared into the snow. Charlie instinctively continued the turning motion that his opponent started. In the process, he pulled an ample knife from his waist and re-extended his right arm.

Turning with the speed and grace of an ice skater, Charlie slashed the front of the man's neck. The billow of bright red spray shocked the white snow. As the man hit the ground, Charlie used his second sidearm and fanned again to cover the ground behind him in case Moreno could not. As he turned, another white camouflaged soldier materialized quietly from under the snow. This time, Charlie did not sense the danger quickly enough. As Charlie began to turn his head to meet the next challenge, Fred opened his door and fired his hunting rifle into the back of the soldier. Falling to his knees, Charlie shot the wounded soldier square in the forehead.

"Fred, FBI! Get in your house and protect yourself. Leave this to us."

Fred disappeared as quickly as he had appeared. Charlie smiled as he turned to head back to the others. Still there was muffled gunfire, the exact location of which he could not yet pinpoint. He could also hear the sound of something like a chainsaw. This made no sense to him.

Fournier met formidable forces behind the house. With the mask on, he killed two men as he materialized through the smoke of the tear gas that Charlie had flung back outside. He continued to the edge of the forest behind the house. Although widely spaced, the sizable tree trunks provided a protective barrier for Fournier. He heard the sound of chainsaws and was initially baffled. From the forest, three snowmobiles camouflaged in white came at him, quickly closing ground.

Fournier flipped off the gas mask and quickly stepped around the tree. Crouching and aiming, he fired three shots as a hail of bullets chipped a flurry of bark and wood.

He hit his mark, and one soldier fell off his snowmobile. Its throttle released, the snowmobile stopped quickly in its tracks, as it was designed to do.

The two other snowmobiles were nearly upon him. Fournier dove and rolled to the other side of the tree to optimize its shielding abilities.

The killers on the snowmobiles crisscrossed and made the shortest turns they could. One went through the smoke; the other rode in the clear. Fournier appeared from behind the tree while the rider in the clear was at the apex of his turning arc. Negotiating such a sharp turn required two hands at that point, and Fournier took his best shot, hitting his opponent and literally throwing him off his vehicle.

Fournier could hear the last snowmobile coming toward him from behind the cloak of the smoke. He ducked behind the tree again. A volley of bullets shredded the trunk before the rider was visible.

Fournier had seconds to make a decision. The assassin could pass him on either side of the tree and kill him. He chose to make a stand.

The whine of the snowmobile engine grew exponentially louder. Blood pounded behind Fournier's ears. He screamed like a warrior and pivoted to the right and out in the open, taking aim. He had taken the logical route, but made the wrong decision. He found himself directly in the path of the fast-moving snowmobile. With a fraction of a second left to act, his luck changed for the worse. The large roots at the base of the tree acted as a snowy ramp, propelling the snowmobile into the air. Not only did Fournier not have a good shot, but also he could not move out of the way of the oncoming vehicle.

The hull of the snowmobile impacted his chest. Reflexively, he grabbed the soaring vehicle in a sort of half bear hug. As the snowmobile fell, Fournier emptied the remaining bullets of his gun in whatever direction his weapon was pointing. At least one penetrated the gas tank, catching both men in an explosive ball of fire as the hull of the snowmobile slammed the earth, padded only by Fournier and snow.

More soldiers had vaulted through the window in Evert's room before she could recover from her wound. As Baker turned the corner and entered the room, one of two soldiers had stood from his roll and was in Baker's face. Baker and the intruder fired at the same moment, killing each other instantly.

Evert managed to kill the other soldier, then empty her gun clip and reload. "Baker's down!" she screamed as she moved toward the window, not sure Moreno would hear her over the screams of the children.

The floor of the room was covered with dead men. The soldiers had been coming with the frequency of the finale of a fourth of July firework show. John wondered how many could possibly be left as he and Cheryl placed their bodies over the children on the floor of the closet. From his view, John could see that Evert was injured, but she seemed to move well. Maybe she did not even know.

"Stay in the room with the Harrises," yelled Moreno.

Charlie moved to the picture window of the cabin and yelled to Moreno: "It's me. You OK in there?"

"Yeah, come back in. Baker's down. Evert needs help. I need to stay here. Did you see any more out there?"

"No, but I haven't seen Fournier. There was that big explosion out back and he never made it to the front of the cabin."

"OK. Go check out the other side of the house."

As Charlie stood facing the house, preparing to turn and carry out his next mission, he was struck by a lone bullet. He felt it, but he did not hear it.

A large-caliber bullet, fired from a sniper's post up in a tree at the apex of a triangle formed by the two homes and the forest behind them, hit Charlie in the back of the neck. He whirled and landed in the snow on his back. He was alive and awake. He could see, and he could breathe. But he could not move his arms or his legs.

The bullet had come from a silenced high-powered rifle. Moreno had not heard it either, but he had seen a small flash from up in a tree. He could just make out the white-clad figure up in the tree.

He looked at Charlie, and Charlie at him. The look of fear in Charlie's eyes pierced Moreno. Moreno allowed himself to be overcome by emotion, but just briefly.

"I'm scared. I haven't felt this way since I was a kid."

"You'll be OK. I'll get him. And you'll watch." It occurred to Moreno that Charlie still *was* a kid.

Moreno had some tough decisions to make. Fournier's side of the house had not been secured. There was a sniper in the trees. Charlie was probably dying. The Harrises were not out of danger. What the hell should he do?

Perhaps he could do it all.

He ran to check on the Harrises. He knew he was stepping over Baker in the hallway but did not look down. At the doorway, he could see that the Harrises were OK in the closet. Evert stood guard beside the window and looked reasonably well.

"You got enough ammo?"

"Yep."

"I'm going to head out front and then circle around to your side of the house and secure it. There's a sniper in the trees in the forest between the two houses, so the front of the house is not totally secure. Wait for me."

"Where's Charlie?"

"He's out front, dealing with the sniper," lied Moreno.

Then Moreno gave up on playing by the book. He handed John a handgun.

"Do not hesitate to use it. It's loaded, and the safety is off," he said to John. "Evert, I'm going out through the garage. Lock the door behind me, and come back to this post."

Moreno turned, stooped over Baker and took the gun from his dead hand, and disappeared. He exited through the door leading to the garage. Before he made his way fully out of the garage, he could hear more gunfire in the house. He prayed that Evert would continue to handle it.

When Evert returned from locking the door, she could see John taking aim from the closet at a figure just climbing in over the window ledge. She fired twice and blew him back outside.

"Stay where you are, but keep an eye on the bedroom door," she said to John.

Outside, more gunfire. She knew Moreno was doing something he did very well. The comfort she got from this notion was short-lived. As she moved toward the window again, another body flew through. She fired. Just after, two men came through the open door of the room. John fired at the first one through the door, but not before the assailant's weapon discharged and hit Evert squarely in the abdomen. She doubled over in pain that she could not ignore.

The second man through the door kicked the gun from John's hand and snuffed out Evert in a salvo of automatic-weapon fire. The soldier turned toward John, who was frozen in disbelief. The children were hysterical as they clung to Cheryl and one another. The man grabbed John by the hair and started to drag him toward the living room. Cheryl managed to free her arms from the children and grabbed John's leg as Eric and the other kids held her tightly. Getting nowhere, the soldier loosened his grip, and John flew backward toward the closet. As the soldier stepped toward John to grab an arm, Cheryl pulled a syringe full of Anectine from her pocket that she had been saving and thrust it into the soldier's forward leg. Finished, she withdrew the hypodermic at lightning speed. In the chaos and adrenaline rush of it all, the soldier did not feel or notice a thing.

"Come with me now, or I will shoot your family," said the man with an Arabic accent, pointing his weapon over John's head.

"Go ahead John. Do it," said Cheryl.

John turned and looked at her. Her eyes pleaded for cooperation, although he could not imagine why.

John stood, knowingly taking the aim away from his family. He raised his arms and walked toward the soldier, causing him to back up through the door, into the hall, and then into the living room, away from his family. The soldier looked back and forth between John and the living room all the way. Neither man knew exactly what was to happen next.

In the living room, the soldier staggered. His face glistened with sweat as he fought to focus on John. To John's surprise, the soldier dropped to the ground and lay there without moving or talking. His eyes were open, but John did not know whether he could see. The anectine that Cheryl injected him with was working. The soldier would now suffocate in a fitting death as he lay paralyzed, but conscious, on the floor.

John grabbed the man's weapon and placed it over his shoulder. He took the soldier's sidearm and put it behind him, under his belt.

John looked out the front window and listened. He could see Charlie and others downed in the snow. No one moved. He did not hear any more gunfire. He decided to go get Cheryl and the kids and get the hell out of Dodge.

Moreno moved from tree to tree behind the house, looking and waiting for lethal action, as he closed in on the tree housing the sniper. Aside from the barely smoking tear gas and the disabled snowmobiles, nothing tripped Moreno's radar. Once he had a good view of the tree in question, Moreno made the surprising discovery that the sniper was gone, and the ground below the tree was clear of dead bodies. As he moved close to the tree, he saw a single set of tracks behind the tree, and another headed in his direction, where they melded with numerous other human tracks. He presumed the tracks leading up to the tree from behind were placed as the sniper found his perch, the other tracks as he left.

Perhaps Moreno had encountered and silenced him on the other side of the house. On the other hand, he had not run into anybody with a sniper's rifle. Maybe the sniper was in the house.

Moreno ran back, taking cover whenever possible and continually fanning his weapon about and above his head. He crouched behind a tree; the clearing between it and the house had to be negotiated. It was not that great a distance, but there would be maximum exposure, with no cover at all. He took a deep breath, jumped up from behind the tree, and ran in a zigzag pattern to the house, through the residual haze of the tear gas. He ended up with his back against the wall of the house, in minimal smoke. He stood and put his ear as close to the broken kitchen window as possible. No sounds. He moved to the other side of the window, then peered inside at an angle. He could not see anyone. He was at a crossroads. Should he sweep to the other side of the house again, go to Charlie's aid, or check on the Harrises in the house?

He moved to the corner of the house closest to Charlie. Again, no one. Moreno made his way back to Charlie. Charlie's eyes were closed, and he did not appear to be breathing.

"Charlie? Hey, Charlie?" whispered Moreno.

Charlie opened his eyes.

"Jesus, I thought you might be dead."

"Almost there. Can't feel my body."

"Any perpetrators come by here while I was gone?"

"Nope. But I saw the sniper get down out of the tree."

"Which way did he go?"

"Back into the forest."

"Shit. He could be fucking anywhere. You hang in there, and I'll be back for you."

At the moment Moreno stood, he heard the most terrifying sound he could imagine: the muffled sound of a sniper's rifle. Any reaction would be too late. Maybe it would miss, he thought to himself. Before the next thought could be synthesized, he felt severe pain in his upper abdomen as a bullet tore into him and knocked him to the ground. He lay within earshot of Charlie, bleeding to death. He sunk his weapon hand into the snow.

"Charlie?" He strained to whisper, careful not to move. "I'm hit. You say when he's close enough for me to shoot."

Some minutes later, the sniper emerged with the rifle slung over his shoulder. He too fanned a handgun as he crossed the snowy divide between the two homes. As he neared Charlie, Charlie yelled.

"Now!"

The sniper immediately shot Charlie in the chest. Charlie gasped, knowing he was hit, but not feeling pain. The sniper and Moreno fired at the same time. All bullets hit their targets. The sniper fell to the snow.

The sniper rose and, dragging his left leg, made his way toward the house. Charlie managed a glimpse of him as he passed by. How could it be? Moreno had only winged him. Must have a bullet proof vest. He realized at that moment, since no other bullets were flying, that Moreno must have been mortally wounded. The Harrises were on their own. Charlie closed his eyes and prayed for the Harrises as he waited for death to arrive.

Back in the bedroom, John took command. "Everybody up. We're getting out of here now." He went to the window and looked outside. He saw only dead bodies strewn about, each in a slightly different position in the snow like human snowflakes. There was blood everywhere. He felt grateful that his family was alive and hoped they would soon be delivered from this hell on earth.

"Where's Moreno?" asked Cheryl. "What happened?"

"I don't know. I'm sure he'll be here any second." He handed Cheryl the handgun from the small of his back. "All you have to do is aim and pull the trigger. No thinking. Just pull the trigger. I'll take the lead. You follow with Nicole and the other kids."

They moved toward the living room. John stopped, peered around the corner, and saw nothing living. The kids closed their eyes and weeped again as they stepped over Baker. Eric was the only one to turn and take one last look at Evert.

"Stay behind me."

When the Harrises were partway through the living room, the injured sniper entered the home. The family stopped in their tracks and gasped. John did not possess the reactions of the trained agents; his gun was still at his side as he stared down the barrel of the sniper's weapon. The children retreated and huddled behind Cheryl as she peered around John. She could see the man was wounded, but it did not look life-threatening. She held her gun behind her.

"Throw your gun over here!" the sniper shouted at John.

John did as he was told.

"Put your hands up, Mr. Harris, and move over to me slowly."

John did not move.

"No, Daddy," cried Erin.

"Don't do it, Dad," said Eric.

Nicole and Michael clung to Cheryl's legs.

"You will do it, or I will kill one of the children."

"No, John. They won't shoot innocent children," said Cheryl.

"Cheryl, kids," John said, "I want you behind me at all times! Do you understand that? He won't shoot me, but he'll do anything to get me to do what he wants, including shooting you. Stay directly behind me." John moved between the soldier and his family, into the line of fire, and slowly pushed his family backward. In the preceding few seconds it occurred to him that his life had never truly been in jeopardy. The real threats always seemed to be made upon his family members instead.

"I'll kill you now!" the man said, pointing his weapon directly at John's head.

"Go ahead, shoot me," John said.

The sniper turned his weapon and fired into the wall, hoping to rattle the Harrises and get Cheryl and the children to separate. They all cried out, but did not move. John closed his eyes, then opened them.

"John!" screamed Cheryl.

"I'm OK! It's OK, kids! Stay right behind me," he said, substantiating that his premonition was true.

Given his injuries, the sniper could not move very well. After pausing with John in his sights, he moved his gun, pointing around John where he might strike a child. John tracked him completely and made sure his torso was in the line of fire. He kept his hands directly behind him to form a sort of shadow for his family to follow from side to side.

They seemed to be at a stalemate. Cheryl inched her gun away from her side and as close to John's back as possible. Michael and Nicole clung to her like abalone to a rock.

"It'll be OK, Nicole. Don't worry, it'll be fine, honey. Johnny, I think you need to move aside as he asks and let us come out."

John looked back and forth between Cheryl and the sniper, unsure.

"Listen to her. She's smart," the sniper said with a sneer. "Do as she says."

John turned back and gave her a longer look. She pushed her hidden gun into his back. Without losing a beat, John turned to the sniper.

"Calm down. Calm down, *everyone*. I'll step aside, only as long as your weapon is only pointed at me. Deal? You cannot harm my family, or I don't move."

"Move now!"

As John moved slowly to the side, he made as strong of eye contact as he could with the sniper, and drew him in with the fingers of his raised hands, gently repeating, "Me … me." The sniper tracked him.

"Children, come out with me. Don't be afraid," said Cheryl.

As Cheryl and the kids moved into the room from behind John, Cheryl brought her weapon from its hidden position and emptied the clip at the sniper. She continued to pull the trigger, screaming like a wild woman, producing only clicks, after the last bullet was spent.

As the sniper fell and struggled to sit up, John moved forward and kicked him in the face. The sniper did not move anymore.

John rescued the sniper's gun and rifle and took a look out the picture window. He saw Charlie and Moreno lying in the bloodied snow.

"Cheryl. Take the children to the door to the garage and wait for me."

"No, John. We shouldn't separate."

"Trust me." He kissed her forehead. "I'll be right there."

She moved the children as he asked without further hesitation.

John picked up another handgun from the floor and headed out the front.

"Moreno! Charlie!"

He shook Moreno's lifeless body. No response. He did the same with Charlie. Charlie managed to open his eyes. Blood slowly percolated from his nose and mouth.

"Take the keys from my right pocket and go," he said in the loud whisper of a dying man. "Trust no one."

"What is this all about?"

"We don't know any more than you do. That's God's honest truth."

"We'll get you to a hospital."

"Don't be stupid. Help will be here soon. I'll be OK. You go. Now!"

"Thank you, Charlie, from all of us. I mean that."

John removed two sets of keys from Charlie's pants pocket. Before leaving, as distasteful as John found the search, he rummaged through Moreno's jacket and found his special cell phone. It was not damaged. He found a big wad of large bills in one of the dead agent's pants pockets. John took his wallet as well and joined his family in the wrecked garage.

John smelled gasoline fumes. The light coming through the broken garage door was enough for them to maneuver. As they approached the rear of the van, they could see that the plow of the snow vehicle had not only pierced the garage door, but also punctured the fuel tank of the van. What they would use for transportation?

Outside the garage, John looked to both sides of the house. He saw nothing more than dead bodies. John climbed awkwardly into the snowplow cab to look for keys. Driving it would be another issue altogether … but he found no keys. Then he remembered the keys he had taken from Charlie—two different sets. He depressed the heaviest clutch he had ever touched and placed the tractor in neutral. He slid one of the most obvious keys into the ignition.

"Move way away from the front of the tractor," yelled John to his family.

He fired up the loud diesel engine. The kids and Cheryl only flinched transiently as they stood huddled and stunned. The glassed-in cabin of the tractor was large. One by one, John helped the kids and Cheryl up as they stood around him in the single driver's seat.

John struggled for what seemed to be the longest time to find the reverse gear and began to curse. "Would it be too fucking much to ask for reverse to be in the same standard location as it is in most goddamned vehicles?" The gearshift pattern had worn away from the shifter knob long ago. With a grind and a clank, John finally accessed reverse, then applying pressure with his right foot while easing out the clutch. The tractor lurched backward and, since everyone but John was standing, his family struggled to keep from falling. As it pulled away, the tractor ripped the garage door off its hinges. The door fell apart in the driveway as the tractor headed for the road. The forward gears were easier to find; the Harrises were on their way. The children closed their eyes and took deep breaths of relief—anything to get them away from the carnage.

Roughly a mile away, they passed a police squad car speeding in the opposite direction. John was heading for the gas station they had passed through on their first day in Stonington. From there, he was not sure where they should go or what they should do.

"Anybody got any ideas?"

One person nodded. "Mm-hmm."

"What's on your mind, Cheryl?"

Chapter 27

The children played in the check-in area of LaGuardia Airport while John and Cheryl talked out Cheryl's plan. They both knew what had to be done; separation from the children was the best plan, regardless of how painful it was going to be. The problem was the mechanism. Who could take the kids? They had a scratch pad with a number of possibilities listed. Who was least likely to be under surveillance right now—and, hence, be in the best position to take and hide the children? Who could adequately care for them? The caregiver's life might be endangered too. Whom could they trust? The answer to these important questions kept coming down to the same couple. They were the best of the choices, though far from optimal. The next question was whether John and Cheryl could live with choosing them. Specifically, could John live with it?

"You've got to be kidding," said John. "Let's go through the list again."

"We've been through it over and over. We're running out of time. Think about it. They found us much quicker this time. We need to get out of here."

"OK. All right. Let me think how we can do this. I haven't ... *we* haven't ... spoken to them in ... Jesus, it's been several years. What makes you think they'll do it?"

"Everyone we know is likely being watched. They're wealthy. Probably retired. There's no other choice. And they will do it."

"What makes you so sure?"

"Because they're your parents. You're their only child, and these are their grandchildren. Their *only* grandchildren. I know they'll do it. Time heals all wounds."

"Thank you, Doctor. Just call them, just like that?"

"Kinda, but it can't be *just* like that. I suppose there's a remote chance that their phone might be bugged. I cannot imagine that they are being watched. But we must take no chances. We need to contact them, arrange a meeting, and make a fairly quick handover. Then we've got work to do."

"Boy, are we fucking desperate. After what they did to you, you're still willing to deal with the two of them?"

"I'll do whatever it takes. I can't believe you would even question it, John—after all the death we've seen. And you know what, if I can forgive your parents, maybe you can too."

"All right. All right. So what are you thinking?"

"I'm thinking there must be some way to contact them without using the phone. We could show up on their porch, but there's got to be an even better or safer way. Come on … think."

"Well … nah, never mind."

"No, what?"

"No, really, it's ridiculous."

"So say it. I'll laugh, and we'll move on."

"Remember at my high-school reunion? I introduced you to Jeff Selig?" Cheryl looked puzzled. "Tall, blonde, balding. My best friend from grade school?"

"No. But go ahead."

"Well, he said he and his family moved back into his childhood home after his parents died."

"OK."

"Well, he lives on the same street as my folks … less than a block away."

"So we call him and …"

"And he goes and gets my dad and brings him down to *his* house …"

"Which certainly can't be bugged."

"I'll bet that old house has the same phone number as when we were kids. I'll remember that number all my life. I mean, I remember it just like when I was a kid. And if it's been changed, we'll look it up."

They spent the next half hour deciding on the rest of the strategy—where they would rendezvous and so on.

"Should I go with you to the phone?" Cheryl asked.

"No. I mean, that would be nice, but you've got to watch the kids."

"Then good luck. I love you. We'll be right here."

"You know, I just can't stop thinking about Moreno, and Charlie ... and Evert, and Baker, and Fournier. As sick as it is, they were starting to become family. Know what I mean?"

"Absolutely, and I'm keeping *this* family alive."

"Yeah," he said as he walked off toward a row of pay phones.

"Oh! Use change ... no calling cards," shouted Cheryl.

John held up an OK sign without turning around.

John stopped at the souvenir store to get change. At the phones, John took a deep breath, put in the change, and dialed his friend's number.

"Hello?" came a woman's voice.

"Hi. I'm calling for Jeff Selig."

"No one here by that name."

"Is this 335-7717?"

"Yes. But no Jeff Selig."

"I'm sorry. I'm calling long distance. Have you had this phone number very long? Because I think I have the right number."

"Oh, about ten years."

"Well, then, I'm sorry. Oh, is this Chicago?"

"No. You've made a mistake. This is New York."

As John hung up the phone, he could not believe that he had forgotten to dial the area code. The next time he dialed, he did it correctly. This time, a child answered.

"Yeah," was the full extent of the greeting. John knew from experience that answers this short from children meant only one thing: the TV was on.

"Is this the Selig residence?"

"Yeah."

"May I speak to your dad, please?"

"Yeah." There was a pause.

"Hello?"

"Jeff?"

There was a pause. "Who is this?"

"Jeff Selig?"

"I'm sorry. Who is this?"

"You are not going to believe this, but this is Johnny," John said, trying to contain his joy, lest he alarm his old friend. "Johnny Harris. I can't believe you have the same number as when we were kids."

"Johnny? Wow. What's going on? How the hell are you? Hey, I can't play right now ... I've got homework."

"Jesus. Remember that shit?"

"Yeah, and you know what? As I get older and I watch my kids grow up, I kinda miss it. So, what's up?"

"I need to speak to my parents, and I can't risk talking to them on their phone. It's complicated, and maybe I'll get a chance to explain why sometime. It's urgent—really urgent. Have you seen them at all … I mean, like when you drive by their house?"

"Sure, just the other day. They were taking a walk. Matter of fact, they take walks all the time, regardless of the weather. Exercise buffs."

"And how did they look?"

"Fit as fiddles, far as I can tell. Why?"

"Well, I kinda lost contact with them some time ago. So, what do you say? Can you help me?"

"Sure. Lay it on me."

"I was wondering if you could walk over there and ask them to come to your phone, and I could call back in, say, fifteen minutes?"

"You bet. Mind if I ask why?"

"Like I said, I can't explain right now, but it's critical that I do not speak to them directly on their phone."

"John, you in trouble with the law?"

"No, of course not. I really can't talk about it, though, but I promise I will share it all with you soon. Will you trust me on this?"

"Blood-brother animal trust?"

"Yeah. Blood-brother animal trust," John answered with a smile. He had not heard that for at least three decades.

"OK, I'll go now. John, if there's any other way that I can help, let me know. All right?"

"Thanks, Jeff. I owe you big time."

"My pleasure, buddy. So call me back in twenty minutes, just to be safe. Hey … maybe we can get together soon?"

"I'd like that."

"I seem to remember from the reunion, don't you have kids?"

"Yep. Four beautiful ones."

"We got a few too. Anyway, talk to you soon. And you take care of yourself."

The next twenty minutes were difficult. John set his watch alarm. He was impatient and nervous. He had the worst case of butterflies. He sat down on the floor by the phones, back against the wall, and looked alternately between his watch and his family. The children frolicked, as they had not done in a long time. They were in a large, open space for the first time in a number of days and ran free. This put a smile on John's face … momentarily. How he would soon miss them terribly. John wondered what the chances were that he wouldn't see them again. He quickly killed that thought. The pain was too great. His mind wandered onto Cheryl's hunch and her associated plan. What if she was wrong?

The watch beeped. He dialed the Selig residence.

"Johnny?"

"Yeah. Jeff, did you … I mean, are they there?"

"Right here, old buddy. Let me put them on."

"Johnny?" said an elderly, but recognizable man's voice at the other end. It cracked, and John was not sure whether it was the result of age or emotion.

"John Junior?" said an elderly woman's voice, also on the line.

"Dad? Mom?" To his surprise, John was overcome by emotion. He had to cover the phone as he wiped away tears and inhaled through his nose to keep it from running down his face.

"Are you OK, son?" asked his father. "We got Cheryl's message, but we were in Europe. By the time we got home, no one answered your phone. I'm sorry. It's horrible … your kidney. Who would do such a thing?"

"Cheryl called you?"

"Of course. So, how are Cheryl and the kids?" This was a pivotal question in John's mind. Years ago, they would not have asked about either. Perhaps Cheryl was right: time, and age, might heal all wounds.

"We're all fine," John lied. "Jeff tells me that you all are in good health."

"Yes, me and Mom are just doing great, Johnny. Just great. So … you're in good health too? I mean, one kidney is … works good enough?"

"Oh. Yes. The body does just fine with one healthy kidney. I just have to keep an eye on my blood pressure."

"My God, the children must be so big now," said his mother, her sniffling audible.

"Eric is eleven, and as tall as Cheryl already. His feet are almost the same size as mine. Can you believe that? Erin is ten and beautiful. Michael is six. Just the sweetest. And Nicole is two and a half, and the most precious. They are all bright, happy, great kids.

"Mom, Dad, I don't have much time. Please listen to me carefully. This is a matter of life and death. Without going into detail, my life and the lives of Cheryl and the children are in danger. It's somehow tied to the kidney thing, but we're not sure how yet. We have been in a type of FBI witness-protection program, although we are witnesses to nothing. Someone wants me, and they've killed a number of FBI agents to try to get at me. They will stop at nothing. I think they would even kill the children. In fact, I'm certain of it." Both of his parents gasped. John tried to visualize their faces. "There are no agents left to protect us, and we have no one else that we can trust. We need your help."

"Of course, son … what can we do? How can we help? Mother and I will do anything."

"Jeff can't hear any of this, right?"

"Yes … correct, I mean. He left us alone."

"Cheryl has a plan, and I think it is a great one, although it's going to be painful for all of us. For the safety of the children, we have to separate from them until this all gets worked out. We need you to care for and hide the children. It will involve you leaving your home very soon, not to return for who knows how long. You won't be able to communicate with anyone you know until it is safe. You'll have to relocate. There would always be the possibility that your lives might be in danger." He paused to let this sink in. But there was no hesitation.

"Just tell us where and when, son."

"Are you sure you don't want to think about it?"

"Unequivocally, Johnny. Unequivocally. Tell us where and when."

"At exactly 10:00 AM tomorrow we need to meet you at the O'Hare Airport. You will have to purchase two tickets—one for you and one for mom—for Delta flight 1098 leaving O'Hare at 11:30 AM at Gate 27a."

"Got it. 10:00 AM, tomorrow, O'Hare, Delta flight 1098, Gate 27a."

"Between now and tomorrow, don't answer your phone or call anyone. You need to make your plane reservations in person. Act as though you were agents yourselves, as silly as that might seem. We doubt that you're being watched. You're probably not being bugged either. But take no chances. It's too risky. We can't risk the children any further."

"We will be diligent. Promise."

"We're going to need some cash too."

"How much?"

"I don't know … five thousand, something like that, if that's alright. Just until we get it all worked out. We can't access our bank accounts or credit cards."

"That's not a problem. Anybody asks, we're just taking another vacation."

"Well, that's a good idea. We need to catch a flight. See you tomorrow."

"Johnny?" asked his mother.

"Uh-huh?"

"We're sorry, and we love you very much."

The tears welled. It was clear to him, at that very moment, that they felt the same way about him as John felt about his own children. Time, issues, diversity, pain, sorrow—the love between a child and his parents transcended it all.

"I love you too."

He hung up the phone wanting to bawl like a baby. He could not, but he did resume his position on the floor against the wall, closed his eyes, and visualized his parents through the years until he last saw them. They were loving, they were loyal, they were supportive, and they were good. How, then, could they have done what they did? Banish their son, their grandchildren, because Cheryl was black? Human behavior sometimes just defied understanding.

John and Cheryl had booked several inexpensive super-saver flights with as many connections as possible. They zigzagged around the states for the next several hours watching airline movies. Despite being pent up, the kids preferred the airplanes to their other habitats as of late. The final redeye got them into O'Hare at seven in the morning. With three hours to kill, they decided to check into a hotel and get showered up.

A change of clothes was purchased for everyone from one of the shops in the airport Hilton lobby. In the sundry shop, Cheryl purchased toothbrushes and toothpaste before heading back to their room to join the rest. Standing in line to pay for her goods, she noted the availability of stationery. In particular, she fancied a package designed for letter writing. It contained paper and envelopes in serially decreasing sizes. She plucked it off the display. She purchased stamps as well.

En route to her room, she about-faced and went to the front desk.

"Excuse me. Do you have a brochure that lists the various Hiltons worldwide?"

She was handed a thick, nifty brochure with minute color pictures of scenes in Europe, Asia, and the rest of the world. Inside was a listing of the hotels by country, with their addresses and phone numbers, and a brief description of accommodations and services available.

She stashed the brochure, stationery, and stamps in her bag and headed upstairs. In the room, she and John would go over the game plan with the kids one last time. They couldn't cover everything in the hours they had to prepare the children, but the three older children would manage. The children acted as though it were an acceptable plan, although they were very frightened. They were to think of it like any other of a number of vacations that Mommy and Daddy had taken in the past.

But John and Cheryl had never left Nicole before. The concept of parents leaving on vacation and then returning was meaningless to her. It was going to be torture for her. The only way John and Cheryl could reconcile it was that even torture was preferable to death.

Chapter 28

The Harrises sat in chairs and on the floor of the lounge in front of Gate 27a. John had purchased boarding passes for the whole family to take advantage of airport security, but with no intention of using them. John was nervous, and Cheryl and the older kids were depressed. What made it worse was that Nicole would not move away from Cheryl's lap. Cheryl fought back tears, not wanting to upset Nicole further.

"You know," Cheryl whispered to John, "when we see your folks, whatever arrangement is made for the switchover, I think we need to play a bit on the floor with the kids and your parents, and then carry the baby down to their car, or whatever their plan is. The separation will be too l-o-u-d," she said, spelling the last word, even for the inside of the airport. "And remember, they can't tell us where they're going."

"Got it," said John. "Hey, you guys. Your grandma and grandpa will be here soon, and then they'll take you on a little vacation, you lucky guys!"

The anticipation was driving him nuts. He stood and started pacing.

"Johnny?"

He turned, and was speechless. They looked so much older than he remembered them ... but, then again, so did he. He reached out and hugged them both at the same time, as Cheryl and the kids just stood and watched. The three of them were crying. Soon Cheryl was crying too.

John looked remarkably like his father, both in stature and thickness. Both men were physically fit for their ages. John's mother was thin, with short, gray hair and a shy smile. Both were dressed in casual, but expensive clothing.

"You look great, son," said John Sr., barely able to speak. His face was flushed, his nose and eyes saturated. John's mother just clutched him, unwilling to release, not unlike Cheryl with Nicole. After a good moment or so, both remembered Cheryl and the grandkids.

Tearfully, their demeanor fully apologetic, they walked quickly around a row of seats and hugged Cheryl. The message was clear. Nicole was snuggled somewhere in between. John was feeling slightly faint, and his legs refused to move, so he just watched. After several moments, his parents let go and turned to the children.

"Well, young man, you must be Eric," said the elderly man, shaking his hand. "I'm Grandpa John II. Your dad and I have the same name. And this is Grandma Audry. And you must be Michael, and you Erin."

"And that little one over there must be Nicole," continued Grandma Audry.

"Oh," said Grandpa. "Johnny, could you please hand me that bag over there?" He gestured toward the large bag John Sr. had dropped while he was hugging his son.

John walked the bag over, his legs having regained power. John Sr. sat down with the bag and continued, "Grandma Audry and I have a gift for each of you before we take you all on a special vacation. Come on over here."

Nicole looked, but kept her ground, as the others moved right on over. They had not had a toy to play with in ages. John was taken with how his parents had changed. He remembered that only his mother would interact with children. Now his parents seemed to have switched places.

"OK. This one says Michael, so I guess it must be yours. Here's Eric's, Erin's. And here's Nicole's."

Nicole preferred to open her gift on Cheryl's lap. John was amazed. His folks had actually taken the consideration and time to help make the children more comfortable.

"Grandma Audry, can you come and share with Nicole and me?" Cheryl said in baby speak.

An hour passed quickly. John thought he might have made a big mistake waiting so many years. Conversely, maybe his folks were able to respond only given the severity of the circumstances. Either way, Cheryl had been right about old wounds. While Grandma bonded with the children, John shared the circumstances as they had unfolded from the time of his abduction as his father listened in shock.

"My God, you're lucky to be alive."

"Well, certainly the rest of them are. These guys want me alive for some strange reason. I've only recently come to realize that they won't kill me."

"I don't know of anything like this. I've been around a long time. I've never read or heard anything like this. You hear a story here and there about people stealing organs over the past few years. Mostly overseas, I think. But nothing like this. This is bizarre. What will you do? How can I help?"

"Cheryl has an idea. But you know what? It's safest if you know nothing about our plans and for us to know nothing of your plans. Know what I mean?"

"Sure. So, how will we get into contact again? How will we know when to come back home?"

"Every day, keep your eye on the news. And I guess we can use the Seligs as a contact if all else fails. Second-to-last resort: take this phone number of the cell phone I have. I will turn it on for one hour every night, between ten and eleven o'clock at night, Pacific time. But these have to be last resorts only."

"Well, I guess Cheryl's not the only one with a plan."

"Despite all we've been through, and maybe because of this, the separation with the kids is going to be more painful than anything we've ever done, especially with Nicole. They're going to need lots of love and attention, communication. Just in terms of Nicole, rather than have her crying and making too big of a scene here in the airport, maybe we can walk you outside. We don't want to draw any attention."

"Sounds good to me," said John Sr.

"Hey, Dad. Let me ask you one thing before we go."

"You don't have to. Your mom and I made a horrible mistake that we've had to live with in pain for too many years. I can't tell you how glad we are that you called."

"I wasn't going to ask that."

"It's important you hear it anyway, son. It was hard for me to say … and I don't, for the life of me, know why. Our stubbornness has caused all of us a good deal of pain, and maybe you too. But now I want to put it out there, and I want you to hear it loud and clear. Mom and I were wrong, and we were too stubborn to admit it. We've learned a lot. I just hope we haven't burned any bridges."

"I hear it, Dad. When this is all over, maybe we can sit down, the four of us, and talk about it. I'd like that." John paused uncomfortably. "Anyway, since time is of the essence, how did you know which child was which?"

"That's all you wanted to ask me? I think you told me on the phone call to the Seligs'. But, to be perfectly honest, Cheryl's mom has sent us pictures over the years. You know, Christmas pictures, things like that. I think she felt we needed to see our grandkids. And we never wrote back once, but she kept sending the cards, bless her," he said. "God, were we stupid."

"Yeah, she's quite a remarkable woman."

John's watch alarm sounded. Both men seemed grateful for the interruption.

"OK. Honey, we've got to get going," said John, changing the subject matter and tone. "Maybe we can all walk outside, even though it's cold, and say good-bye before we each go on our separate vacations."

"That's a great idea, Johnny," said Cheryl. "Maybe Nicole can walk, and I can hold one hand, and Grandma Audry can hold the other."

Nicole smiled. She liked that idea. Temporarily.

As they walked, the mood was somber. No one knew what lay ahead, but they certainly knew the tragedies that had befallen them. They were quiet as they neared the airport annex exit.

"OK. Let's all put on our coats and go outside," Cheryl said sweetly.

Outside, it was chilly, although none of the Harrises noticed. The inevitable had come to fruition; the unthinkable was about to transpire. Cheryl and John were about to experience the separation of parent and child. No stronger bond existed in the universe. No wonder parents rallied behind their children, even under the worst of circumstances.

Cheryl got down on her knees to face the smaller ones. John stood behind them, his hands and arms touching each of them.

"Now listen, kids. This is hard, but you know what? We've been through harder things these last few months. Did you hear that? Harder. And now we're going to go on vacations. Mommy and Daddy won't be gone long," said Cheryl, fighting back tears. "And when we see you next, we'll be back in our own home, with all of our friends, having fun and growing up, just like it used to be. Look at me. Look into my eyes. You know I'm telling you the truth. I want you to help Grandma and Grandpa take care of you. We need the bigger kids to help with the littler kids. Try not to fight. Try, instead, to make each other feel better. When you're thinking of us, remember this. At that exact moment, at the very exact second you are thinking of us, you know what? Mommy and Daddy will be thinking of you too. So you know we will be with you, up here and over here, every day," she said pointing to her head and heart. "Give us a hug, so we can go, so we can see you all soon," she finished, her cheeks sore from forcing smiles and staving off tears.

They huddled into one hugging mass. Grandma Audry wiped her tears as she and John Sr. viewed the love and desperation before them.

"Nicole, you stay with Grandma Audry, real close. She'll make you feel safe and warm until Daddy and I come back. Love you. Love you all," Cheryl said, prying Nicole from herself and attempting to transfer her to Audry.

Nicole began to scream and struggle. The sound of the shrill cry and the terror in her eyes as she reached out to her Mommy would be seared in Cheryl's and John's minds from that day forward. John helped Cheryl to break away as he helped himself. They walked briskly in the opposite direction as John's parents hung onto the kids. Nicole tried desperately to get to the ground and run to her mother. John and Cheryl turned once and waved, blowing them all a kiss and forcing smiles. And then they were gone.

Cheryl swore she could hear Nicole's scream inside the airport. John reassured her that it was an impossibility, although he looked about to be sure.

"This is what it's come down to," John said bitterly. "They've made us give up what we love. I'm ready to fight … and die, if necessary."

There was no response. Cheryl was too numb to answer.

Chapter 29

Russ Marley was almost used to his cell phone ringing in the wee hours.

"Marley here."

"Russ. This is John Harris."

Marley glanced at his wife and whispered, "I'll do this in a different room. Hold on a second … OK, what's going on? You got me all riled up from your other call."

"They're all dead."

"Who? Who are 'they'?"

"All the FBI agents. Killed. Me, Cheryl, and the kids escaped."

"Are you absolutely sure?"

"Marley, I've seen more death in the last couple of weeks than a thousand people see in a lifetime."

"So who's protecting you now?"

"No one."

"You're on your own?"

"Yes."

"Oh my God. We've got to get you somewhere safe. Where are you?"

"We think we have a plan. Meet me at Cheryl's office building on Rossmore in thirty minutes."

"You're here?"

"There's underground parking. The keycard will be left for you on the top of the sensor box. Just bring it up to the third floor with you. And Russ … you have to come alone. We just don't trust anyone else."

The Harrises held major stock in the Larchmont Pediatric Group, and a large chunk of the three-story building belonged to them. They used Cheryl's parking card to enter the underground parking lot.

"I wish we could have waited until Sunday to do this, when there was a zero-percent chance of running into anybody," Cheryl said wistfully.

"What can we do? We're screwed if we do and screwed if we don't. Time hasn't been our friend so far. Now let me ask you this."

"What?"

"You sure you can do this?"

"You've already asked me that a dozen times. Cold feet, eh, Mr. John Harris III?"

"I don't think that's unreasonable for a person in my position," John said.

"Look, we can stop at any point if it's too difficult. No harm, no foul. Just relax."

Inside, the first thing Cheryl noticed was that familiar medical-office odor: some combination of rubbing alcohol and whatever had been indelibly imprinted in everyone's olfactory memory during their first doctor's office visits. Cheryl had never liked it before, but now she inhaled through her nose, slowly, and savored it.

"Hello ... anyone here?"

As they walked through the waiting room to get to the treatment and office areas, Cheryl squeezed John's hand and stopped.

"Oh, look at the toys. God, I sure hope Nicole is doing OK."

"You know what I think?"

"No, what?"

"At least what I hope. You know how sometimes in the beginning, when we'd leave the kids at preschool and they'd cry and carry on, and it ripped our hearts to shreds when we had to leave?"

"Boy, do I."

"Well, remember how we would return five or ten minutes later and watch them, and they'd be playing like nothing ever happened? Well, I'm hoping that was how it was for Nicole after the airport."

"I hope you're right."

John followed Cheryl down the hallway to her office, where preparations could begin.

True to his trade, Marley circled the block twice to be safe before parking in the underground parking structure. Panzer was suddenly in his mind. He removed his weapon, found the elevator, and went to the third floor. Once the elevator opened, he scanned the hallway before exiting. Nothing. He made his way to the waiting room. The office was not well lit. He could hear muffled conversation nearby.

"Hello?" called Marley.

"Down here. It's Cheryl and John."

John met Marley in the hall and extended his hand.

"Dr. Harris? Where are you?"

Cheryl poked her head out of the office and smiled. Marley holstered his weapon and shook hands with John. It immediately became a hug, and Cheryl joined them.

"We know you took a big chance coming here," said John. "We're so grateful."

"We had no one else to turn to," said Cheryl.

"Where are the kids?"

"Tucked away for safekeeping. We don't even know where they are. That way, they can never be touched."

"Are you sure you've thought all this through?"

"We've thought this thing through as clearly as we can," John answered.

"From the peace-officer perspective, it just seems way too risky for you take matters into your own hands."

"God knows how many FBI agents are dead," John said. "If you'd seen what we've seen, you'd do exactly what we're doing. No one can help us at this very moment. We're asking for you to trust us. When we've got a better handle on it, we'll fill you in. Promise."

"Enough talking," said Cheryl, changing the subject. "Right now, we've got work to do and not a lot of time. I need to take a single KUB x-ray film of John's abdomen."

Marley looked at John in confusion. He knew what an x-ray was, but a KUB? Exactly what "work" Cheryl was talking about?

John went to the x-ray and minor surgery room and lay supine on the table. Cheryl placed a needle on the skin of John's abdomen, pointing to the center of his umbilicus. Another needle was placed on his belly, pointing to the bottom of his breastbone. Finally, a small lead apron was placed over John's groin.

"What's that for?" asked Marley.

"Protects the testicles from x-ray exposure."

John winked gamely.

Cheryl slipped a large x-ray film cassette under the table and adjusted its position under John's body. She pushed a button on the movable machine above John, and a light came on in the shape of a rectangle over part of John's body.

"They teach you this in medical school?" asked Marley.

"No, you learn it in private practice—HMO 101. Follow me."

They walked behind a leaded wall. Cheryl adjusted the knobs, then pushed a button. "I'm just going to develop this. Meet me in my office."

Cheryl walked into her office and placed the developed x-ray on her wall-mounted lightbox to scrutinize it. John and Marley stood behind her.

"What are all those small white things?" asked John.

"Those are metallic clips from your surgery. Like staples. Metal shows up white on x-rays. OK … a few more films, and we'll be ready."

"What exactly are you looking for?" asked Marley.

"Maybe nothing, just a hunch. I'll tell you if and when I find it."

John lay on the x-ray table once again, this time on his side. Two needles were placed on the skin at each end of his surgical scar. Now the x-rays would go through his body in a direction perpendicular to the first x-ray.

Moments later, Cheryl joined the men in her office once again. With sweaty palms, she placed the second x-ray next to the first. She took a breath and focused.

"Bingo, boys."

"What the hell is that?" asked Marley. He pointed to a white square with a complex pattern of minute lines and circles within.

John closed his eyes.

"I'm no electronics buff," said Cheryl, "but that sure as hell looks like a transmitter to me."

"Now, why didn't they see that in the Kansas hospital?" Marley felt for his weapon instinctively as the ramification hit home.

"Well, two reasons. They had absolutely no reason to take a lateral film—one from the side, like this one. Maybe they didn't even take the first view. But even if they did, the doctors—if you want to call them doctors—who placed this transmitter placed it perpendicular to the anatomical plane of your body. Very smart. Take a typical flat plate KUB x-ray, and you might just fool someone, seeing this thin thing on end. Put a few clips around it for camouflage, and voila, you have a missed foreign body, in our vernacular."

"Can you get it out?" asked John.

"Well, that's what I'm looking at now. See this shadow or line here?"

"Mm-hmm."

"That's called the abdominal fat pad stripe. The device is right on the edge of that, which means that it's outside the peritoneum and retroperitoneum."

"Meaning?"

"It's fairly deep, but it's in fat or muscle, outside of the cavities that contain your vital organs. So, the chances of hitting a vital structure are minute, and the risk of introducing serious infection is also small."

"Jesus. You gonna have to put me out to get it?"

"I don't think so. We can't put you *out* anyway. We just do minor surgeries in the office. But don't worry. I think I can get it under local."

"And what do we do with it when we're done? Destroy it?"

"I've got some ideas. Let's cross that bridge when we get to it."

"One last thing," John said. "Doesn't this violate something somewhere in the Hippocratic oath?"

"Trust me. There's nothing about doing minor surgery on a spouse—or major surgery, for that matter—in there. Relax. I'm going to need your help. In fact, I'm going to need both of you to help."

John and Marley looked at each with controlled fear.

John lay on his right side in the surgery suite. Cheryl washed the area around his surgical scar with dark iodine soap.

"Let's let this sit for a moment. I'll be right back. Don't touch it, either of you."

"What should I do?" asked Marley.

"Just sit tight, and make sure John doesn't touch it. I'll be right back."

Cheryl went to her office, closed the door, and quickly found her anatomy book. She blew the dust off the top of it, opened it, and rapidly thumbed through it until she found the flank anatomy. After a moment, she closed the textbook, having confirmed the anatomy and convinced herself that there were no significant structures she had to be concerned with. She had done her share of suturing, and foreign-body retrievals occurred frequently in the pediatric trade. But this foreign body was quite a bit deeper than what she was used to. In fact, it might just be out of her league. She offered herself the consolation that if she could not retrieve it herself, she had a surgeon friend she could call upon in a pinch for a favor.

"So how's the patient, Marley?" asked Cheryl when she returned to the surgical suite. She set up a tray with a number of supplies on it.

"Oh, just fine."

Neither of them looked well.

"John," she said, filling a large syringe. "I'm going to inject the skin all around your scar. It burns, and it hurts. It's just xylocaine, like when you cut your leg and when you had your lip repaired."

John winced and moaned as she slowly injected the entire scar. Next Cheryl injected the skin and tissues below the scar. The numbing complete, Cheryl inserted a three-and-one-half-inch spinal needle into the middle of the scar. She sunk it an estimated two and a half inches. Marley's jaw almost unhinged.

"You know what? We're going to need one more x-ray when I'm done numbing this up, before we begin the surgery."

"What can I do, Doc?" asked Marley nervously.

"Relax, Nurse Marley. Your time will come soon. OK, John. I'm going to roll you onto your back for another flat x-ray. We need to keep this sterile, and you need to keep your hands away, OK?"

Ten minutes later, Cheryl put another x-ray on the lightbox. John's back remained turned to it.

"What's the verdict, Doctor?" he asked.

"We're ready."

"But what's the x-ray tell you?"

"John, honey. I know you want to know all this stuff. I know that you're nervous. It lets me see how deep the transmitter is. Now I'm gonna tell you something that I've always wished I could tell some of my patients since medical school, but never could. And I mean it with all sincerity: shut the hell up!"

She did not want to tell him that the transmitter was about three inches down.

"OK, we need to get started. You'll feel pulling, and that's OK. If you start to feel discomfort, let me know, and I'll give you some more medicine. Marley, I think you need to stand guard by the door until I need your help."

Marley moved to the door.

"Discomfort … is that the same as pain?"

"You know what I mean. Marley, watch how I put on these gloves. The key is not to touch anything nonsterile. You'll need to help me eventually. Think you're up to it?"

Not waiting for Marley's reply, Cheryl put disposable sterile surgical drapes around the old scar. She removed the spinal needle she had placed earlier and used a scalpel to cut out an ellipse around the scar. Marley walked over, peered over her shoulder, and then walked back to the door. The skin bled, but not very much. Cheryl took her sharp-pointed scissors in one hand and toothed forceps in the other and snipped out the entire old scar.

"Boy, this is so weird," John commented. "I feel like you are cutting but there's no pain."

Marley started to blanche and feel faint at his position by the door. No one noticed his embarrassing moment—able to shoot and kill, but the sight of minor surgery completely unglued him.

"Good stuff, that xylocaine," murmured Cheryl.

A thump sounded on the floor.

"What was that?" asked John.

"Don't move. It's just Marley. He'll be OK. Happens to just about every medical student. Happened to me too."

Marley lay dazed on the floor, but not unconscious.

"Marley. Lie there for a minute. When you feel better, sit up and wait five minutes. Then stand up. You'll be OK. Trust me."

Cheryl resumed her work. The tissues below the removed scar were bluntly dissected, or pulled apart without cutting, until the wound gaped. The edges of the wound oozed blood over tiny clusters of glistening fat. Cheryl used the pencil-like cautery device to zap all the surfaces until the wound remained dry.

She continued the blunt dissection slowly, deeper and deeper, until the first problem arose. Right in the middle of the huge hole she was cutting in John's side ran a sizable vein. If she cut it, it would bleed like stink, and she lacked the proper instrumentation to pull it out of the way. It would have to be cut, but in a controlled fashion.

"Hmm, you know what, guys? We're going to need some good-sized retractors, which I know we don't stock, since we're not in the habit of removing transmitters from our patients. Can you think of anything we can use?" Cheryl was thinking out loud without expecting much help from the men. "Got it. I'll be right back. John, don't move. Marley, don't touch a thing."

Cheryl returned with two plastic vaginal-exam specula in sterile wraps. She opened them and regloved.

"Hey," said Marley, "aren't those …"

"Yep. We see plenty of teenage girls in the office too."

"Just what do you have in mind?" asked John, straining to look over his shoulder.

"Relax. Don't worry. And don't move, for crying out loud. John, no more joking for now, OK?"

Cheryl knew that finding the transmitter would be tricky. The layers of tissues that composed the human body had a disturbing way of hiding things.

The wound ran some ten inches in length and gaped about four inches wide. The vein traversed the crevasse, visible along the full width of the gape. Cheryl tied suture ligatures around the vein, twice on each side to be safe, and then cut it in the middle. The vein fell away like a broken bridge. Thankfully, she saw no hemorrhage.

"OK, you're up, Russ. I think you're better off if you don't look, but I need you to hold these specula apart, so I can see what I need to see. Go ahead and put on your gloves. Then move on the other side of John, but don't touch anything with your gloves except for what's on the inside of the surgical drapes."

Cheryl thought that were Dr. Ginsberg, of the Utah University Medical Center, to see her surgical technique, he'd have a shit fit. Nonetheless, the specula worked perfectly, as they spread the wound and held the tissues apart for better visibility. Cheryl introduced the spinal needle into the wound and measured off the same distance she had produced on the final x-ray. They were within an inch.

Unfortunately, the blunt dissection at this depth became harder, as the instruments were relatively short. But Cheryl continued, the transmitter itself providing all the urgency she needed. Finally she heard a perceptible click—like metal touching metal with a bit of something in between. Cheryl's pulse quickened.

Methodically, she noted her position within the wound and took her time dissecting, millimeter by millimeter.

"It should be right around here—"

"Uh! Excuse me, I can feel that."

"I'm sorry, honey. I'll put some more medication in."

She injected the deeper tissues with more xylocaine, but purposely stayed way from the area of focus. She did not want to chance distorting the anatomy with the fluid of the injection. She dabbed the bottom of the wound with a clean piece of gauze.

By this time, Marley was looking into the wound with less difficulty. "Hey … what's that?"

A barely detectable glint of metal shone at the bottom of the wound.

"Looks like gold to me." Cheryl tapped it with her hemostats and verified a hard surface. No bone in this area ... that left only one possibility. "Now what do we have to grab that with?" It was too large for her small instruments to grab. "This ought to do. Let's take her home, Mr. Sulu."

The ring forceps were long and could grasp pretty large objects without destroying them. They were designed to plumb the full depth of the vagina and carry out a variety of procedures. A little improvisation in John's flank was not unreasonable.

One overriding concern remained at this point. The transmitter was embedded in the next tissue layer, which was muscle. Muscle was quite vascular and could bleed heavily, with no distinct vessel to tie off. Even if there were a single vessel to tie off, Cheryl had neither the instruments nor the experience to get that job done at this depth. She hoped and prayed that this would work.

The small, rough surfaced rings at the end of the forceps grasped the transmitter and clicked to lock in that position. There would be no further concern now about finding or losing the needle in this haystack.

Cheryl attempted to pull out the electronic device first with slight force. She tugged a little harder. It would not move. For the life of her, she could not imagine what tethered it.

"Doesn't want to budge. Maybe some scar tissue has formed around the base of it or something."

The body normally reacted in this way; objects recognized as foreign evoked a response. Plastic and metal didn't faze the body too much; it simply walled the object off with scar tissue to keep it harmless and then, essentially, forgot about it.

Cheryl held the forceps in one hand and dissected with the blunt hemostats in the other hand—first down one side, then down the other. She dabbed up the minimal bleeding produced by ripping tissue away from the transmitter. She was having trouble with the scar tissue on one side. She switched to sharp, pointed scissors and continued the dissection, careful to keep the scissors along the surface of the transmitter. She put down the scissors and pulled on the ring forceps with a rocking motion. Again she applied moderate force and actually felt the tissues giving way as they tore to release an object they had not wanted to begin with.

"Almost there." She gave one last tug.

Out came the transmitter and forceps as one unit. She held it up and looked at it with pride. It was one inch by one and a half inches, a few millimeters or so in thickness, mostly encased in clear, hard plastic and metal, and quite bloody. She wiped it off with a four-by-four gauze and could see the micro-technology within.

"We got it!" she said as she set it down on a tray.

"Ahem," grunted Marley, trying to get Cheryl's attention inconspicuously.

She turned her attention back to the incision and gasped with horror. The wound was nearly filled with a rising tide of dark-red blood. "Oh goodness!"

"What?" asked John.

"Nothing, just a little bleeding," she said.

She took a whole pack of four-by-four gauze and thrust it into the wound. That absorbed about fifty percent of the blood. She pulled the saturated wad out and replaced it with the second, sopping up the rest. Pulling it out, she looked for the site of the bleeding, but the bleeding itself was too brisk to see anything.

Cheryl felt herself descending into panic. As she had feared, the muscle was bleeding. She put in half of the last pack of dry gauze and then removed it quickly. She fired up the cautery pencil and began aimlessly cauterizing; it was to no avail. The blood overwhelmed the cauterizer, rendering it useless. Cheryl reinserted fresh gauze.

"So what's the good news, Cheryl Lynn?" asked John with understated concern.

"Be with you in a minute, Johnny, OK?"

She took a deep breath and let her mind search for a solution. She hit on a traditional saying learned by all medical students: "All bleeding stops with pressure." She took the ring forceps and pressed it firmly against the four-by-fours in the bottom of the wound. The bleeding slowed substantially.

"Marley, I'm pushing hard here, and it's working perfectly. I want you to continue while I go get something. Johnny, I'll be right back. Don't move, OK?"

"Ten-four."

Cheryl took off her gloves and left, rushing back in less than a minute. She emptied the small packet onto the surgical tray, got out more gauze, and regloved.

"Found this Surgicel on the epistaxis tray."

"What's epistaxis?" asked Marley.

"Nosebleed, in doctor talk. The Surgicel is a synthetic material that promotes blood clotting. I'm gonna put some in here, hold pressure for a good ten minutes, and then close up."

"Sounds good to me," said John.

Cheryl took the pressure off the gauze and plucked it out. The bleeding had slowed dramatically. Nonetheless, she placed the Surgicel at the base of the wound, shoving a sliver of it in the sleeve previously occupied by the transmitter. She put a pile of new gauze in the bottom of the gorge, on top of the Surgicel, and again used the forceps to put substantial inward pressure on the packing.

"I do feel that a bit, by the way."

"Just ten minutes, and I'll let up the pressure. Then we'll close this baby up and have you lie down somewhere for the next twenty-four hours and ice it. Honey, do you have a view of the clock?"

"Yeah."

"Then let me know when ten minutes passes, OK?"

"Sure."

Cheryl spoke with authority and confidence she did not have. She was in over her head, and she knew it. But why scare the patient? The next ten minutes felt like an eternity to her.

"Ten minutes. Can we go now?"

"Well, let's take a look. OK ... there isn't too much blood in the gauze. That's good. I'm going to remove the gauze now. Let's all cross our fingers." She teased the wad of gauze from the depths of the wound ever so gently, closed her eyes and took a deep breath, and looked. "Yes! So, let's give it five minutes of watching without pressure, and if there's still no bleeding, we'll close it up. You up for watching the clock again, John?"

"No problem, Dr. Harris."

Cheryl had already begun to relax. Why should John's wound start bleeding again, especially with the Surgicel in there?

Marley seemed impressed, both by the size of the cavity and the fact that the heavy bleeding had stopped. "Strong work, Doc."

"Thank you. But we still have a bit more to do."

Cheryl closed each layer of the wound with an absorbable suture that the body would break down in a few weeks. When she finished, Cheryl removed her gloves and flung them across the room. She bent over and kissed John softly on the cheek and whispered into his ear.

"Thank you for trusting me. I love you."

"I love you too."

"Before I forget, we need to give you some antibiotic before we leave. This is what I want you to do right now. Very gently, turn onto your left side, so as to put pressure on your surgical site. We leave in one hour."

"Good idea, given this." Marley indicated the transmitter. "What's the plan?"

"As you can imagine, the less you know, the better," answered Cheryl. She hugged him. "Thank you so much for helping."

"Yeah, Russ. We owe you big, buddy."

"There's got to be something more I can do to help."

"We need some time to sort this out, and we know how to get ahold of you when we need to," Cheryl said. "I think the most you could do right now is just make sure it's safe for us to leave. We're gonna be here another hour, and it's late. You need to get home to your family."

"I'll make sure it's safe and then go. Where will you be going?"

"Just can't tell you. Meanwhile, we've got a redeye flight to catch. Mum's the word, right?" replied John.

"When you coming back?"

"You'll be the first to know. You've got to trust us. You're all we have."

Marley shook hands solemnly with John. Cheryl walked him to get his things. When he'd left, she returned to John with her purse.

"Think you can move a pen while you're lying there?"

"Sure. What do you have in mind?"

Cheryl pulled out the series of envelopes, as well as the stamps she had purchased in the Hilton. She handed him the brochure of Hilton's international hotels.

"What's all that stuff?"

"We're going to send our Arabic friends on a wild-goose chase that they are not going to believe. Watch this."

Cheryl took the smallest envelope and addressed it to one of the European hotels in the brochure. On both sides of the envelope, she wrote in capital letters, INTERHOTEL MAIL. She put the transmitter into this envelope and sealed it.

"OK. That was Germany. Your turn. Pick out another continent and country from the brochure and address this envelope," commanded Cheryl, handing him the envelope next in size.

"That's ingenious! You're something else," said John. "One envelope into the next, with no return address, and this little baby gets mailed all around the goddamn globe. And at no charge. They just enter it into their interhotel mail!"

"There may be a time factor here, in terms of getting the transmitter away from ourselves. In one hour we go to the airport and drop it off in the mail there. That way it gets processed as fast as the U.S. Postal Service can manage."

"Pediatrician. Surgeon. Agent. Saboteur. You are unbelievable, Cheryl Lynn."

Chapter 30

It was the perfect time and scene for them to do it: late and dark. After swinging by the airport to drop off their transcontinental mail, they headed out of the city. They had each made the drive so many times in their lives, they could almost do it in their sleep. They were heading back to the ranch, back to the homestead they had missed so dearly. They reasoned that no one would ever suspect they would return home. Besides, they had work to do and did not have a lot of money left. Their computer was there. It was the right thing to do.

They pulled onto the entrance of their property.

"Stop!" said John as they pulled into the drive of their ranch.

"Why?"

"What if that transmitter thing is still attached to the beam across the drive? We don't need Marley or anyone else up here right now."

"Why would you think it might be on?"

"Well, the light on our sign is on. That means the utilities are still on, and that means the sensor might be working."

"I wonder how much longer the FBI is going to keep paying our mortgage and utilities?"

"We don't need them to pay the utilities, and we don't want them to know we're here. We have a few Honda generators that I bought last year, right? We have plenty of firewood, right? We've got camping stoves, right? We've got Moreno's FBI cell phone, right? We got groceries, right? Then we're relatively OK for a while, as far as I can tell, should they turn off the electricity."

"Excellent points," Cheryl said. "Hmm. We still need to get up to the house with this vehicle. We can't let you walk … Got it. Let's just take that back road that gets us near the barn."

"You mean the fire road?"

"That's the one."

"Good thing there's not much snow on the ground."

The gate blocking the fire road was not locked; fire departments, by law, needed twenty-four-hour access to it. Although bumpy, for the most part the road was manageable. Patches of snow presented a small problem. The major concern centered around the jostling of John's new wound.

Finding the barn was going to be a little more difficult. A gradual, off-road hill had to be navigated in the dark. Once they were over the crest, the exterior lights of the house, set on timers, would be visible. The barn stood near the house. They'd park inside the barn and be well hidden.

At the barn, Cheryl made the executive decision to drive John down to the house before she returned the vehicle and tucked it away in the barn. He certainly did not need to risk falling and opening his wound—and maybe even bleeding to death.

John sat on his favorite rocking chair on the porch and waited for Cheryl to return. When she did, they sat together and held each other tightly for a moment. They were finally home ... but far from it. They hoped the nightmare would soon be over. It was late. The next day, they had work to do.

"How are you feeling this morning?" asked Cheryl, bringing coffee to John in bed. She knew he was waking up by the funny noises he made in his sleep. She had lain awake for a few hours, thinking and planning.

"Oh, great." He grimaced as he turned.

"Let's take a look at your wound, shall we?" She lifted the sheet. "Not much going on in that bandage. Fantastic. By the way, there was nothing on the AM news regarding Stonington."

"So nothing last night, nothing this morning. Next time we go into town, we can check the newspaper. But you know what? They gotta be covering this whole thing up. There's no other possibility. I wonder what BS they're going to lay on those poor agents' families?"

"Listen, I've been doing a lot of thinking. Let's jot down what we know and what we don't know, so we can chart our course. What do you say?"

"I say I go pee before anything. Go get your notepad."

"Take your time getting up. Seriously, easy does it."

"Hey, Cheryl. Did you notice that there wasn't any yellow tape around the house marking off the crime scene? And there wasn't any chalk around where Marley nailed that guy near the entrance ... not to mention a lack of blood?"

"No. I didn't even think about it."

"Think about it while I hit the bathroom."

John walked very carefully into the kitchen to get himself breakfast and another cup of coffee. He slowly sat himself at the table. Cheryl's laptop was plugged in and booted up.

"I'm lost," Cheryl said. "What's your point about the yellow tape and all?"

"Well. This was the scene of a crime, right? Far as I know, until cases are closed, the property remains roped off and is kept untouched pending resolution. So this crime has apparently been solved. Anybody tell you about it?"

"No. Of course not," she pondered as she sat at the PC.

"All right, let's get to it."

Cheryl created three columns. The left-hand column she labeled KNOW, the middle DON'T KNOW, and the right PLAN.

"Here we go," Cheryl said. "Know. One. We know they took one of your kidneys. Two ... and let's discuss each one after we're done making these lists, OK?"

"Fine."

"Two. They want you stone quiet on the entire subject of your kidnapping and surgery. That has been made abundantly clear. They are willing to kill to achieve that end."

"Three," continued John, as Cheryl typed. "Arabic people seem to be involved. Lots of them. Well resourced. And, this of course, leads us to number four. The FBI is involved and not talking. CIA possibly too."

"All right. Anything else?" Cheryl asked. "Oh, obvious. Number five: you were handpicked. They had to have the ability to access your medical data in order to determine, presumably, that you were the kidney donor they somehow desired."

"Discussion on number one: I was not a random event. I was the intended victim donor and likely the best match. The perpetrators are extremely organized, trained, and financed ... that smacks of some governmental sponsoring, although it is not inconceivable that a rich, sleazy entrepreneur type could finance and use mercenary types. Which brings up another point. Make it number six. Just type in capital letters, 'MEGA IMPORTANT.' These people are *willing to take on the FBI, one of the largest U.S. governmental agencies, head-*

on. Head-on! This was not your run-of-the-mill kidney theft, if there is such a thing."

"Discussion on number two," said Cheryl, taking over as they both looked at the computer screen. "Well, that ties in with your discussion on number one. I don't think I would have anything to add to that."

Cheryl typed in "Why mega important?" in the DON'T KNOW column, next to number six of the KNOW column, and numbered it six as well.

She typed in the DON'T KNOW column next to number two, "Which Arab country?"

"So that leaves us with number five," said John. "Why me, and how the hell did they pick me? What makes me the apparent kidney donor of choice?"

Cheryl typed that next to number five in the DON'T KNOW column.

"Let's be clinical here," Cheryl said. "Dr. Harriman already told us that you had to be a good match to the person needing your kidney, or they wouldn't have bothered with you. I mean, they could have taken anybody off any street, in any country, at very little time and expense. So, that begs the question: How then did they find you?"

"How does someone become a donor?" John asked. "I mean, how does a professional determine, mechanistically, that my kidney might work in someone else's body? How is the matching process actually carried out?"

"It requires a blood specimen from you. That way certain genetic markers in your blood are matched to the one needing your kidney. This is called tissue typing and we know that the better the match, the less the chances are that the person receiving your kidney will reject it. Nobody wants a rejection. It's pretty hairy surgery, as you well know."

"So I had to give blood somewhere, right?"

"I don't remember. Did we ever have you donate at a blood drive?"

"I don't think so, but who the hell remembers?"

"Well, my educated guess would be that the typing would have had to be done within the last five years, likely less. And you wouldn't forget the experience of donating blood. They lay you down and use a huge needle, so there's a pain component. They give you something to eat and drink after they take a bag full of blood from you. And then they watch you for a while. So when did all that happen to you?"

"I can honestly say never."

"Now the same can be said for donating plasma and white cells as well, so they're out too."

"Wait. I did donate blood for Eric when he was born so prematurely."

"Oh, yeah. But that was eleven years ago. So that's out."

"Whoa. Wait a minute. What are we, stupid? What about Shelly?"

"Shelly Vitullo?"

"Remember when I was typed in case she needed a transfusion when she was sick with cancer two years ago? Come to think of it, we both were."

"Wow … since she died, I've totally put that out of my mind. But you're right. We were both typed, although I don't think we went at the same time. As a matter of fact, they took a pint of blood from each of us at the hospital, and damned if they didn't turn it over to the Red Cross when Shelly died before ever needing to be transfused."

"The Red Cross has got to be the biggest blood handler in the U.S.," John mused, "and probably the entire world. Correct me if I'm wrong."

"Right, but the Red Cross doesn't tissue type."

"They're not involved with organ donations?"

"Nope. So someone has to have access to the blood and the confidential records regarding whom the blood belongs to, and *then* have access to a lab that can do the tissue typing. We're talking well connected, well financed, with a ton of employees … and I use the term 'employees' loosely."

"Sounds like the people who've been on our asses for the past several weeks."

"Yeah."

"And there are Red Cross chapters probably in every state, right?"

"Like we said: well connected, well financed, and well organized. Sound familiar?"

"Can you imagine the amount of work that went on over who knows how many months to find me? The resources alone are mind-boggling. Big bucks."

"So, we're talking about calculated, exacting work over at least a year, possibly a little longer. The only time-limiting factor other than finding the best match would be the health of the recipient … that is, whether or not there was some rush for the recipient to have the transplant."

"Is there such thing as a perfect match?"

"I would think so. I'm guessing it's very rare, if it exists, but I don't know for sure. Hey, except for an identical twin, of course."

"OK, for the moment let's assume perfect matches exist, outside of identical twins," John said. "So, if you've got the resources these people do, why take a less-than-perfect match? And why take all the risks they have taken—FBI, CIA, whatever—unless it were for the perfect match? Put this on the computer."

"Put what?"

"Start a number seven, and in the unknowns put, 'Who is the recipient?' and 'Perfect match.' I mean, all the unknowns are tied together, but we now have a few pieces of the puzzle to attack here."

"Well then, unless there's more discussion, why don't we make some concrete action plans, if we can? You take the lead. You're on a roll."

They both studied the first two columns, hoping to fill in some more of the space of the third column.

"Boy, slim pickings in terms of viable plans," John said

"I say we call that lady over at ... ROPA, was it? What's her name?" asked Cheryl.

"I think we've still got her card somewhere."

"See if she can assist us in finding an appropriate recipient."

"In what way?"

"In finding important Arabs in need of a kidney."

Chapter 31

By the time the Harrises returned home, it was late. They had found a battery charger for their spy cell phone, along with some connectors that would allow modem activity over the cell phone. And they'd managed to avoid running into anyone they had known in their previous lives.

The next morning, John fetched Mrs. Dennison's card. On the bottom of her business card was the ROPA Web site address, as well as her personal e-mail address.

John attached the modem of their laptop to a connector he had purchased last night, then attached it to the cell phone. They would soon be using their dial-up internet service connection through Moreno's untraceable cell phone. John was day dreaming about the perfection of his improvisation when Cheryl called him to breakfast.

"Be right there."

Both of them sizzled with newfound energy and optimism. They knew they were on the right track. They held hope for some answers to questions that had burned deep inside. They wanted their normal lives back. They ached for the squeals of four children to set their home aglow.

"What if she won't help us?" asked Cheryl as John walked into the kitchen.

"She will. I think she'll be so pissed by what happened to me, given her status in the transplant community, that she'll stretch the rules. I'm banking on it."

"And if she doesn't?"

"Maybe Dr. Ginsberg will be sympathetic to the point of helping us. He seemed pretty moved by it all, didn't he?"

Something caught John's eye, and he looked out the kitchen window to watch deer in the yard. He watched how gracefully they stepped as they grazed. So beautiful and fragile, and respectful … much like *most* humans. He prayed for the deer and all of God's creatures. And for Cheryl and the rest of his brood. He asked nothing for himself.

They sat at the PC. If John's suspicions were correct, owing to the cell phone, no one would be able to track their transmission.

"So far, so good," said Cheryl.

"Yeah. Let's hope Dennison is as compulsive as we think she is."

Cheryl sent an message to Dennison's e-mail address:

Ms. Dennison, do you have time to chat? You can reach me at this IM screen name …

In less than a minute, Dennison responded.

"Bingo!" said John.

DenROPA: This is Dennison of Utah ROPA. How may I be of service?

Dr. CHarris: We desperately need your help. You, in particular.

DenROPA: Do we know each other?

Dr. CHarris: We met several of weeks ago. My husband and I came to visit, with many questions regarding transplants, specif. kidneys, after seeing Ginsberg. You were tied up at the time.

DenROPA: Oh. Know your predicament well. I did speak with Dr. Ginsberg and he filled me in on your situation. Unbelievable. Tragic.

"See, I told you!" said John.

DenROPA: So what can I do for you?

"That's just like her … right down to business. My kind of lady," remarked Cheryl.

Dr. CHarris: We need your help. Private. Totally confidential.

DenROPA: To do?

Dr. CHarris: We'd like to find out how many requests for kidney transplants have been logged in from the Middle East over the last five years and how many have been met.

DenROPA: I won't violate patient confidentiality of course. Doable. Will

take time. Need to contact UNOS, online. Why important?
Dr. CHarris: Not sure if it is important. A hunch. Let's see.
DenROPA: I think I can do that. Back to you in half hour. OK?
Dr. CHarris: Thank you. We know this could put you in a bit of a bind &
apprec it :-)

The Harrises signed off and waited the next half hour nervously. In twenty-nine minutes, they logged on again. She was online.

DenROPA: 7 total, Here's the breakdown: Kuwait 1; Saudi Arabia 2; Iran 1; Jordan 2; Syria 1. Bear in mind that requests from less developed countries are unusual, as you can imagine, and that the requests are almost exclusively from the elite. Royalty. They have no precedence over U.S. citizens, regardless.

"Uh, wait a minute," said John. "Kuwait, Saudi, Iran, Jordan, and Syria … We're missing a few. Ask her about Iraq and Turkey."

Dr. CHarris: Excellent, thank you. Anything from Iraq or Turkey?
DenROPA: None.
Dr. CHarris: Which, if any, have been fulfilled?
DenROPA: Kuwait 1; Iran 1.

"OK, put it to her," John said. "We gotta ask her. The worst she could do is say no."
"I don't think she'll—"
"Do it, or I will."

Dr. CHarris: Mrs. D. we have a bigger favor to ask. Could you, would you, cross check the tissue types of the outstanding 5 (7–2 = 5) against my husband's tissue type?
DenROPA: We don't have your husband's tissue type

"That sounds like a yes to me," said John.
Cheryl grabbed a piece of paper with Dr. Walter Harriman's header on it.
Cheryl had already asked Dr. Harriman to type John—another clinical hunch.

Dr. CHarris: John's type: B pos; Loci A(43,69), B(67,77), DR(52,53)
DenROPA: Are you serious?
Dr. CHarris: I've rechecked. That is it.

DenROPA: In my fifteen or so years with this company, I have never seen a type close to that. It's very rare. Now, with regards to the cross check. I believe that would be a violation of patient confidentiality.

"Here, scoot over," said John. "Let me try this."

Dr. CHarris: Mrs. D, this is John Harris III. I'm trying to think of how we can give you more comfort. The questions we need answers to are twofold: A. Any matches? B. If so, what country? No names. Nothing else. Confidentiality not violated. Please, I need your help. There is no one else to turn to.

DenROPA: I'll see what I can do. But don't you get your hopes up. I'm skeptical about the existence of another rare tissue type like yours. Let's talk again in one hour.

Again the Harrises signed off. The next hour was going to be torture.

"Hey, Cheryl Lynn. Don't the kids have an atlas CD?"

"Yeah?"

"Can you run and get it?"

Although she had successfully avoided going to the children's rooms thus far, Cheryl went to get the CD. Once in Eric's room, she felt overwhelmed. Monster posters and posters of high-tech villains and saviors hung on the walls. A few trophies adorned his dresser. The typical array of dirty clothes decked the floor, and some clean clothing draped out of open dresser drawers. She smiled, the faint scent of dirty socks catching her. The bunk bed brought tears to her eyes. His teddy bear, which he had kept since the days when he would not consider parting from it, perched among pillows on the top bed. She did not need to close her eyes to see and feel him as a baby. It was the same bed that he had used for sleepovers on the weekends. He was shaping up into a wonderful young man.

"I was wondering what was taking so long," said John, startling her. "I might have guessed." He hugged her as she wept.

"I put them out of my mind for a few days. Out of mind, out of sight. I mean, out of sight, out of mind," she said, laughing and sniffling. "Oh, Johnny …"

He wiped her tears. "Let's go look at the atlas and try to keep our minds off the children and focused on the task at hand. It's up to us to pull it all together and deliver ourselves from this fucking abyss."

They found the CD, returned to the computer, and inserted the atlas.

"OK, let's see what we have here," said John with a cheeriness magnitudes above what he was feeling. "Here it is, Middle East, in all its grandeur. Do you know the big question, madam?"

"No." She blew her nose.

"Why would the FBI … and, let's presume, the CIA … cover up anything to do with this region?" He chuckled. "Can you imagine it? My kidney is somewhere in the goddamn Persian Gulf right now."

"Oops," Cheryl said. "Time to get back on with Mrs. D."

Cheryl logged on. This time, her palms were sweaty. "Please, God, let this be the answer!"

Dr. CHarris: Mrs. D?
DenROPA: Yes, I'm here. You're not going to believe this.

John and Cheryl sat forward as if they could possibly glean more information that way.

DenROPA: One perfect match Saudi Arabia. No other matches past or present with even 4 of those loci. One thing more. It is a child. Aristocracy.

Mrs. Dennison ended her message with no salutation or further comment, clearly unwilling to remain involved any longer.

Cheryl and John were floored.

"Uh, well," Cheryl said slowly, "I suppose we could go to the library and look at the microfiche of newspapers gone by for something involving a child from Saudi Arabia."

"We'd need a team of investigators helping us. It might take a few days with all that help. Us, maybe a week if we were lucky. And then, of course, there would be the risk of us seeing someone we know at the library …"

"So what are you suggesting?"

"There must be search engines out there now that would allow a search of the archives of major newspapers."

"Have you used them before?"

"No."

"Well, how do we go about giving it a try?"

"Let's see." John took her seat. "We need to search the Web for a major newspaper. Let's try the *New York Times*. Wouldn't you think that would be our best bet?"

When he signed off his internet service with Mrs. Dennison, the map of the Middle East reappeared. Something caught John's deep attention and his eyes danced about, not focusing on anything in particular. He was lost in thought.

He looked at Cheryl at last. "It's so obvious. What, are we stupid? Why is the FBI sweeping up, sweeping under actually, after this failed operation? Why does anyone do anything? Money. Dollars, buckaroos, greenbacks. The Middle East means oil. O-i-l. It fuels their economy, literally and figuratively … as it does every nation, directly or indirectly."

"How's that help us ID the sick kid?"

"It doesn't, but it's a fact we can't ignore. We're not just up against some rich sheikh … we're up against a powerful, geopolitical ally of our own United States."

"I would agree. But are we gonna let that stop us? Can we focus? Are we gonna look at the *New York Times* archives or what?"

"I can tuck that away for the time being and focus. But we're going to have to come back to it Cheryl."

He pulled up the archives for the *New York Times*. The costs of searches, by time, and how and when billing was to occur was determined up front. They elected just to bill it through their credit card. Damn the risk.

"OK, what do you think? Two years ending … oh, about six months ago?" asked Cheryl.

"Sounds good to me."

A search box requested a keyword or article title.

He entered "Saudi Arabia, kidney transplant."

A little hourglass appeared, followed by a message that there were no such citations.

"Let's try … let me see, uh, 'transplants, Saudi Arabia.'"

Another hourglass. No citations.

"We're doing just great, so far," Cheryl said sarcastically. "Try 'Saudi Arabia, kidneys.'"

Nothing.

"Kidneys, Saudi Arabia."

This went on and on with mounting frustration. Cheryl took to entering each trial phrase in writing on a notepad to avoid repeating each futile attempt.

They broke for lunch to clear their minds and gain a fresh perspective.

"It's there. The information's there," said John. "We just need the right buzzwords to tease it out. We're close, Cheryl Lynn. I can feel it."

"I feel it too."

They finished their drinks and walked back to the computer, hand in hand.

"All right … seven-eleven, seven-eleven," said John, as if at a craps table.

"Wow. Wouldn't that be nice?"

"What?"

"We go to Las Vegas with the kids when this is all over. I hear the place is just one big family playground now. Fun for all ages. Key word being 'fun.'"

"Deal." They shook hands and then refocused on the PC. "Let's be methodical and creative, shall we?" Cheryl said. "What haven't we tried that is still logical?"

"Got it. How about 'Arabian donor?'"

"Yeah. OK."

Cheryl got back on the Internet, surfed to the *New York Times* archives, and entered the phrase.

No citations.

"Arabian recipient."

No citations.

"Arabian kidney donor."

No citations.

"Arabian kidney recipient."

No citations.

"Saudi donor."

No citations.

"Saudi kidney donor."

No citations.

"Saudi kidney recipient."

No citations.

The couple continued searching for another half hour, to no avail.

"We're getting nowhere here," John said. "And correct me if I'm wrong, but we're running out of possibilities. Let's try another tack."

"Like?"

"How would you expect to see a headline in the newspaper, or how would you write it if you were a reporter?"

"Oh, I don't know. Something pithy and catchy like 'Renal-failed rajah requires replacement,'" said Cheryl.

John wanted to laugh, but did not want to take the chance of their search deteriorating into giddiness.

"I'm sorry," said Cheryl, biting her tongue. "OK, serious. How about 'Saudi requires transplant.'"

"Go for it."

She typed it in and hit the Return key.

No citation.

Without discussion, she typed in 'Saudi needs kidney.'

No citation.

"Wait a minute. What if it's not for the Shiekh himself? Didn't Dennison say it was a child? Try 'Saudi's son needs kidney'.

The number "1" appeared in the box next to the word "citation." They had seen so many zeros in that box in the last couple of hours that neither of them noticed it initially.

"Shit. OK, try—"

"Wait!" exclaimed Cheryl. "There's a citation!"

"What?" John stared at the screen in disbelief. "Get it! I mean, let's pull it up! I don't fucking believe it … the simplest entry, the simplest!"

"It's not that easy, but we can do it. First, it looks like they want to give us some data," said Cheryl. "Let me click here and see what it is."

She moused to and clicked the prompt. A new screen appeared.

Number of words: 96
Location: B 5

The screen then asked whether the viewer wanted to see the article.

"What do you think?" asked Cheryl.

"Yes! What are you, nuts?" asked John, rapidly writing down the date of the article.

She moused to the prompt and clicked. A new screen came into view with the article as it originally appeared:

Saudi Sheikh's Son Needs Kidney

The son of Sheikh Fawzi Aswad, suffering chronic kidney failure, was said to be in need of a suitable donor for a transplant, according to an unnamed family member. An evaluation was recently undertaken in Chicago's famed Children's Hospital,

according to a hospital spokesman.
The United Network for Organ Sharing
(UNOS), a U.S. agency, confirms that it has
been contacted by the Aswad family. The
10-year-old heir has been battling
worsening kidney disease for most of his
life. Sheikh Aswad is the president of
the United Arab Emirates.
ASSOCIATED PRESS

John and Cheryl were stunned into silence. Suddenly much of it made sense … a sick sense. There it was. That was the connection. There was no question.

"Well, that explains the funding, the elite forces, the resources, and the accents, doesn't it?" John asked. "And I'll bet the child doesn't even have a clue. They come to America for help, to take advantage of our medical superiority. Then they fuck us. The whole thing reeks."

"Yes, it does, Johnny."

"It's hard for me to imagine why the FBI didn't make this connection. That's the scary thing. Why wouldn't they act to stop all this? Why would they sacrifice you, the kids … even Moreno and the others? And why would they tell Marley that we were all dead and close the crime scene at our house?"

Cheryl nodded, following his thinking.

"I'll tell you why," John said. "Saudi Arabia has the oil. Plain and simple. I submit that if the Saudis want me so bad, then so does the U.S."

Cheryl nodded again but didn't quite get it right away.

"We know they want me alive. This heir needed my kidney, but they still want me alive. Why?"

John watched Cheryl look away and say nothing.

"Cheryl? What are you thinking?" John took her hand. "I need to know how a doctor thinks right now. I've exhausted what a broker can come up with. Why do they still want me?"

Tears began to well over Cheryl's lower lids and run down her cheeks.

"What? Tell me, honey."

"It's obvious, medically. Kidney transplants fail. It can happen in the first few months, or maybe years later."

No more needed to be said. John understood.

"It's sickening ... disgusting," she said through the tears. "They want you to be a human kidney incubator in case their little prince has problems with the first one you 'donated'. What a sick notion."

Wait a minute! If that is true, why'd the Arabs bother sending me back to the U.S.? Why not just keep me until they need me?"

"I don't know." Cheryl contemplated the question further before continuing. "How long did Harriman say perfect match transplants last?"

"Good matches, perfect matches? Years. I think that's what he said."

"Then it just gets back to basic science. Don't animals live longer and healthier in their own environment versus captivity?" It did not take long for Cheryl to process this concept to it's natural conclusion. "That makes total sense. So then why do they keep coming after you?"

"We need to break down exactly who 'they' arc."

"I'm not following you. What do you mean?"

"Well, if 'they' are the Arabs, then maybe it's because things got messy."

"Like what? You stopped talking to people like they told you to."

"A police officer was killed. Panzer. That's pretty goddamn messy."

"Yeah, and?"

"I don't know. Let me think this through ... If 'they' is our own government, then yeah, this is it. If 'they' is our own government then they would want me too. They just might want to have me to dangle over the heads of the Arabs."

"Leverage?"

"Sure. Perfect word, Cheryl Lynn. John Harris' kidney could be the short term key to our oil problems. Leverage over the Arabs for oil for a decade or more to come. So maybe that's why they want me. They know the FBI, the US, will use me as leverage, if they don't get me. What did Moreno say, the FBI wanted to put us on a base somewhere? It's been a bloody race, literally, for John Harris."

"So what do we do next?"

"We call Marley, get the name of his current FBI liaison, call them or get them online, and go from there. Agreed?"

"Sounds like a deal. What happens if we verify it all?"

"Well, then, we've got some major thinking to do. Because if we don't do something major, nothing's changed, and they still will both come after us and likely find us, one way or another."

"Do you think the chiefs are in on this?" Cheryl asked.

"Which chiefs are you referring to?"

"The director of the FBI, the director of the CIA, higher?"

"Yes and yes, without a doubt. If you're talking about the president, maybe, but in no way would he be allowed to be culpable. You know, arm's length type of thing. But that's all academic. It would not be out of the question for the CIA to pull something major off like this without the White House's OK."

"Alright … so we've got the beginning of a plan," she said. "Right now, can we just hold each other a minute?"

New Delhi Hilton. The posh hotel belied the poverty nearby. In a back-room, out of sight behind the reception desk, an Indian grabs a large zipper-bag from Sydney, Australia out of the box labeled "Incoming Inter-Hotel Mail". He opens it to find a number of documents and starts to sort them. One item is a peculiarly thick sealed mail envelope. He opens it to find another envelope within, addressed to 'Stockholm Hilton'. He holds it up to the light unable to see what is inside, then tosses it into the "Outgoing Inter-Hotel Mail".

Chapter 32

Cheryl got online and found the FBI Web site. After a short wait, she was able to access an FBI representative in real time. At this point, John took over.

FBI: How may I help you?
Dr. CHarris: I'm looking for …

"Cheryl, quick. What did Marley say the FBI guy's name was?"
"Breslow."

Dr. CHarris: … Mr. Breslow
FBI: I have no way to connect you with him.
Dr. CHarris: Do you have a directory? He's high up in the bureau.
FBI: Even if I did find him in a directory, I would have no way of connecting with him.
Dr. CHarris: One step at a time. Could you please verify his position in your organization?
FBI: I have that information.
Dr. CHarris: Big cheese, right?
FBI: How can I help you?
Dr. CHarris: Please inform Breslow of two things: (1) John Harris is online and pissed and (2) it is a matter of national security.
FBI: Sir, we do NOT deal with pranks. Pranks of the order you are suggesting are against the law. We have the right to contact your online service and have them terminate your membership.
Dr. CHarris: That would be reasonable, if only I were joking. I am dead serious. You must have a mechanism for dealing with calls like this. You

are the FBI.

FBI: I will contact my supervisor. Stand by.

Three minutes lapsed before transmissions continued.

"You think they're somehow trying to trace our location?"

"Wouldn't matter, with Moreno's cell phone they don't have a chance," answered John.

> **FBI:** I am Agent Singleton. We'll need a whole lot more info than that to stick our necks out.
>
> **Dr. CHarris:** Sir, I can tell you nothing more. I can guarantee you that if you use the name John Harris, no matter where Mr. Breslow is, he will make it his business to get online. Can contact him by phone as well. His preference. But Mr. S, if you fail to contact him, it will be your ass.
>
> **FBI:** Give me some time.
>
> **Dr. CHarris:** How much?
>
> **FBI:** Five minutes, maybe ten?
>
> **Dr. CHarris:** Fine.

"OK, here we go," said John, rolling his eyes at Cheryl. "Definitely trying to trace us. Calling our online service provider. Good luck, eh?" A few minutes passed, and then another message popped up on the screen.

> **FBI:** Breslow asked that you call him directly at the following number: it's a secure line.

The Harrises signed off. John disconnected the cell phone from the modem.

"You ready, Dr. Harris?"

John dialed the number and put Moreno's cellular on speakerphone.

"Breslow here."

"This is John Harris."

"How do I know you are who you say you are?"

"Moreno, Baker, Evert, Fournier, and Charlie … all dead in Stonington."

"OK. What's on your mind?"

"I was just going to ask the same. What's on your mind?"

"You're in serious danger out there by yourselves. You need to let us help you."

"Fine. Tell me what it's all about, just so we can make sure we're all up to snuff."

"The people who took your kidney don't like you talking to the news media."

"Why would that concern them?"

"Public opinion, I presume."

"You have several excellent agents dead, and you *presume* it's because of what the public opinion might be over my kidney? I am not stupid. I would venture to say that at this point, you are not operating on presumptions."

A pregnant silence filled the line.

"Who took my kidney, Breslow?"

"I don't know. Do you?"

"If you don't start communicating two-way with me here, I'm getting off. I've been on long enough for you to know that you cannot trace this call."

"I don't know."

"I'll tell you what you know, so you know how much I know. Then no more bullshit. The answer is Saudi Arabia."

The next silence was significant.

"What are your plans for me?"

"To get you out of harm's way."

"Moreno and his people were eminently qualified to do that, and they failed."

"Quite honestly, we underestimated our needs. We won't make that error again."

"So we'd be able to go back home, continue at our jobs, and have our normal family life back again ... just with triple or quadruple the security?"

"Basically."

John mouthed "Bullshit" to Cheryl.

"Would you guarantee it?"

"Yes."

"In writing?"

"If necessary."

"Why can't you just tell the Saudis to knock it off?"

"They are, how should I say it ..."

"Say it like it is. We're two grown men, intelligent, and Americans. We have faith in the American way."

"Their ways and customs are much less advanced or developed. They play by different rules."

"But there are certain rules that everyone understands ... universal rules. Destruction of person and property, to be exact. Like, 'We're the U.S., and we're not going to tolerate what you're doing. And just to show you how serious we are, in one hour, we're going to blow the shit out of one of your air bases and blame it on Iran.'"

"Please, Mr. Harris."

"How far does it have to go? How far will *you* let it go? They come to America, get one hell of an education, and reap the benefits of our advanced technology. And how do they thank us? They take whichever one of us they want for our organs, without a second thought. Maybe they sanction it as a decree of Allah. I call it the most serious human-rights incursion that you've ever dealt with."

"You're angry because it happened to you. Don't lose sight of reality—"

"Reality! I'm talking reality. You all need to take a closer look at what *you* are calling reality. It's not just me. It could be any one of us next time."

"We hear you, John. We're not far apart. There's just so much more that we must balance at the same time."

"Well, I question whatever else you're putting on the scales."

"Our sources tell us that more foreign agents have entered the U.S."

John looked at Cheryl, covering the receiver of the phone and mouthing "More bullshit." She understood, as did he, that the Saudis were more likely focusing their efforts in Germany and points east at that moment, following their ruse.

"Would Mr. Kelly and Mr. Freeman agree with that assessment?" John asked, using the CIA and FBI director's names.

"Yes, I feel secure they would," he said after a strategic pause.

"Well then, that does it. I'll contact you in the next forty-eight hours at this same number. At that time, I'll advise you of our location, and you will have precisely two hours—one hundred and twenty minutes—to bring us in. It will have to be you and Mr. Kelly and Mr. Freeman. I know exactly what they look like. Anything else is too risky."

"Don't be ridiculous."

"Are you suggesting to me that the FBI and the CIA do not have the ability to reach any point on this globe at supersonic speeds at a moment's notice?"

"No," replied Breslow tentatively.

"I think there are leaks from within your organizations," John lied, echoing Moreno's misguided sentiment. "I would be ignorant if I risked my family's lives and gave you any more time. I suggest that you all be within a stone's throw of your private jets for the next forty-eight hours."

"And if we don't hear from you in the next week or so?"

"Then they got to me first."

John hung up. He and Cheryl had their answers, as little as they liked it.

"Moreno must have confided in the family," said Director Kelly.

"Moreno didn't even know. I have no idea where they got their intelligence," responded Breslow.

Freeman was seething. "Look, you've been in on this from the start. You've known every step and condoned it. We need to clean this up and get the upper hand. Now."

"Do you honestly think he'll come in?" asked Kelly.

"Without question," said Breslow. "What are his choices? He's dead without us, and he knows it. He's an American."

"I'm not so sure. He's desperate, but he's clearly not stupid."

"They're smart and educated people," said Freeman, his temper no longer showing. "They will come to the right conclusion. There is no better option. Nothing even close."

Kelly shifted in his seat and looked out the window. "I hope you're right, or everyone here is out of a fucking job. What's this … he'll only come in if the heads of the CIA and FBI are there? Who the fuck does he think he is?"

Martin Breslow shook his head.

"Can we can be frank for a moment?" asked Freeman. "You know as well as I do that poor bastard's remaining kidney is our salvation for decades to come. Against overwhelming genetic statistics, an American is a perfect match. Our best minds could not have engineered a better situation. There will never be a chance like this again. I'm ready to do as he says … take the appropriate precautions, of course, but we'll take full advantage of an opportunity like this."

Chapter 33

John and Cheryl made their next call to Breslow from a pay phone. That day, it did not matter that they might be traced. In fact, they preferred and expected it. It was part of the plan.

"John, how are you?"

"We're ready to come in."

"Good, good. Give us the specifics. We're ready to move immediately."

"In exactly two hours, you, Freeman, and Kelly are to meet me in downtown Larchmont, on the west side of Sparrow Street, between First and Second. I'll be watching for you. When I recognize Freeman and Kelly, I'll join you."

John dropped the phone and left it to dangle purposely, not waiting for a response. He turned and hugged Cheryl. "The ball's in motion," he whispered. "We've got exactly two hours."

John used Moreno's cell phone to make one last call. "The deed is done. Two hours to contact. May God be with us all."

Within twenty minutes of the call, U.S. federal agents began arriving in downtown Larchmont. They systematically scoped out the site and located themselves strategically, heavily armed. Each carried two family photos of the Harrises that had been wired from Central, along with an enlarged facial photo of John. More agents would be arriving over the next hour.

On the west side of Sparrow was a single large building complex with a few small storefronts to one side. To the east stood a number of small shops and private businesses. Ironically, this city block was, itself, only blocks from the city courthouse and other governmental buildings.

At both ends of the block, two government sedans parked to occupy each corner. Agents reached rooftop positions, taking orders from transmitters in their ears. The area had been secured.

At twenty-five minutes before the witching hour, a small military aircraft landed at Larchmont International Airport. At precisely five minutes before the predetermined rendezvous, a Brinks armored truck pulled up to the northeast corner of Sparrow. Inside, Breslow, Freeman, and Kelly put on their bulletproof vests and readied their weapons. A small, flesh-colored disc went onto all six of their earlobes, receivers into one of each of their ears. For the sniper's benefit, the discs emitted a special coloration visible only through their high-tech, rifle scopes.

FBI agents opened the heavy back doors of the Brinks van like the doors of a vault, then scanned the perimeter. Breslow, Freeman, and Kelly stepped down, all sporting sunglasses. Pedestrians seemed not to notice them. They crossed the intersection and walked to the west side of street. The plan was to walk back and forth until they were intercepted. Walking slowly in a southerly direction, they attempted to make eye contact with everyone they passed. On occasion, that eye contact met someone with the same employer, the same earlobe beacons, disguised as a civilian. As they strolled, they heard intermittent communications regarding tactical information, most of which did not involve them. When they reached the south corner, they turned and headed back. About midway down the block, they passed a large set of glass doors. As they passed, a dark-haired man with a closely cropped beard, a Hawaiian hat, and short pants came out and walked behind them. He had three pairs of binoculars hanging around his neck. In plain clothes, Detective Russ Marley stepped in right behind him.

"Mr. Kelly? Mr. Freeman? Mr. Breslow?"

All three men stopped and turned slowly. At first they saw only a vague similarity. A closer look made them certain. They extended their hands to John and introduced themselves. He reciprocated, his palm less sweaty than Mr. Breslow's. Marley stood nearby.

"Interesting costume," said Kelly. "Tourist theme, eh? Three binoculars in case the first two fail?" He laughed.

"Works for me," said John, without humor.

"Where's the rest of the family?" asked Breslow.

"Nearby. So how do we do this? Are we safe here?"

"For the moment. You come with us to the Brinks truck over there. Then we pick up the rest of your family, and everything else is set up."

"Hey, tell me something. I just gotta know. Do you really think you'll get away with it?"

"With what?" said Breslow.

"Come on. You know. Using my remaining kidney as some sort of bargaining chip with the Saudis. You thought you had them by the balls. And no one would ever know. I disappear and, whammo, Saudi Arabia's in our corner. No need to worry about the next war in the Middle East. No more messy battlefields with American bodies and all those painful apologies. No more uncertainty. And plenty of petroleum products for everyone."

Breslow shifted his stance. Kelly looked about suspiciously but kept an ear on the conversation. Freeman stared at John like a poker player deciding whether to raise or fold.

"We only just learned the source of the threat," hedged Freeman.

"I don't think so," said John. "And Moreno? The others? God rest their souls. You never told them, did you?"

"Think about it, if you can," said Kelly. "The Middle East is horribly unstable." His voice went from a whisper to a hiss. "What would have happened if Saddam Hussein had prevailed in the Gulf in 1991? What will happen if Osama bin Laden prevails today? Such scenarios are unacceptable. What if the OPEC decides to put a major clamp on their exports? What do you think will happen when the prices go up through the roof? And then, what will happen when our reserves run out? Imagine that. No petroleum products. What will Americans want? When a million or more Americans lose their oil-related jobs, what will *they* want? Oil. Almighty oil. What will they be willing to pay to get it? Anything. Anything."

"So, the life and kidneys of a John Harris are small potatoes. Do you think the American people will accept the bartering of organs, life, and liberty so that they can have oil?"

"Without hesitation."

"You're the FBI and the CIA. You represent the American people. The very foundation of this country is freedom. When did that change?"

"We better get going," said Breslow, looking at his watch.

"Where do you possibly keep someone like me? The little Saudi prince might not need another kidney transplant for ten years. Maybe never."

Breslow signaled for agents to move in as Kelly's voice turned conciliatory. The cobra charming the rat.

"Close it down. Close it down," said Breslow into his microphone.

"There are places. You'll be very comfortable and perfectly safe," continued Kelly.

"Safe! Jesus, you guys are unbelievable."

Two agents on the sidewalk and another one from across the street approached the group.

"What gives you the authority to do all this? Does the White House possibly know?"

"John, don't make this ugly," said Freeman.

At that moment, John was surrounded. Six hands were placed on his body. Breslow started to speak into the receiver in his lapel to order the Brinks truck over.

"Wait!" John said, getting their attention.

Marley stepped up behind the group and placed one gun in each of his hands at the back of the heads of two of the agents.

"Gentlemen, behind you is Detective Marley of the Larchmont police. Also an American."

"Is that true, sir?" asked Breslow.

"Yes, it is. Please don't do anything that we'll all be sorry for."

"If it is, and you are a police officer," said Kelly, "then you know that you are interfering with a matter of national security. That's a capital offense. Let us finish our business. Stand down."

"I can't do that, sir."

Marley kept his head well hidden behind the agents, so as to avoid sniper fire.

Breslow shouted into his transmitter, "Plan B! Repeat, Plan B!"

Two sedans came from each end of the street, screeched to a stop in front of the group of men, and unloaded suited agents, brandishing automatic weapons as they surrounded the group. Two held weapons to Marley's head.

Civilians on the street began to scramble and scream, many of them dropping to the sidewalk and street. At the same moment, a number of Larchmont police and SWAT members exited from buildings, pointing their weapons at the group.

Not one gun-toting person from any of the law-enforcement divisions knew what to do. The standoff heightened as all involved looked between those they had their weapons trained on and those with weapons trained on them. One slip, and there would be a mass annihilation.

Kelly spoke into his transmitter. "Hold your fire. Repeat, do *not* fire."

"Detective, have your men stand down. You are in way over your heads. Leave this to us," commanded Freeman. "Let us do our work."

"Is this official business?" asked Marley.

Silence.

"Dammit, Detective. Look at the rooftops. We have the upper hand physically and by jurisdiction, for Christ's sake."

"Ask your snipers to look above and around them," said Marley, his voice transmitting through a white collar mike of his own.

SWAT troops came out of rooftop hatches and doorways and showed themselves from atop antennae and utility towers. A SWAT helicopter could be seen approaching in the distance. Breslow, Kelly, and Freeman could hear the report in their earpieces.

"Gentlemen," said John. "Think this over. And while you're doing that, take these." He removed all three pairs of binoculars. "One for Mr. Kelly, one for Mr. Freeman, and one for Mr. Breslow," commanded John calmly as he pointed.

"What?" asked Breslow.

"Put on the binoculars and look across the street into the storefront with the widescreen TV, second floor." The circle slowly opened in the direction John pointed.

"What are you talking about?" Kelly took the field glasses.

Freeman did the same. Both men put the binoculars to their eyes and looked for the TV through one of the large picture windows on the east side of the street.

After a moment to focus, they gasped in unison. What they had seen was themselves on TV. Next to the TVs stood a woman behind another set of binoculars, peering back in their direction, Chief Gordon Weeks at her side.

Kelly spoke first. "Oh, Jesus."

Breslow looked and dropped his binoculars.

"Turn off the camera now," continued Kelly, "or—"

"Or what? You'll have one of your henchmen take out a perfectly patriotic America-loving guy like me? Besides, I can't turn it off."

Breslow clearly understood, but Freeman hadn't yet caught on.

"It's a live, public broadcast," said John. "I have no control over it. Hell, your wife and kids might be watching right now."

"Check him for a goddamn wire! Right now!" commanded Kelly.

Marley did not interfere as one of the assisting agents reached inside of John's shirt and fished out a microphone and its transmission wire.

"You have no idea of the damage that you've done," said Kelly.

"No. *You* have no idea how much damage *you* have done. To this country. You sold me out, and you sold out all the good people of this country. You guys are vermin!"

"Goddammit," said Breslow, not knowing what to do. The other agents were confused and waited for a command.

"What will you do now?" Freeman had a small smile on his face. As a shadow soldier, he realized and appreciated in some sick way that he had been defeated.

"We're going back home, where we belong."

Read on for a preview of the upcoming thriller

The Hacker

by

Ken Corre

Chapter 1
March

He is a knight in shining armor, his head shrouded in a black helmet with a heavy faceshield. His arms are covered in heavy protective gear that project into the glass booth. He is ready, masterful, and undaunted. Or so he thinks. Any King and Queen would be honored to have this fierce soldier at the head of their army. *Fuck the King,* he says to himself. *I should be King. They do not appreciate my magnificence. They will see. And fuck the Queen, the biggest bitch in a realm of bitches.*

The room itself is dark, but the glass booth radiates an incredible incandescence. It is so bright that without protective eyewear it can obliterate the retina of the eye and blind a man, perhaps permanently, in less than a few seconds.

The initial flare up of the welder in the oxygen-free environment yields the most intense and pure white light. The Knight views it with deep religious reverence. As he begins welding, explosions of extraordinary color take place, dancing into the air as they fly off the tubular titanium joints being melded. It is a ballet of colors and shapes reminiscent of the aurora on the sun's surface. The images often change dramatically in tenor without warning. Unimaginable shapes of hate and evil suddenly dominate over the bright white light and colors. The images of hate appear dark against the blinding, white light. Sometimes the images are so intense that he has to stop welding, catch his breath, and allow the sweat to evaporate. Increasingly, he hears voices, words, and names accompanying these horrific images. Sometimes the words and names coalesce into a command, a mission from the highest source. At times, he looks to the source for guidance and receives no reply. He has to be patient.

The foreman enters unnoticed and approaches Mr. Vitrelli. There is no response to his voice. When he taps Mr. Vitrelli's shoulder the Knight stands from his stool with the speed of a cornered animal, extricates his arms from within the glass booth, and turns to meet his attacker. A large knife materializes from nowhere and the foreman fights for his life. During the scuffle, the flap of the welding helmet flips up and the ambient light from behind the open door catches Mr. Vitrelli in the face. He immediately becomes limp.

The foreman wriggles out from underneath the paralyzed Knight and runs to the parking lot, never to return. In later statements, the foreman will swear he heard Mr. Vitrelli utter the words "mother" and "cunt" repeatedly. Since no skin was pierced and Mr. Vitrelli has no record, no formal charges are ever lodged against him.

Chapter 2
June 8

The peaceful morning is interrupted as a tall middle-aged man runs up the long and gradual grade of Starlight Drive. His gray sweatshirt has deep water-rings on both the front and the back. Nearing the end of the five-mile run, he has found his stride. Although the headband does not help his thinning blonde hair to stay in place, it does keep the sweat from pouring down his face. About ten feet behind him, and quite winded, is his dog Luke, named after one of the Apostles. His tongue fans widely as it drapes far over the edge of his jowls and undulates with his panting.

As they proceed, an occasional neighbor picking up a newspaper gives a wave or thumbs-up sign. The suburban habitat is filled with all the charm of an old neighborhood, replete with the lush vegetation of grand old trees and no sidewalks. Beautiful Jacaranda line the street and their fallen flowers form a bed of purple matted to the road by the morning dew. The two lunge toward the driveway of a small two-story home in a final spurt of energy.

The beauty of Great Pass, Colorado stands in stark contrast to the metropolis of Denver that looms roughly twenty minutes away. Unlike suburban Great Pass, Denver has to deal with a rapidly growing population and the attendant problems of poverty, crime, tension, filth and decadence.

Crawford stops abruptly in his driveway and begins walking briskly in circles, hands on his hips, to keep his aging and exhausted muscles from cramping up. He pants, while Luke does the same lying on the cool grass like a pot-belly pig. As soon as Crawford catches his breath, he begins his post-exercise stretching. Standing, he twists in each direction to stretch the expansive muscles that line each side of the spinal vertebra. Taking a sitting position, he straightens his legs and bends forward to touch his toes in order to stretch his hamstrings. As he bends forward, his baggy sweatshirt pulls up his back and off his hips, revealing a holstered handgun. Luke starts barking, as he always will, when Crawford does this particular exercise.

His wife, Claire, comes out of the front door. Her bathrobe covers the short nightgown on her mildly pudgy body. Because her dark brown hair is unkempt from the night's sleep, her gray roots are more obvious. She carries a small silver plastic object in her hand.

"How'd you know I was back?" asks Crawford.

"Luke's barking is a dead giveaway. You got called about ten-fifteen minutes ago," she says coldly as she holds his cellphone out to him.

"Who was it?"

"I don't know. I didn't look," answers Claire, knowing very well who it was. "But I'm getting tired of this, you know?"

Crawford stands up quickly and takes the cellphone. Claire turns abruptly and goes back inside. He depresses one of the buttons and a phone number comes up.

"Oh, no. Not on a Saturday."

Luke follows Crawford into the house as he walks to the coat rack in the entrance hallway. He removes the pistol from his back holster and places it in the holster hiding under his jacket. Claire is within earshot in the kitchen.

"Where's Paul?" he asks.

"Either sleeping or studying, as usual. Where else?"

"Did he go out last night?"

"No. Why?"

Crawford turns and moves to the kitchen as he continues to talk: "After everything we've been through with him, don't you still get the feeling he's avoiding us?"

"No, but I often get the feeling he's avoiding *you*."

Crawford pauses for a moment looking at Claire and then turns to his cellphone and dials.

At that moment Paul walks into the kitchen. His hair is short and he is handsome despite the numerous piercings in his ears, one in his left eyebrow, another in his tongue. Not exactly what Crawford, or Claire, for that matter, had in mind. But he is gifted, doing very well in his first year of college. They hope that he is close to the end of the transition through the touchy phase. How and when and why their only child physically morphed is much more troublesome to Crawford than Claire. Paul assumes his father just isn't proud enough to bring him to his work anymore, where everyone is straight-laced like him. Even the undercover guys aren't allowed piercings. There is also the issue of the sole tuft of facial hair located just below his lower lip.

"Crawford here. What? Yes I do. What's the address?"

Crawford snaps his fingers and Claire reluctantly fetches a pad and pencil for Crawford. He writes down the number and ends the phone call.

"Ruff, ruff," mocks Paul. "She's not a dog."

"What street?" asks Claire looking at the pad, trying to ignore Paul and hoping Crawford will do the same.

"Monroe."

"My God, that's not too far from here."

"Is it your impression, over the years, that I treat your mother like a dog?"

"Whatever."

"I gotta go." Crawford grabs his things and heads out. "Hope this doesn't take too long."

Chapter 3

Nothing bad ever happens in Great Pass, ever. This explains the gathering mass of gawkers in front of 537 1/2 Monroe in the early afternoon of June 8th. There are marked and unmarked police cars from Denver as well as the familiar local Sheriff's car. The entire lot is roped off with a neon yellow plastic tape from the curb to the two adjoining properties. Although no one has a clue about what has happened, they all know something bad has finally befallen their cherished Great Pass. A few whispers are heard in the crowd: "It must be that strange girl." "I told you she was bad news." "Poor child." The predominant sound, however, is that of silent concern. The children are kept indoors.

Under normal circumstances, the scene of grown men in suits groping about a front lawn with surgical gloves would have been funny sight. Not today, not even for the kids who were lucky enough to catch a glimpse.

"The big boys from Denver sure know what they are doing," someone murmurs as they watch as the lawn is meticulously dissected for evidence.

While the boys do their combing, the flash of cameras from within 537 1/2 Monroe is seen behind the drawn curtains. Inside is a macabre scene. Death looms with its slight putrid scent despite open windows and the backdoor.

"Don't move her, dammit, until all photos are taken, and I am there right beside the DB," yells the chief of Denver Homicide, Detective Crawford. Per usual, he had arrived on the scene within thirty minutes of the call for damage control and most of the morning had already passed quickly....

978-0-595-40659-3
0-595-40659-9